THINGS COULD BE WORSE

The Pastor Kastenmayer Stories

Virginia DeMarce

Cover designed by Laura Givens

Printed in the United States of America

First Printing: Nov 2020
1632, Inc. & Eric Flint's Ring of Fire Press

eBook ISBN-13 978-1-953034-19-9
Trade Paperback ISBN-13 978-1-953034-20-5

Dedication

Margaret Wilhelmina Angela (Jongebloed) Easley (1909-2006)

I grew up on a farm in Boone County, Missouri. Part of the reason that I ended up as a historian, I believe, is that my utterly urban mother, born, reared, and employed in Lower Manhattan until her marriage at age 30, provided a kind of Greek chorus in the background of my childhood, pointing out that not everybody in the world did things the way that the people who surrounded me did them and, moreover, that there was no particular reason why they should.

ACKNOWLEDGMENTS

The major acknowledgment, as always, is to Eric Flint for writing 1632, which spawned this fictional universe, and for inviting me to be a part of it.

Many thanks to Kerryn Offord and Bjorn Hasseler for generously sharing some of their characters with me for the stories that required them.

I am grateful to all the historians and researchers who spent time in early modern European archives and publish their results.

Many thanks to Walt Boyes, the editor in chief of the Ring of Fire Press, for struggling with my manuscripts, and to Gorg Huff for turning them into something that is e-book friendly.

CONTENTS

FOREWORD

"...all at once, and nothing first, just as bubbles do when they burst." Oliver Wendell Holmes (1809-1894), *The Deacon's Masterpiece, or, the Wonderful One-hoss Shay: A Logical Story.*

"Eternity isn't time that goes on forever. It is a place without time, where everything is all at once. Everyone knows that." Salome Piscatora, verh. Kastenmayer (1593-), "The Woman Shall Not Wear That" in: *Things Could Be Worse.*

If, for some random reason, you have picked up this little volume titled *Things Could Be Worse* as your first introduction to the universe of Eric Flint's 1632 series (also known upon occasion as the Ring of Fire), you'll need a bit of introduction to what is happening.

The West Virginia mining town of Grantville, a sphere of territory extending three miles from its center in all directions, along with its approximately 3500 residents, arrived in the middle of largely Lutheran Thuringia, Germany, in April 1631, courtesy of a science fiction device named an Assiti Shard. As the town had no Lutheran church, as German refugees from the Thirty Years War flooded into the town, the local *Landesherr*, Count Ludwig Guenther of Schwarzburg-Rudolstadt, saw his duty. For more background, you may go read "The Rudolstadt Colloquy" (set in April 1633) in the *Grantville Gazette I* anthology from Baen Publishing. After the end of that story, having consulted with the consistory of his territorial church, the count proceeded with the building of St. Martin's in the Fields on land he owned just outside of the Ring of

Fire, along the road leading to his little capital city of Rudolstadt, and appointed Ludwig Kastenmayer as its first pastor.

Since this series is alternative history rather than fantasy, things do not occur instantaneously. You make the acquaintance of Our Fictional Protagonist a year after the colloquy. He is not a hero of romance, but rather in his mid-sixties, born in Saxony, a Lutheran of the Phillippist ilk who endured the controversies with the Flacians there until, being on the losing side, he had the luck some twenty years prior to the "Grantville miracle" of being appointed to a parish in the Thuringian town of Ohrdruf, located in the extinct County of Gleichen, where he remained until called to Grantville. He comes accompanied by his pragmatic wife, whose given name of "Salome" was quite popular at the time, having nothing to do with the dance of the seven veils (the name of that woman is not in the biblical narrative, but rather transmitted by Josephus) and everything to do with the "righteous Salome," wife of Zebedee and mother of the disciples James and John. He also arrives with numerous children from two marriages, the eldest aged thirty and the youngest a toddler.

The various seventeenth-century intra-Lutheran theological controversies follow him from both Saxony and Ohrdruf into the culturally and ecclesiastically diverse town from the future.

Most of the stories collected here were originally published in the *Grantville Gazette* and were separate and independent. Consequently, they are not a sequential narrative, but overlap chronologically.

* * *

For quick reference, here is a chronology of some of the mainline events in the changed history of Europe that has resulted from the Ring of Fire, and to which the characters in the stories make passing references, without explanations, because they are happening in the background of their preoccupations within their own lives.

Late 1634, pan-Lutheran theological colloquy in Magdeburg

4 March 1635 assassination of Dreeson and Wiley in Grantville

June 1635 USE transition from Stearns to Wettin administration

Summer 1635 plague epidemic on the western borders of the USE

June 1635 start of Gustavus Adolphus' campaign against Saxony and Brandenburg

September 1635 John George of Saxony, his wife, and one of his sons killed in the Vogtland

October 1635 Gustavus Adolphus seriously injured in battle at Lake Bledno and doesn't make sense for four months; Oxenstierna and the reactionaries

Late November through December 1635 Grantville quarantined for a measles epidemic

February 1636 Gustavus Adolphus recovers significantly; death of Oxenstierna

Summer 1636 USE transition from Crown Loyalists to Piazza FoJP administration

Summer 1636 Ottomans invade Austria

When you read these stories, please understand. Basically, they are not sequential, but rather simultaneous. From Sabina Ottmar's flashback to coming into Grantville in 1631 to the dedication of Countess Catharina the Heroic Lutheran School in the spring of 1637, they span the time thus far covered in the mainline books of the 1632 series. However....

However, the characters in these stories are not involved in great USE imperial or international political events. Most are not even directly involved in politics on the level of the State of Thuringia-Franconia

(SoTF). Those events do, at some remove, affect them. They do not, by and large, affect those events. Their lives and primary concerns are local.

* * *

The core portion of "Pastor Kastenmayer's Revenge"[1] starts and ends in April 1635 with Pastor Kastenmayer's thinking about the events of the previous year. However, the action takes place between April 1634 and April 1635, with a couple of mental flashbacks to even earlier events, so this story should be read first. The seven individual mini-stories contained in it overlap with one another.

* * *

"The Woman Shall Not Wear That"[2] starts in summer 1634 and ends on Christmas Eve of the same year. It is simultaneous with the "middle" chronology of "Revenge."

* * *

"Or the Horse May Learn to Sing"[3] starts during Christmas vacation 1634 and ends in late August 1635, so the first part is simultaneous with the latter part of "Revenge." The 1632 series has numerous other stories

---

[1](*Grantville Gazette* #3; Baen Publishing *Grantville Gazette III.*)

[2]*Grantville Gazette* #6.

[3]*Grantville Gazette* #28.

involving the Reverend Albert Green, by other authors, particularly Terry Howard, which have appeared in the *Grantville Gazette*.

"The Truth about That Cat and Pup"[4] starts in January 1635 and ends in September 1635. It overlaps with the latter part of "Revenge" and is essentially simultaneous with "Horse." For this collection, I have split the story as published in the *Grantville Gazette* into two parts, with a new story inserted between them.

* * *

"Clothed with the Imperishable" is a new story, not previously published, set in April-May 1635. Chronologically, it occurs in the middle of both "Horse" and "Truth." Those who are curious about how Phillip Gribbleflotz and Dina Kastenmayer met, as well as Pastor Kastenmayer's reaction to the improbable match, should read Kerryn A. Offord, "The Doctor Gribbleflotz Chronicles, Part 3; –Doctor Phil's Distraction," *Grantville Gazette* #8, or Chapter 16 in~~in~~ Kerryn Offord and Rick Boatright, *1636: The Chronicles of Dr. Gribbleflotz* (Baen Books, 2016), before moving on to this story. Ideally, readers should read Kerryn's story first whether they are curious or not. The ladies of the Fortney, Kubiak, and Drahuta families who appear in this story have been introduced in other of Kerryn's Gribbleflotz stories published in the *Grantville Gazette* and also appear in the *Chronicles*.

[4]*Grantville Gazette* #27.

The other previously unpublished story, "Things Could Be Worse," starts in May 1635 and concludes in March 1636. The earlier part overlaps somewhat with "Horse" and significantly with "Truth." The major part of the action takes place in early November of 1635. For background concerning Neustatter's European Security Service (NESS) and its activities, the curious should read several of Bjorn Hasseler's stories that show interaction between his characters and others that appear in the stories in this book. For example, the original group of employees generally attend church at St. Martin's in the Fields. They eat at Cora's City Hall Café. In "A Cold Day in Grantville," *Grantville Gazette* #40, the date being 14 Nov 1634, Neustatter excommunicates Pankratz Holz.

* * *

"Waking Up in Heaven"[5] begins in February 1636 and ends in November 30, 1636.

"Angels Watching over Me"[6] takes place in May 1637 and concludes the Pastor Kastenmayer sequence. His widow, Salome Piscatora, and his children will reappear in the future in Kerryn Offord's Dr. Gribbleflotz sequence.

---

[5]*Grantville Gazette* #84.

[6]*Grantville Gazette* #85.

CAST LIST

Adams, Jeffrey (fi u-t), physician, general practitioner in Grantville

Altschulerin Hedwig "Hedy" (fi d-t), refugee from Saxon Henneberg, married to Jarvis Beasley in Grantville

Arnim, Hans Georg von (hi d-t), Saxon general

Baker, David Perry (fi u-t), son of Ryan Baker and his wife Meg Heunisch

Baker, Ryan (fi u-t), husband of Magdalena "Meg" Heunisch; Lutheran convert

Barthin, Catharina (hi d-t), wife of Friedrich Hortleder

Bates, Cheryl Ann (fi u-t), divorced second wife of Zane Baumgardner

Baumgardner, Carly (fi u-t), daughter of Zane Baumgardner and Tina Marie Hollister; half-sister of April Lafferty; girlfriend of Anthony Green

Baumgardner, Mildred (fi u-t), mother of Zane Baumgardner, grandmother of Carly

Baumgardner, Ronnie (fi u-t), son of Zane Baumgardner and Tina Marie Hollister

Baumgardner, Zane (fi u-t), father of Carly Baumgardner

Beasley, Buster (fi u-t), late father of Denise Beasley

Beasley, Denise (fi u-t), best friend of Minnie Hugelmair

Beasley, Jarvis (fi u-t), employee at MaidenFresh Laundries; husband of Hedwig Altschulerin

Beckworth, Staci Ann (fi u-t), former girlfriend of Lew Jenkins; married to Arnold Pflaum

Blocker, Crystal (fi u-t), married to Walt Dorrman; friend of Megan Collins

Blount, Derek (fi u-t), husband of Ursula Krause; Lutheran convert

Blount, Donnie (fi u-t), brother of Derek Blount

Böcler, Johann Heinrich "Heinz" (hi d-t), private secretary to Duke Ernst of Saxe-Weimar

Booth, Manning (fi u-t), proprietor of goat dairy outside of Grantville; married to Myrna Wright

Brunswick, Georg, duke of (hi d-t), moderate Crown Loyalist, head of the USE Province of Brunswick

Canzler, Margaretha (fi d-t), lady-in-waiting of Erdmuthe Juliana, countess of Gleichen-Tonna

Carissimi, Giacomo (hi d-t), musician

Carpzov, Benedikt (hi d-t), lawyer in Saxony

Carstairs, Liz (fi u-t), successor to Henry Dreeson as mayor of Grantville

Chabert, Anthony "Tony" (fi u-t), SoTF military officer; Catholic

Chabert, Ludwig Anthony (fi u-t), infant son of Tony Chabert and his wife Andrea Kastenmayer

Collins, Mariah (fi u-t), sister of Megan Collins

Collins, Megan (fi u-t), fiancée of Ronnie Baumgardner

Conrath, Barbara "Barbel" (fi d-t), stepdaughter of Margaretha Krause

DeVries, Henny (fi u-t), public health nurse

Dreeson, Henry (fi u-t), mayor of Grantville

Ennis, Cora (fi u-t), proprietor of City Hall Café and Coffee House, Grantville

Fischer, Sebald (fi d-t), employee at Lothlorien Farbenwerke; brother of Thomas Fischer

Fischer, Thomas (fi d-t), mailman in Grantville, route including St. Martin's in the Fields; recent immigrant from Nürnberg

Fritz, James Anthony "Jim" (fi u-t), husband of Maria Krause; Lutheran convert

Gerhard, Johann (hi d-t), dean of the Faculty of Theology, University of Jena; Lutheran

Gleichen-Tonna, Erdmuthe Juliana von Hohnstein, countess-dowager (hi d-t), widow of Johann Ludwig, the last count of Gleichen-Tonna; convert from Lutheranism to the Stiefelite heretical sect

Green, Albert (fi u-t), Baptist minister in Grantville

Green, Allen (fi u-t), older son of Albert and Claudette Green

Green, Anthony (fi u-t), younger son of Albert and Claudette Green

Green, Claudette (fi u-t), wife of Rev. Albert Green

Gribbleflotz, Phillip Theophrastus (fi d-t), alchemist in Jena; proprietor of HDG Industries

Griep, Oswald Georg (fi d-t), Flacian Lutheran minister at St. Thomas the Apostle church, at the border of the Ring of Fire on the northwestern side

Hardegg, Johann Georg (fi d-t), pompous young attorney

Henneberg, Katharina von, countess of Schwarzburg (hi d-t), late staunch Lutheran who resisted the Duke of Alba, for whom Countess Katharina the Heroic school is named

Hercher, Elisabetha "die Hercherin" (fi d-t), widow, mother of Ursula and Else Krause

Hercher, Elisabetha "Lisbet" (fi d-t), Quittelsdorf village girl, member of St. Martin's in the Fields parish

Hercher, Walpurga (fi d-t), Quittelsdorf village girl, member of St. Martin's in the Fields parish

Heringen, Clara von, née duchess of Brunswick, widowed countess of Schwarzburg (hi d-t), elderly noblewoman; much older sister of duke Georg of Brunswick

Heunisch, Magdalena "Meg" (fi d-t), Quittelsdorf village girl, member of St. Martin's in the Fields parish

Hobbs, Mitch (fi u-t), son of Joe and Gloria Hobbs, husband of Walpurga Hercher; Lutheran convert

Hoë von Hoënegg, Mathias (hi d-t), Lutheran theologian in Saxony

Hohnstein, Erdmuthe Juliana von, see Gleichen-Tonna

Hollister, Tina Marie (fi u-t), divorced from both John Lafferty and Zane Baumgardner; married Lucas Sartorius and moved to northern Germany, leaving her adult and near-adult children from both marriages to the care of her second husband's mother

Holz, Pankratz (fi d-t), orthodox Lutheran, errand-runner for Superintendent Melchior Tilesius

Horst, Simon (fi d-t), candidate to succeed Ludwig Kastenmayer at St. Martin's in the Fields

Hortleder, Anna Catharina (hi d-t), daughter of Friedrich Hortleder

Hortleder, Friedrich (hi d-t), chancellor of Saxe-Weimar

Hudson, Willie Ray (fi u-t), head of the Grange organization in Grantville

Hugelmair, Minnie (fi d-t), singer, adopted daughter of Benny Pierce

Immanuel Renatus (fi u-t), adopted son of the widowed dowager countess of Gleichen-Tonna

Jenkins, Joe (fi u-t), becomes a leader of the Anabaptists in Grantville, had been ordained in some "off-brand" Baptist body up-time

Jenkins, Michael Lewis "Lew" (fi u-t), husband of Sabina Ottmar; Lutheran convert

Jordan, Bitsy (nee Elizabeth McDougal)(fi u-t)–, musician; wife of Fred Jordan; children Daniel and Leah

Jordan, Fred (fi u-t), SoTF, deputy sheriff in Grantville, assigned to Ohrdruf

Kastenmayer, Andrea (fi d-t), older daughter of Ludwig Kastenmayer by his first wife

Kastenmayer, Johann Conrad "Cunz" (fi d-t), third son of Ludwig Kastenmayer by his first wife

Kastenmayer, Jonas Justinus (fi d-t), infant son of Ludwig Kastenmayer and Salome, born October 1634

Kastenmayer, Ludwig (fi d-t), pastor of St. Martin's in the Fields Lutheran parish; Phillipist

Kastenmayer, Maria Blandina "Dina" (fi d-t), second daughter of Ludwig Kastenmayer by his first wife

Kastenmayer, Martin (fi d-t), second son of Ludwig Kastenmayer by his first wife

Kastenmayer, Peter (fi d-t), thoroughly precocious son of Ludwig Kastenmayer and Salome

Koch, Carol (fi u-t), mathematician, mother of Ronella Koch; ELCA Lutheran

Koch, Ronaldus (fi u-t), mining engineer, up-time German, husband of Carol and father of Ronella; vaguely secular Lutheran

Koch, Ronella (fi u-t), teacher at St. Katharina the Heroic elementary school; ELCA Lutheran

Krause, Anna (fi d-t), Quittelsdorf village girl, younger half-sister of Maria Krause

Krause, Elisabetha "Else" (fi d-t), Quittelsdorf village girl, younger sister of Ursula Krause

Krause, Margaretha "die Krausin" (fi d-t), widow, remarried to Burton Vandiver, member of St. Martin's in the Fields parish

Krause, Maria (fi d-t), Quittelsdorf village girl, member of St. Martin's in the Fields parish

Krause, Ursula "Ursel" (fi d-t), Quittelsdorf village girl, member of St. Martin's in the Fields parish

Lambert, Gary (fi u-t), business manager of Leahy Medical Center; Missouri Synod Lutheran

Lowe, Hugh (fi u-t), president, Railroad and Tramway Corporation

Luther, Johann Ernst (hi d-t), last surviving grandson of the reformer Martin Luther

Mansfeld, see Reuss

McDonald, Beulah Ann (fi u-t), registered nurse; faculty of medicine, University of Jena

Mercer, Eric (fi u-t), husband of Lisbet Hercher; Lutheran convert

Meth, Ezechiel (hi d-t), leader of a heretical sect

Mittelhausen, Ursula (fi d-t), HDG Enterprises, housekeeper for Herr Doktor Phillip Theophrastus Gribbleflotz

Muselius, Jonas Justinus (fi d-t), teacher at Countess Katharina the Heroic Lutheran elementary school, attached to St. Martin's in the Fields parish

Neustatter, Edgar (fi d-t), head of NESS security services

Oldenburg-Delmenhorst, Emelie countess of, wife of count Ludwig Guenther of Schwarzburg-Rudolstadt

Olson, Sheila (fi u-t), wife of Gary Lambert, left up-time

Onofrio, Emmanuel (fi u-t), mathematics teacher at Calvert high school in Grantville; Catholic

Ottmar, Sabina (fi d-t), Keilhau village girl, stepsister of Rahel Rosina Dornheimer; member of St. Martin's in the Fields parish

Penzey, Anne (fi u-t), profoundly curious teenager

Pflug, Julius von (hi d-t), deceased; last Catholic bishop of the diocese of Naumburg in Saxony; renowned scholar and book collector

Piazza, Ed (fi u-t), president of the State of Thuringia-Franconia (SoTF)

Piscator, Ernst (fi d-t), brother of Salome Piscatora

Piscatora, Anna (fi d-t), sister of Salome Piscatora; wife of Heinrich Schlosser

Piscatora, Salome (fi d-t), wife of Ludwig Kastenmayer, pastor at St. Martin's in the Fields

Prüschenk von Lindenhofen, Zacharias (hi d-t), lawyer, suitor of Anna Catharina Hortleder

Pflaum, Arnold (fi d-t), farmer, married to Staci Ann Beckworth

Piscatora, Salome (fi d-t), second wife of Ludwig Kastenmayer

Quiney, Richard and Thomas (hi d-t), grandsons of William Shakespeare, doing drama in Grantville

Rawls, Vesta (fi u-t), managing director of MaidenFresh Laundries

Reimarus, Ludwig "Lutz" (fi d-t), organist in Weimar; cousin of Salome Piscatora verh. Kastenmayer

Reuss, Anna von Mansfeld, widow (hi d-t), elderly noblewoman, granddaughter of Katharina von Henneberg

Richards, Preston (fi u-t), chief of police, Grantville

Richards, Mel (fi u-t), wife of Preston Richards; child protection officer, Grantville police force; former special education teacher

Rosenbusch, Joachim (fi d-t), steward of Erdmuthe Juliana, countess of Gleichen-Tonna

Rothenmaler, Johann (hi d-t), Lutheran superintendent in Schwarzburg-Rudolstadt

Saxe-Altenburg, Johann Philipp, duke of (hi d-t), cousin of the dukes of Saxe-Weimar; has also become a wealthy industrialist since the arrival of Grantville

Saxe-Weimar, Albrecht, duke of (hi d-t), administrator of the Wettin family estates

Saxe-Weimar, Ernst, duke of (hi d-t), administrator of the Upper Palatinate for Gustavus II Adolphus

Saxe-Weimar, Wilhelm, duke of—see Wettin, Wilhelm

Saxony, Hans Georg and August, dukes of (hi d-t), sons of Elector John George of Saxony

Schlosser, Heinrich (fi d-t), teacher at Countess Katharina the Heroic Lutheran School; brother-in-law of Salome Piscatora verh. Kastenmayer; children Heinrich Hektor, Catharina Diana, Anna Penelope (among others)

Schwarzburg-Rudolstadt, Ludwig Guenther, count (hi d-t), married to Emelie; father of Albrecht Karl; involved in Lutheran diplomacy on behalf of Gustavus Adolphus

Schwarzburg-Sondershausen, Anton Heinrich, count (hi d-t), cousin of Ludwig Guenther, administrator of his branch of the family's properties within the SoTF, morganatically married

Selfisch, Blandina (fi d-t), deceased first wife of Ludwig Kastenmayer

Selfisch, Johann Georg (fi d-t), attorney, half-brother of the late Blandina Selfisch verh. Kastenmayer

Smith, Joanie (fi u-t), English teacher, Countess Katharina the Heroic school

Stiefel, Esaias (hi d-t), heretic, "false prophet," founder of a Thuringian sect that broke away from Lutheranism

"Stiefelin, die" (hi d-t), sister of the late Esaias Stiefel; widow of Matthias Meth; mother of Ezechiel Meth, the current leader of the Stiefelite group in Ohrdruf

Stone, Gerry (fi u-t), son of Tom Stone; studying to become a Lutheran minister

Szymanski, Garnet (fi u-t), registered nurse; divorced from Duane Fritz, mother of Jim Fritz; Catholic

Thomas, Harley (fi u-t), SoTF Marshalls' Service

Tilesius, Melchior (hi d-t), Lutheran district superintendent in Langensalza

Vandiver, Burton (fi u-t), mechanic, second husband of Margaretha Krause

Walsh, Bernita (fi u-t), sister of Lew Jenkins; children David and Ashley

Werthern, Georg von (hi d-t), Saxon nobleman; sons Dietrich and Wolfgang

Wettin, Wilhelm (hi d-t), oldest of the brothers who are dukes of Saxe-Weimar; renounced his title so that under the USE Constitution he could run for the House of Commons in parliament and become prime minister

Wiley, Enoch (fi u-t), Presbyterian minister

Worley, Roland (fi u-t), machinist; husband of Rahel Rosina Dornheimer; Lutheran convert

Zuehlke, Johann Friedrich "Hans-Fritz" (fi d-t), bureaucrat; stepson of Lucas Sartorius from his first marriage

PASTOR KASTENMAYER'S REVENGE

April, 1635

Ludwig Kastenmayer would never forget the day. April 11, 1634, by the reckoning of these up-timers, who had adopted the pope's calendar. The day that one of them had stolen his daughter. It was the worst thing that had happened to him since Count Ludwig Guenther assigned him to the new parish of St. Martin's in the Fields after the Rudolstadt Colloquy.

The man should not even have been in Grantville. He was an officer in the military of the New United States and should have been in Erfurt, where he was assigned.

Jonas—Jonas Justus Muselius, the youngest teacher at the Lutheran elementary school attached to the church and a friend of several of the up-timers—had said that he was on "R and R." Even after Jonas had explained it to him, Pastor Kastenmayer found it peculiar. There was far more to do in Erfurt than in Grantville. Theological lectures by guest professors. Organ concerts. Choral performances. Sermons by visiting pastors. The man should have stayed in Erfurt for his holiday. Erfurt was a magnificent city. He had greatly enjoyed all four of his visits there.

That man should not have come to Grantville and, within less than two weeks, seen Andrea on the street, walked up to her, introduced himself, persuaded her to accompany him to a public restaurant for a meal, and—married her!—six weeks before the end of the school term at Countess Katharina the Heroic School next to St. Martin's, leaving Maria Blandina to manage all of the youngest children by herself. Still, there were only eighty-three of them, after all. There had been little reason for her to complain so bitterly.

Barbaric, this idea that couples could marry in three days' time and without the consent of the parents. Especially when anyone who thought about it should have realized that the parents would not consent. The man was—well, ultimately, to put it plainly—

Catholic.

At least he hadn't insisted that Andrea convert to his church. That would have been the final embarrassment. Nonetheless, it had been difficult to explain to the consistory in Rudolstadt. Extremely difficult, to say the least. Better yet, they had not married in the Grantville Catholic church. Pastor Kastenmayer had derived some minimal satisfaction from discovering that St. Mary's forbade such an absurdity as manifestly disastrous mixed-confessional matrimony on three days' notice, even if the civil laws did not. They had married before the mayor at the *Rathaus*, the man saying casually (Pastor Kastenmayer had heard second hand; he had not been there in person) that they "could get the religious stuff sorted out when they had time."

Additionally, Salome, his second wife, suggested that it was his own fault for not having arranged marriages for the daughters of his first marriage in a more timely manner. Indeed, she had commented that it would not be entirely surprising if Maria Blandina chose an equally unsuitable spouse. She hadn't *quite* said that the girls were both self-centered young snips with pretty faces...not—quite. It would not have been true, and she was fair-minded.

Pastor Kastenmayer had duly sounded out Jonas about Maria Blandina. It would have been quite suitable; the father of young Muselius had been his second wife's half-brother. But he had received a courteous refusal. Too bad. God had blessed Pastor Kastenmayer greatly—five children from his first wife, all surviving (and the two oldest earning salaries, one as a city clerk and one as a junior pastor, which was also a great blessing). Eight children from his second wife, seven surviving. And, ah, of all those, currently, three sets of board, room, and tuition at the university in Jena; two sets of board, room, and tuition at the Latin school in Rudolstadt, and two boys still not old enough for Countess Katharina the Heroic. All on the salary of a parish pastor, with a bit of tutoring here and there. Salome had recently informed him that they were to be blessed again. I am supposed to find a dowry for Maria Blandina *where?* he asked himself. He sighed gloomily and considered lengthening his morning prayers.

But Jonas, although refusing the offer of a wife, had suggested an alternative. What he called a "payback."

Jonas felt responsible for the remainder of the village he had led into Grantville. A few old people, a couple of young mothers, and quite a few children. Well, some of the children had been adolescents in 1631, and most of the adolescents had been girls. The older boys had stayed behind with their fathers to fight the delaying action against the mercenaries from Badenburg. The boys lay dead with their fathers, in a mass grave next to the burned-out church. Now, in 1634, the older girls were becoming—at least at the ages the up-timers considered suitable—marriageable. Also without dowries. The arable lands of Quittelsdorf had been removed to West Virginia, Herr Gary Lambert had told Jonas. At least, that was the up-timers' best guess as to where God had chosen to put their fields. God moved in most mysterious ways. If they had not fled from the mercenaries, they too, presumably, would have been removed to West Virginia. It had been a good day to work in the fields.

"So," Jonas had said, "if the Habsburgs can do it"—he quoted the proverb about "happy Austria" waging matrimony rather than war, in Latin, of course—"then so can we. We must ask '*die Krausin*'." Margaretha Krause, widowed with three children, had gone into service as housekeeper and cook for a middle-aged American whose wife had been left up-time and shortly thereafter had married him.

Before the construction of St. Martin's in the Fields, be it known. Pastor Kastenmayer had had nothing to do with it. The man was not Lutheran. On the other hand, he was a skilled artisan with a regular position, owned a house, and did not interfere with her church attendance. He had allowed her to have their daughter baptized Lutheran at St. Martin's. Things could be worse.

"But," Pastor Kastenmayer had protested, "I do observe the truth that the different churches and their pastors of this Grantville appear to survive in this parity arrangement without excessive conflict. But still—if we try to pluck away their members, that will certainly cause offense. Count Ludwig Guenther does not wish to cause offense. They are his allies. He is part of their confederation."

Jonas cocked his head to the side a little. "More than a third of these up-timers belong to no church at all."

"You mean that they do not enforce attendance?"

"No. People who do not belong to any of the churches in the town. They are not only not Lutherans. They are not even *heretics*." The honest sense of scandal that had enveloped Jonas when he first discovered this was still plain to be heard in his voice. "But, anyway. We steal their men, but we don't steal them from any of their churches. How can the other pastors complain if we convert the heathen?"

From the perspective of his sixty-five years, the first forty-five of them spent among the feuding theologians of Saxony, Pastor Kastenmayer predicted grimly, "They'll find a way."

But it had been irresistible. He called upon "*die Krausin*," now known to the Grantville public as Mrs. Burton Vandiver. He did not overreach. The weapon that God had forged to his hand consisted of, after all, a dozen quite ordinary village girls, even though they had been given two or three years more schooling in Grantville. His requirements were basic. He needed a list of up-time marriage candidates: his only limits were "no constant drunkards, no brawlers, no lazy louts who will expect their wives to support them."

One more year. Palm Sunday, 1635. Harvest time coming in the spring. He smiled upon his congregation from the pulpit. "Today we welcome into fellowship through the rite of adult confirmation Herr Ryan Baker, Herr Derek Blount, Herr James Anthony Fritz, Herr Mitch Hobbs, Herr Michael Lewis Jenkins, Herr Errol Mercer, Herr Roland Worley...."

The men stood in front of him, closely shaved, their hair cut short with the exception of Herr Mercer, who had grown his to a respectable length for an adult man since leaving the army, wearing "neckties" and, most of them, the semi-stunned expression of guys who have not fully analyzed the process by which they got themselves into their current situation.

According to Herr Lambert, the "neckties" were a good omen, indicating that the men were taking their oaths seriously.

The girls of vanished Quittelsdorf had done well in the service of their Lord. Indeed, one was also betrothed to the stepson of "*die Krausin*," but that young man, like his father, was a church member elsewhere; another was betrothed to a colleague of Ryan Baker, but that man also belonged to an up-time church. Still, he had seven. *"Seven at one blow,"* he thought, as the story of the brave little tailor flitted through his mind. Four of the Quittelsdorf girls, prompted by Jonas, had even made their chosen husbands go back to school and get the magic "GED" before they agreed to marry. *Jonas was, after all, not merely* a *school teacher, but their own former teacher, from their lost village; they listened to him.* Pastor Kastenmayer proceeded through the liturgy in a dignified manner, but part of his mind was on other things.

THINGS COULD BE WORSE

Ryan Baker and Meg Heunisch
May, 1634

Ryan Baker had gotten out of the army—stupid amount of paperwork involved with that, it turned out—and gone for a beer. Where he had found the girl. Magdalena. He called her Meg—Magdalena didn't come off his tongue well. Four hours later, he asked a little doubtfully, "Don't you need to go home, or something? Won't somebody be worried if you don't turn up? What about your mom and dad?"

She wasn't any more than five feet tall, if that. Narrow little shoulders; flat little chest; tiny little waist; a bit more in the way of hips, but not a lot. Now she crossed her arms on the table, put her chin on them, looked at the mug of beer he had bought her, and said, "Dead."

"Ah? Dead?"

"Father dead. I was little girl. Had stepfather. Dead when the soldiers came. Had brother. Dead when the soldiers came. Mother bigger than me. Strong. Worked hard. Stayed to fight the soldiers. Brave. Dead." She picked up the beer mug.

It was dawning on Ryan that there might be situations in the world worse than the one in which he found himself. He had never been particularly fond of Dayna Shockley, who had already been his stepmother for ten years as of the Ring of Fire. It wasn't that she was awful, but if Dad hadn't married her, he would never have talked to the woman. But his mother was left up-time, so there hadn't been much option except to move in with Dad and Dayna after the Ring of Fire until he finished high school.

He graduated in 1633, did his basic and one year in the full-time military, and really, really, didn't want to move back in with Dad and Dayna now that he was getting out and had a job as a trainee at the Grantville-Rudolstadt-Saalfeld Railroad and Tramway Corporation.

Meg was continuing. "Things maybe worse. Have little sister. Half-sister. Still alive. Lives with me. No—lives with Maria. I live with Maria. Maria is stepsister. All live in "refugee housing" with Maria's aunt. She is alive, too. She has two daughters still alive."

She lifted her chin. "Things maybe worse. If everybody else dead, much worse."

Ryan admired her for being so upbeat about it all.

"Maria's aunt not worry where I am. Too much work, too many girls, too busy. I am the end one to worry about."

Ryan put his arm about her shoulders, in what he intended to be a friendly and comforting manner. She cuddled her head against his neck. Her light brown hair was slick and smooth. He realized that he had a key to Mitch Hobbs' parents' empty house.

The next morning, she was quite friendly and cheerful. Which was good, all things considered. She'd been a virgin, and she might have gone all tearful on him. Instead, she climbed out of bed, fixed porridge, and said, "I go to work."

"Where?"

"Kitchen at Cora's. Peel vegetables. Peel fruits. Peel, wash, peel, scrub. Peel more." Her hands moved descriptively.

"Ah." Ryan paused. *What next?* "Ah, what time do you get off?"

"When done. Cora pays overtime." Meg beamed brightly.

"Ah. I'll be off first, then. If I come pick you up...."

He stopped rather awkwardly.

"We could go see Maria's aunt. Give her this address. Tell her where you're living now."

He wasn't one hundred percent sure of that, but he was pretty sure that Mitch wouldn't mind having him rent a couple of rooms. The upstairs in the Hobbs house had two bedrooms that you got to on a really narrow and steep staircase. Mitch probably wouldn't be using them after he got out. There was only one bath, and it was downstairs, but at least there was a bath. Some rent would help pay Mitch's taxes. And Meg would be a *really* good reason not to move back in with Dad and Dayna. Once Dayna found out.

He thought he'd tell Dad first. Maybe let Dad tell Dayna. When he wasn't there.

September, 1634

Maria Krause looked at her stepsister with exasperation. "You're urping in the morning because you're pregnant, that's what."

Meg nodded quite cheerfully. "Ja, okay."

"You're pregnant and you are *not* married."

"I told Ryan. He says we'll go to the *Rathaus* and get married right away. It's all okay." Meg was not about to admit to her stepsister that she had been happily surprised by her boyfriend's reaction to the news.

Walpurga Hercher said, "No!" Forcefully.

Maria looked at her reproachfully. "No? She is lucky that she will not be suffering for what she has done. Why not?"

"Because it won't help Teacher Muselius' project. Pastor Kastenmayer's project. Magdalena is one of us. We must make our husbands Lutheran for them. If Magdalena marries Ryan at the city hall, it won't help."

Maria's answer would have been better placed in the barnyard.

"She can always fall back on City Hall if he won't go along with it," Walpurga conceded.

* * *

Ryan was startled to discover that although Meg was (when not morning sick) as friendly, cheerful, and pleasant as ever, she didn't jump at the prospect of immediate marriage. Meg, truth to tell, would have preferred to jump at it, but she found Walpurga Hercher rather intimidating. So she said, "Want to marry by Pastor. See Teacher Muselius. You be Lutheran."

It was weird, really. Hugh Lowe, the big boss at work, had thought it was a good idea to see this Teacher Muselius. "You might as well find out what you're letting yourself in for, kid. Besides, they outnumber us. They're most of our customers. It can't hurt us to have an in with them, when we're looking for workers and supplies."

April, 1635

Ryan had quickly come to the conclusion that Pastor Kastenmayer moved through life at a stately pace. The confirmation instructions had been excruciatingly step-by-step. It looked like this wedding was going to be a prime example of what Hugh called just-in-time scheduling. Meg was so little, to start with. As the months went by, there had seemed to be more and more baby, with less and less Meg to go around it, like she was shrinking. He'd had the marriage license for three weeks, just in case she started popping before today. And he'd called the mayor, who had agreed to run over to the hospital and marry them off before the kid showed up, in an emergency.

He stood in the front of St. Martin's, his mind wandering as the liturgy flowed over him.

Dad and Dayna were here for the confirmation and wedding. Well, Dad came and dragged Dayna with him. They *never* went to church. Plus his sister Sam, who never went to church either. Plus Dayna's two kids. Plus, somehow, Dayna's ex, LeVan Jessup, and his wife, who was German and went to church here, plus her kid and their kid. Teacher Muselius had been glad to see them. He'd led them to one of the front pews; introduced them to several officers of the congregation.

If it's a little girl, Meg says she wants to name the kid for her mom. Heroically dead in the defense of Quittelsdorf and all that. Ottilia? *What do you call a kid named Ottilia? Ottie, nah. Tillie, well, maybe.*

At least she wants to call a boy after her brother, not her dad. David's better than Hermann any day. David's a sort of nice name....

Things could be a lot worse.

WE'RE ALL COUSINS, SOMEHOW

Derek Blount and Ursula Krause May, 1634

The circle around the Vandiver kitchen table looked at Margaretha's list. "*Die Krausin*" had outdone herself. Pastor Kastenmayer had expected her to select one up-time man per girl and start to arrange marriages. Two years of marriage to an up-timer had taught her that this would not work. She had a list with twice as many men as there were girls from Quittelsdorf. This had not been hard, even limiting herself to heathen men who were of a social class that might be expected to marry undowered girls such as these. Quittelsdorf had never been the largest of villages. By stretching the definition of "marriageable" from seventeen to thirty-five and including a widow, plus Rahel's stepsister who was not even from Quittelsdorf, her list of potential brides was still less than a dozen.

Ursel Krause was standing behind Margaretha, looking over her shoulder. Ursel's little sister Else, the youngest of them all, was standing on the other side of the table, looking mulish. There was a stubborn streak in Ursula and Elisabetha Krause. Of course, their mother was born Elisabetha Hercher. There was a stubborn streak in the Hercher family as a whole.

"I," Else said, "will not do it."

"You," said Margaretha, "have the best chance of all. You have had almost three years of school here. You speak English best. And," she paused to evaluate the possibilities, "you are prettiest."

In the words of the Lutheran catechism, "this was most certainly true." No voice rose to dispute this assessment. Else Krause had curly auburn hair and a set of teeth that a princess would envy. She also, thanks to the Grantville Chapter of the Red Cross, had a toothbrush and baking soda with which she cared for them.

Plus, Else, and Ursel, of course, since they were sisters, still had a mother to watch after her. "*Die Hercherin*" watched her own daughters a perceptible degree more carefully than she watched her husband's nieces, assorted more distant cousins, and the other girls who had fallen into her care since the day that Quittelsdorf burned to the ground and its fields disappeared. And she had let her own daughters stay in the up-time schools the longest. Too long, maybe.

"I know the one I want," said Else, "and he is not on your list, because he is not a heathen. A heretic, yes, but not a heathen. If I need to become a heretic to marry him, I will. Pastor Kastenmayer must do without me. That is final."

It turned out to be final.

Ursel, from behind Margaretha, reached down and put her finger on the list. She wasn't as pretty as Else—hair more a reddish brown than auburn, and straight; body a little less well proportioned; nose a little less perfectly suited to the face on which it found itself. "I know *him*," she said. "At least, I already know who he is. If I can have that one, I will do it. If not, not. I will not take a second choice from this list."

That turned out to be final, also. There was a *really* stubborn streak in the Herchers, and "*die Hercherin*" had passed it on to her daughters in full.

But, perhaps, it was not only that Hercher streak. Barbara Conrath, only three months older than Else Krause, also with a living mother, also with three years of school in Grantville since the Ring of Fire, said, "Not me, either." Then she grinned at Margaretha, making full use of her innocent round face, wrinkling her pug nose, and making dimples. "I get Benton. I know he's not on your list. 'Sorry, Pastor Kastenmayer,' and all that sort of thing. I'll make Benton go back to school and get his GED before I agree to marry him, though. Promise. *Schwiegermutter*." She threw her arms around *die Krausin*.

Margaretha was startled. Barbel would be a fine daughter-in-law, certainly. In eight or ten years. But the look in the girl's eye indicated that she was not announcing long-range plans. And her stepson was not on the list because he, like her own husband, was already a member of an up-time church.

She sighed. This was not going to be as simple as Pastor Kastenmayer expected.

* * *

Ursel Krause worked at the Freedom Arches. Not because of any commitment to the Committee of Correspondence's ideology nor, in fact, because she had even the slightest interest in it. She had applied for jobs in several inns and taverns. She picked this one because she liked the idea of staying behind a counter where the customers couldn't grope the rear end of the waitress. That was worth doing without "tips." Her mother had agreed.

Every morning she watched Derek Blount come in, get his breakfast, look up forlornly at the blank, black, screen in one corner where there was nothing on TV at this hour, reluctantly pick up the newspaper, and try to struggle his way through the front page. Finally, she realized that he had as hard a time reading it as she did. But??? He was an up-timer. He spoke English, after all. Why couldn't he read it?

Since she was still taking ESOL classes in the evening—that was why she worked the shift at the Freedom Arches that began at five o'clock in the morning—after several weeks of smiling at him (real smiles, not simply the "here's your order" smile), duly authorized by Pastor Kastenmayer and *die Krausin*, she asked him for help with her English....

June, 1634

By this time, of course, Magdalena Heunisch was living with Ryan Baker, so they would have met one another, anyway. As Ursel explained to Derek, "We are not all just from the same village. We are all cousins, somehow. I am not related to Meg, really. She is sort of out on the far end. But I am related to her little half-sister, Anna. On the Krause side of the family. Anna is my first cousin. So we are connected. And Mrs. Vandiver is my aunt on the Krause side, so her children are my cousins, too. And Lisbet and Walpurga are her first husband's nieces. Plus, they're my cousins on the Hercher side. Their dad was my mom's brother." She paused for breath.

Derek had followed this discourse without the slightest trouble. He thought that it was kind of nice. After all, lots of people in Grantville were one another's cousins, too. The town had been around for a long time. In addition to his brother Donnie and the two German boys his parents had adopted after the Battle of the Crapper, he had one first cousin on the Blount side who came through the Ring of Fire, and three on the Stewart side. Plus, Stew and Lesley had three kids; Cherilyn and Bob had one, plus, now, two German orphans they had adopted after the battle at Badenburg. Plus, he supposed, Pam's kids would get married one of these days. They were both working down at USE Steel toward Saalfeld and both dating a couple of Frenchies they had met there—Walloons, they called themselves.

That didn't count the Blount and Stewart cousins who had been left up-time.

Derek found it hard to imagine a world without cousins and family picnics. It was really nice that Ursel had a bunch of cousins, too. It sort of gave folks something in common. If you ran out of other things, you could always talk about what your cousins were doing. Especially what they had done that they shouldn't. Like Meg moving in with Ryan Baker.

That was where this conversation had started. Ursel's mom didn't approve. At all. Derek somehow figured that he could forget about lucking out the way Ryan had. At least, with Ursel. And, right now, he was dating Ursel. Which sort of meant that he could forget about.... He had a suspicion that he'd been given a message.

July, 1634

Derek drew a picture on the Formica table with his finger. He'd dropped by the Freedom Arches to see Ursel on her lunch break. He was out of the army now. Since yesterday. He'd been supposed to get out in May, with the other guys, but they'd asked him to stay a couple more months. He'd said okay, but that meant that he'd missed getting on the crews when the road work opened up in the spring. He'd have to go see Mickey Simmons, he guessed, he explained to Ursel. Mickey was doing the training for the Department of Transportation now. See if someone had dropped out. See if he could get on. Road work was about all he was good for, out of the army. Not having a diploma. And it paid pretty good.

"Why did you drop out? Doesn't your family go to school? When they could?"

Derek looked a little uncomfortable. "Actually, Dad does have a high school diploma. And he wasn't real happy about it when Donnie dropped out first, and then me."

"Well, why did you?" To Ursel, the question seemed reasonable enough. Her view of school was that it had been easier than work, any day. She had been glad, when they first came to Grantville, that the people had sent her back to school. And that her mother had let her go. This would not have been necessary. She had already been sixteen, old enough to leave school by Grantville's laws, and her family had needed money, certainly. And it had been not the regular classes for the up-time students her age, so she had not met many of them. But still.

"School is great." Ursel's endorsement of school was unrestrained. That was why she kept taking the classes three evenings each week. "If I could, I would go to school forever and ever and *ever*." She threw out her arms, as if embracing the whole Grantville school system at once.

"Ursel, first of all, you've got to understand. One thing, Dad's *always* had a job. He's never been unemployed, not once. But jobs are sort of scarce around here, so we moved a lot when I was growing up. Not a long ways, but from Grantville to Fairmont, to Shinnston, then back to Fairmont, then over to Clarksburg for a while, then back to Grantville. May have been a couple more in there, but I remember those. So Donnie and me—we changed schools every time. Every time, the classes were doing something that wasn't exactly what we'd been doing before."

He looked down. "I can't read, Ursel. Not really. I can make out some words, but not to sit down and read something all the way through. So I couldn't catch up when we moved. If I stayed in a class long enough, I could pick up what the teacher said and do pretty good in the class discussions. Good enough to squeak by, even if I bombed every test. Which I did. But it got harder and harder. I was flunking junior year flat. So I quit."

"Dad? Well, he couldn't really say much about it—not too much—without upsetting Mom. She's a dropout, too, see. And we were no good in school, Donnie and me. We're no good."

He went back to drawing on the Formica, not looking at her. "You ought to forget about me, Ursel. Take yourself back to school. Go all the way. Be a teacher. You could, you know. Then you could be in school "forever and ever and *ever*." Forget about me. I'm a loser."

July, 1634

Derek sighed. He should never have mentioned teaching to Ursel. Never.

She had not forgotten about him. She had announced, "If I have learned it, you can learn it. The same way."

She had kept every damn work sheet from the remedial-and-ESOL program at the middle school. Every damn one of them. He wondered where she had found to put them, given how crowded the refugee housing was. She said that she had tied them in a bundle with string and hung them from a wooden hook that she nailed to the ceiling.

After a day working road construction for twelve hours, a guy didn't want to go to school. But a guy did want to see Ursel. And, on the nights she didn't go to class, there she was. Waiting at the Freedom Arches. With work sheets.

And, after the first week, with other stuff. On her lunch break, she had marched over to the police department, found Mel Richards, who had been her first teacher here in Grantville, and somehow got a whole set of lesson plans.

Then after the second week, she was waiting there with Mel. Mel was the child protection officer now, but she still had that teacherly look in her eye. And a stack of stuff. "Look, Derek, I didn't get that degree in special education for nothing. It's just diagnostics. We're going to find out what's the problem. It's likely a learning disability, since Donnie has it, too, Ursel tells me. Bring him tomorrow, if he'll come."

Donnie came. Partly because he had this thing for Britney Yardley, and she had a high school diploma plus a VoTech course. She was assistant to the lab technician at the methanol plant. He didn't think that a loser was in her plans. But mainly because they were meeting at the Freedom Arches. He had promised himself, the day he dropped out, that he was never going to go inside a school building again. He could handle talking to a teacher, but no way was he going back to school.

Mel Richards could live with that. There were a lot of people around who had had a bad experience with school. She had a little talk with Andy Yost and the Grantville Committee of Correspondence.

October, 1634

It wasn't a school. No way. It was an extra room, added onto the Freedom Arches. No school desks, no teacher's desk, no looming shelves full of threatening books. You could bring in your food; bring in your drinks. No schedules. Regular tables and benches. Everybody did his own thing, when he had the time. Mel came in the evenings, after work, and wandered around, apparently sort of aimlessly. She'd sit down a few minutes, first at this table, then at that one.

Ursel practically lived at the Freedom Arches, now, except for the three afternoons and nights she went to school. From five in the morning till two in the afternoon, she dished up food. From three in the afternoon until the place closed at midnight, she dished up work sheets.

And happiness. Since the day that Quittelsdorf died, her brothers Hans and Conrad along with it, she had never been so happy.

Until Walpurga Hercher reminded her sternly that she was supposed to be turning Derek Blount into a Lutheran, not teaching him to read his own language.

That night, she cried herself to sleep. When Derek came in for breakfast the next morning, her eyes were still bright red. She was so miserable. He could see it. "Hey, Ursel, what's wrong?" He'd never seen her like this.

Ursel looked at the morning manager, said, "Deal with it," came out into the restaurant part, threw herself into Derek's arms, and in the middle of many more tears, told him. Pastor Kastenmayer and *die Krausin*'s list and Teacher Muselius and catching husbands to make them Lutheran and all of it. It was a full confession. Ursel was spilling a really big bag of beans. Derek was glad that he had on his flannel shirt. It was a lot more absorbent than a cotton tee would have been. A tee would have been drenched and once this was over he had to go back out into the chilly October wind and build a road.

Ursel cried herself out.

Derek said, "Aw, kid. Tell you what. Bring me this Shorter Catechism thingie. If I can read it now, I'll go talk to your teacher guy."

He could read it. Sort of. Not without Ursel's help, but he could read it.

The best thing, though, after he talked to the teacher guy, was that he found out that he wasn't really expected to read it. To memorize it, but not necessarily to read it. It would be fine if Ursel read it out loud to him and he memorized it that way.

Ursel reading out loud was almost as good as TV.

April, 1635

So here he was, about to be confirmed and married. With all his family watching. Not just Mom and Dad, but Donnie and Britney, too. Britney wasn't a church member anywhere, either. Plus all the cousins. Pastor Kastenmayer and the teacher had been real interested in talking about cousins—that Cherilyn didn't go to church, and Bob had been brought up Catholic, but he had lapsed. Lapsed Catholics sort of appealed to Pastor Kastenmayer, it seemed. He thought that lapsing was a good thing for a Catholic to do. The pastor seemed willing to live with the fact that Mom's sisters were Presbyterian, and Mom was the only one who had dropped out of the Presbyterian church because Dad wouldn't go with her.

Teacher Muselius was standing there, a little to the side, watching the whole pew full of people. He looked more like a cat about to pounce than anything else Derek could think of.

Derek didn't think that reading was ever going to be his thing, but Mickey had promised him a promotion once he finished his GED. That meant that Ursel could go back to school full time after they were married.

Ursel would make a great teacher, some day.

They could have lots of picnics and family reunions, with all the cousins there. Their kids would have lots of cousins. On both sides of the family. He hadn't been exactly wild about the Ring of Fire, but things could have turned out a lot worse.

A REALLY GLOOMY TUNE

Errol Mercer and Elisabetha Hercher
Late June 1634

Walpurga had an almost irresistible impulse to clean something. The several months of neglect that the poor house had suffered between the deaths of Mitch Hobbs' mother and father had not been helped by a couple more months with Ryan and Magdalena (how Walpurga hated that "Meg" nickname Ryan had given her) living there, and certainly not by the addition of two other young ex-soldiers.

She had heard that the army of the New United States required that soldiers keep their things neat. Why did this custom not extend to soldiers who returned to civilian life? *Was it her problem to figure out the mystery? Probably not.* She sipped at her mug of beer.

In one corner, her sister Lisbet was demonstrating something to the young man with the brass musical instrument.

"To dance to." Lisbet stamped her feet. "Dance like this. Can you play it?"

She grabbed three of the other girls and they linked arms. First to the right; stomp. Then to the left; stomp. Move in; stomp. Move out; stomp. Village dances had little in common with the elaborate patterns of the court dances. The Hobbs house was far from new; the living room quivered under the impact of the girls' sturdy shoes. Walpurga winced. *The floor, the poor floor.*

Errol Mercer was grinning. "Yes, lady, I can play it. If you want me in your band, I'm in." He put the clarinet to his lips.

"Yes, sir, that's my baby;
No sir, I don't mean maybe;
Yes, sir, that's my baby now."

Stomp, stomp, turn and stomp, stomp; stomp, stomp, turn and stomp, stomp; move in, turn and stomp, stomp, stomp. Ursel Krause grabbed Derek Blount and pulled him into the pattern. Lisbet clapped with utter glee.

Every Lutheran wedding in Grantville. She promised it to herself. Well, maybe not every one. Probably not if the pastor's other daughter got married, and maybe not the up-time Lutherans. But most of them, definitely most of them. This up-timer would be able to play every dance tune she knew, dragging the rest of her little band along with him.

By early August, the dance band was getting bookings. Errol, on the theory that the lady was the boss, had firmly resisted all impulses to lay hand on Lisbet. Hitting on the boss would bring a guy nothing but trouble. His day jobs had never been anything to write home about—bagging groceries back home in Fairmont before he got caught up in the Ring of Fire; then two years as a soldier; now back in Grantville, basically as a stock clerk at Garrett's Supermarket. At least it worked with the band. Play in the evening; go to work after the dance; stay as long as it took to get the stuff out on the shelves for the next day, sleep, rehearse or play in the evening; repeat. So he wasn't setting the world on fire—it beat blowing himself up with explosives, which had been his other post-army job offer.

By the end of the month, when the regular school term was about to start, the group—it had become a regular *Stammtisch*—kept meeting at the Hobbs house; Lisbet's new band kept rehearsing there. The mothers and stepmothers who had survived the evacuation of Quittelsdorf didn't really like these gatherings, but then they wouldn't really have liked the barn dances and *Spinnstuben* the girls would have been attending with the Quittelsdorf boys back home, either. That's what mothers and stepmothers were for: to put on gloomy faces and look disapproving. Walpurga sighed. *How did they expect the girls to get these men as husbands for Pastor Kastenmayer's project if they didn't spend time with them?*

At Tuesday's rehearsal, Lisbet looked at Errol and announced, "I need a new tune. A really gloomy tune."

"Gloomy?"

"Yes. Like this one, but new." Lisbet launched into a series of musical notes that Errol, if he had happened to be Presbyterian, would have recognized as "Old 124th" from the 1551 Genevan Psalter. Since he was totally innocent of all connection with any established religious body, he shrugged and nodded his agreement that it was indeed a really gloomy tune. He picked up his clarinet and played along a bit.

"Mitch, this isn't a clarinet piece. Didn't I see a sax back there in the rec room one day?"

"Yeah, but I can't play it. That was my brother Arvie's. Ain't been played since he got out of band."

"*You* don't need to play it, man. I need to play something gloomy on it. I'm no sax player, but I can finger it."

Sax? Did that have anything to do with the Saxons? Meg Heunisch found that living with Ryan Baker perpetually confronted her with new and perplexing questions. The "sax" appeared in Walpurga's hands, bright and gleaming (she had polished it the week before), and turned out to be another brass musical instrument.

Errol started fingering it, leaning against the right arm of the sofa and propping his boots up on the coffee table. Walpurga cleared her throat in a meaningful manner.

Errol didn't exactly ignore her—he didn't even notice her. He hitched the lanyard over his neck to help him hold the weight, placed the sax next to his knees (its bell extended to his right in front of the sofa, almost to the floor), put it to his lips and started to produce a really gloomy tune.

He pulled it out of his mouth and started to make a rude comment about, "how long has it been since anybody took care of this mouthpiece?" when he was severely jolted. The lanyard, thank heavens, kept him from dropping the sax. He found that he had a lap full of Lisbet, who was enthusiastically hugging and kissing him. It wasn't a particularly erotic hug and kiss but provided him with full opportunity to determine that every one of her rounded curves was quite solid and not in the least flabby. She was deluging him with German, of which he got only, "*wunderbar.*"

Then, without further verbal communication, he was being dragged by the hand out of the house and down the road toward St. Martin's in the Fields Lutheran Church. Which was okay, given how long it stayed light at night around here in summer, even without Daylight Saving Time. They went around the church, up to one of the teachers' cottages, and Lisbet banged on the door.

Jonas Justinus Muselius could hardly believe it. The tune was perfect for the new hymn he had written, which the children of the school would perform. It was not too complex for them. It was not pitched too high, which had a tendency to cause untrained voices to squeak. It was ideal. Herr Mercer should play it with them, of course. But a musician was expected to be a member of the church. Perhaps Pastor Kastenmayer would make an exception in this case, however. A potential catechumen. A potential fiancé. A potential convert. He laid out his argumentation in the classic debate form as he hummed.

September, 1634

The treble voices of the first through fourth graders lifted at the early morning service.

We're sorry;
Sorry for our sins;
Sorry we have done so wrong.

Errol Mercer on the saxophone carried them along, as the strains of "Moon River" rose to the bare rafters of St. Martin's in the Fields.

During the weeks after the children performed the hymn, Errol experienced a blinding revelation. Down-time Lutherans hired church musicians. They actually paid them.

He also discovered that singing a hymn to "Begin the Beguine" was no challenge at all to a congregation that could produce "A Mighty Fortress Is Our God" in its original irregular meter, *a capella*, if need be.

St. Martin's didn't have an organ yet. It was delighted to have a clarinet and sax.

He stopped by the school every morning, after he got off at Garrett's. "*Jesus liebt mich, dass weiss ich.*" He was no church lady, but everybody knew how to play "Jesus loves me." It went over real good, too. "*Du bist mein Jesus, mein liebster Jesus.*" Muselius wrote that one new for the kids, after Errol played, "You Are My Sunshine" for him.

Lisbet said, though, that *full-time* church musicians must be qualified. First, that they must be Lutheran.

That, Errol figured, was doable. Muselius, the teacher, said that it was doable. He furnished Errol with a copy of the Shorter Catechism in English (he had forethoughtfully had a hundred of them printed in Jena, from a copy borrowed from Gary Lambert).

Church musicians must also, Lisbet said, be learned. He should return to school and get his GED. All boards of church elders were impressed by pieces of paper showing academic qualifications.

He was less enthusiastic about that prospect.

But she kissed him.

Going back to school would be a lot more work than stocking shelves.

She kissed him again. "Going back to school will be one year. Stocking shelves can go on forever. Do you want to do that?"

She kissed him a third time. "Or do you want to get paid for your music? More than our little band pays?"

By this time, Errol had a fiancée. He also had a sax, having traded his late grandmother's engagement ring with its tiny diamond to Mitch for it (at the time of the Ring of Fire, he had been wearing it in his left ear; the army made him take it out and the hole had closed up). Lisbet agreed fully that it was more important to have a sax than to have an engagement ring. Errol was therefore quite certain that Lisbet would be a perfect wife.

Lisbet would have been less sanguine about the trade if the result hadn't been that the ring went to Mitch. However, she assumed that if all went as one could reasonably expect, pretty soon Walpurga would get the ring, and Walpurga was, after all, her sister. But she didn't see any need to mention that.

March, 1635

Errol set Jonas' new Good Friday hymn to "Mood Indigo." It caused a sensation. Well, at least it caused a sensation in the Lutheran churches of Grantville, Badenburg, Rudolstadt, and Saalfeld, plus assorted villages in between.[7]

April, 1635

Errol obediently recited memorized passages from the *Shorter Catechism* in reply to Pastor Kastenmayer's questioning. In between, looking at the line-up while the other guys said their parts, he started to wish that he had never played in that "golden oldies" band in Fairmont before the Ring of Fire, because he was having trouble keeping his face straight. He couldn't help suspecting that any minute now, Howard

---

[7]It wasn't performed in Jena, Weimar, Stadtilm, Ilmenau, Arnstadt, Eisenach, Erfurt, and Suhl until the following penitential season. By 1636, it had reached Strassburg, Nürnberg, Leipzig, Königsberg, Copenhagen, and Stockholm See: Muselius, Jonas Justinus. *New Directions in Lutheran Church Music* (Jena, 1637).

Keel's voice would start rolling in with the music from "Seven Brides for Seven Brothers."

He wondered how a performance of that would go over with the down-timers. He thought he remembered all the tunes. And they had seven brides. It was lucky the numbers had come out even. Things could have turned out a lot worse.

WHAT NEXT?

Mitch Hobbs and Walpurga Hercher
June - October, 1633

Walpurga Hercher worked at the MaidenFresh Laundries. That was her regular job and she liked it, even if the boss did yell at her for wanting to stop and remove every little spot and tiny stain. "Not commercially feasible," Frau Rawls said. "Look, girl. Get it in, get it washed, get it out. If they wanted that kind of finicky care, they would hire their personal laundress."

Walpurga found it distressing. She would like for every piece of clothing to come out of the tubs exactly the way it should be. But Frau Rawls was the boss. Some day she would have her own house. With her own washing machine. And her laundry would be perfect.

Once upon a time, she had not been a "refugee." She had not been a plain village girl, either. When she was fourteen years old, she had gone into service in the town of Rudolstadt, as a maid in the household of the second *Bürgermeister*, no less. She had learned about tile floors and chairs with legs that had been turned on lathes. She had stayed until the week before Lent in 1631, when her father brought her home and betrothed her to Wilhelm Conrath. His father had died the year before the Ring of

Fire; Wilhelm was the only child and needed a wife for the farm. It would have been a good match; they would have married in the summer. Now Wilhelm was dead, and she was a "refugee" in Grantville, along with her sister, her aunt, and various cousins.

They always needed money, of course. There was rent. With so many of them, they needed a lot of food. Living in a city, if you needed more food, you could not go out to the garden and pull some more. You had to pay for it right away. Walpurga had decided that Garrett's Supermarket was best, so she shopped there.

She always took extra jobs, when she found them. The Hobbs job was on the "bulletin board." A woman was sick. Her husband wanted a cleaning lady, once a week. Walpurga gathered all of her recommendations and applied. They were all glowing. She had learned a lot during her years in Rudolstadt. When Walpurga Hercher set out to clean something, she *cleaned* it. Herr Hobbs, "Call me Joe," hired her.

Frau Hobbs, "Call me Gloria," looked really sick. But she was not too sick to stop worrying about a dirty house. Not in the summer.

It was an old house, the way the up-timers saw things. Not big, really. Not too big for a single servant to clean. Downstairs, a "living room," a "dining room," the kitchen, the bath, a funny room on the side, an "old porch" Frau Hobbs called it, that they had surrounded with walls and windows, that they called the "rec room." Two bedrooms. Upstairs, on a steep little staircase that started in the pantry, there were two more rooms under the roof. But the carved woodwork. The hardwood parquet floors. The beautiful ceilings with designs on the squares.

Frau Hobbs wanted her to run the vacuum over the surface and clean up the kitchen and bathroom. That was all. But the treasure trove in the kitchen cabinet and the pantry. The waxes, the polishes, the "spray bottles" with their magical contents. While Frau Hobbs was resting, Walpurga had managed to get some of the house really clean. The two rooms upstairs; the staircase; the extra bedroom downstairs. The ones that the gentleman and lady didn't look into any more. They were almost perfect by the time she was done.

In September, Frau Hobbs was too sick to care. In October she died.

Joe Hobbs didn't care about the house, any more. He thought that he was letting the cleaning lady go. He did not know that he was breaking a heart and ending a passionate affair. Walpurga mourned her lost love deeply.

April, 1634

Pastor Kastenmayer was thinking about payback.

Walpurga was reading the obituaries in the *Grantville Times*. Herr Hobbs, "call me Joe," was dead. The house? Walpurga's heart leaped. Would someone who wanted a cleaner live in the house now? "Survived by his parents, Ken and Ada Hobbs. Survived by one son, Mitch, serving in the army of the New United States, and two sons, Arvie and Burt, who were left up-time."

She read carefully. She compared it to other obituaries. She had Else and Ursel and Barbel, who read English much better than she did, compare it to other obituaries. There was no mention that this Mitch had a wife. There was no mention that Herr and Frau Hobbs had grandchildren.

If God were gracious, this Mitch would want his house cleaned.

However, it seemed that this Mitch was still somewhere else with the army. He had told his grandparents to lock the place up until he got out in a couple of months. Walpurga found that out. She knew who Ada Hobbs was. She talked to Ada Hobbs sometimes when she bought food at Garrett's Supermarket. She mentioned to Ada Hobbs that she had cleaned the house, last summer, for "Call me Gloria."

Ada, who had not been looking forward to dealing with the mess that Joe had left behind during his last six morose months, hired her to clean it again.

It was a wonderful reunion. She had the house all to herself for three whole days. But the kitchen was a mess and the bathroom was worse. She had to scrape gooey stuff off the beautiful "linoleum" with a "putty knife," before she could even mop it. She hadn't had time to even start making the living room and dining room and the bedroom that Herr and Frau Hobbs had used perfect. She had hardly touched the "rec room."

May, 1634

The name was on *die Krausin*'s list. Walpurga saw it. Neatly printed, right there on the Vandivers' kitchen table. Mitch Hobbs.

Walpurga promised herself that she would never be impatient during a church service again. She would never complain that Pastor Kastenmayer prayed too long, or preached too long, or reviewed the catechism too long. She would never complain that they sang too many verses of too many hymns. She would never try to skip church on Sunday. Maybe, she would even go on Wednesday. Perhaps, she would even attend Teacher Muselius' catechism review classes for adults on Saturdays.

Maybe all of them should go to church more diligently and take communion more frequently.

It was clear to Walpurga that Pastor Kastenmayer had, as the up-timers said, a "direct line" to God.

Walpurga was not at all sure that having Magdalena Heunisch live with this Ryan Baker in the upper two rooms of the Hobbs house counted as Divine Providence. After all, they were not married. And Magdalena was not a neat cook. Still, it ensured that she would meet this Mitch, even if he did not want a cleaning lady.

June, 1634

Mitch thought it was really weird to be sleeping in his parents' bedroom. But that was how it had worked out. He had Ryan and his Meg upstairs, where he'd been living himself before the Ring of Fire. He was renting the other downstairs bedroom to Errol Mercer, right now. Once Derek Blount got out, he and Errol would go shares on that room. The bunk beds had been in there, and it didn't seem worthwhile to do all the heaving and hauling to switch the beds around. So here he was in a double bed in his folks' room. All by himself. Once he found a job, the money end ought to be okay. But he didn't know what he wanted to do. Not go back to hauling human manure for O'Keefe's, that was sure. He hadn't been sorry to quit that job three years ago when the army had called for every able-bodied guy who could be spared. He hadn't wanted to re-up, either—couldn't figure out why Lew Jenkins and Jim Fritz did. It was the reserves for good old Mitch, from here on.

But he didn't know what he was going to do next. There weren't a lot of choices, even in a boom town, when you were a dropout. But he was not going back to O'Keefe's. That much, he knew for sure.

* * *

Walpurga watched Lisbet and the Mercer man in the corner of the living room, fooling with the musical instruments. It was strange, being in the house with so many people. She felt like she ought to be cleaning something. Her fingers practically twitched.

Between the times when she watched them, she watched Mitch Hobbs.

Who said that he was looking for a job.

She had heard her boss say it so often, to people came through the laundry. To people from whom she was trying to get "investment capital." Frau Rawls wanted to go away from Grantville, build more and more MaidenFresh Laundries in other cities. The boss wanted to move to Magdeburg. Her mouth opened. "MaidenFresh Laundries is a growth industry. Anyone who gets in on the ground floor will make his fortune."

The rest of them stared at her. She ran through the rest of the spiel. She didn't even know that she knew it all. It even sounded like Frau Rawls, the way she said it. Then she blushed and said in her normal tone of voice. "My boss wants to go to Magdeburg. She will need a manager for the laundry here in Grantville. Ask her. Frau Vesta Rawls."

What was that girl's name, anyway? Mitch asked himself. What he said was, "They don't hire dropouts to manage businesses."

"You have been in the army. Your grandmother works at a business, at the supermarket. I know her. Your grandfather is in the UMWA, and that means that he knows the important people. You can go back to school. And clean laundry is important. Very important."

It turned out that Walpurga had memorized another spiel from listening to it so often. This was Frau Rawls' "sanitation prevents widespread epidemics and will save many lives" talk. She delivered the whole thing.

A sister less exuberantly extroverted than Lisbet would probably have been deeply humiliated. Even Lisbet was looking a little surprised. What would Walpurga say next?

Walpurga was saying, "Come tomorrow. I will introduce you."

* * *

Vesta Rawls was a little doubtful. But Mitch was a vet; they owed the vets. And Ken Hobbs' grandson. Not to mention that anybody vouched for by that spot and stain fanatic Walpurga was bound to be the right sort to take an interest in laundry, she guessed. Though he had never shown any sign of it before the Ring of Fire. Maybe the army had matured him.

"I'll try you as my assistant manager. Three months probation. If you're catching on, then I'll try you as temporary manager when I go up to Arnstadt for a month. If that works, then for six months temporary while I go up to Magdeburg. But get yourself out to the VoTech Center this afternoon. You're going to have to learn bookkeeping, at a minimum."

September, 1634

The minimum of bookkeeping had turned into a whole GED. Mitch wasn't sure how, but first he had talked to the business teacher, and the business teacher had talked to the adult education coordinator, and the adult education coordinator had talked to someone in the superintendent's office. They had all agreed that he could finish in a year, in his spare time. It was a done deal before he could even open his mouth. Listening to them, he had an awful feeling that the concept of "spare time" had gone flying out the window. Where was the idea of spending his evenings nursing a beer in the Thuringian Gardens, eyeing the girls? He had dreamed of that, while he was still in the army.

Instead.... He was increasingly aware that he was still sleeping single in that double bed. He also was developing this strange suspicion that Walpurga Hercher intended that he should keep right on sleeping single in that double bed. Meg lived in the house, of course and her sister Lisbet spent a lot of a time there, rehearsing with her band. So Walpurga had plenty of excuses to be there. Talk about having your own personal chaperone. Any other girl he brought in, somehow, only came once. And never got anywhere near the bedroom.

February, 1635

It was ten o'clock at night. There was something wrong with the books, which Mitch discovered at six o'clock in the evening. He had stayed late at MaidenFresh, and then later. He had pulled out his textbook from the VoTech Center. Finally tracked it down. Then started to fix it. Finished fixing it. Management wasn't all it was cracked up to be.

The house was pretty near empty. Ryan and Meg were upstairs, he guessed—the lights were on. Derek was probably over at the Freedom Arches with Ursel. He'd passed Errol on his way in, walking Lisbet home. He'd not bother to eat. Not bother with a shower. Just drop into bed. He walked into the bedroom and...Walpurga was what?

In his bed. Well, standing on it. Fully clothed.

"What on earth are you doing?"

She blushed. "Putting furniture polish on the headboard of your bed." She caressed the wooden curlicues. "It is so beautiful. I want it to be perfect."

He had never thought of Walpurga as sensuous before. All of a sudden, other things that people might want to have be perfect flashed through his mind. In connection with Walpurga.

Well, maybe it was not perfect. But it had been very, very, nice.

During the months while Walpurga had been watching Mitch to make sure that he did not make an unfortunate choice of a wife ("unfortunate" being defined in her mind as "anybody else"), she had also been watching Mitch. She had concluded that marrying this man would be no hardship at all on his wife. Her reaction to his new initiative had been quite cooperative. Now she rolled over and started to play with the hair on his chest, twisting it around her finger into neat little ringlets. "On Sunday," she said, "I will tell Pastor Kastenmayer that we are betrothed and arrange for you to start confirmation class."

"*We are?*" Luckily, he hadn't said that out loud.

He thought a minute. He had a really strong feeling that if they weren't betrothed, this wasn't going to happen again. Not with Walpurga. His body was hinting that it really should happen again. Preferably fairly soon. Walpurga finished the first row of little ringlets and started on the second. He had a vague recollection that down-time girls were perfectly happy to sleep with their fiancés. His body filed a memo to the effect that whatever might be going on up at headquarters, at least one regional office voted in favor of getting betrothed to Walpurga Hercher.

"Where's your dad working?" he asked. Her mom had died three or four years before the Ring of Fire, but he knew that her father was around somewhere, one of the few men who had survived the massacre at Quittelsdorf. Because he'd gone to Rudolstadt, that day, to sell a donkey. Come back to find the bodies. Dug the mass grave by the burned-out church. Looked for the survivors for six weeks, before he found them.

But he hadn't stayed in Grantville, even though old Matthias Dornheimer had wanted him to. Walpurga's dad would never start over, not now. He had hired out as a hand on a farm, somewhere. Not too far away. "We probably ought to look him up and tell him, too."

"He is in Lichstedt. He is working for old Johann Pflaum. I will ask Arnold to tell him. Pastor Kastenmayer didn't see how he could possibly get this young man ready for confirmation by April. He was starting much later than the rest of the class. They were many lessons ahead of him.

"His grandfather," Muselius said, fighting not to clench his teeth, "is in the UMWA. Trust me. I'll get him there."

On one of the nastiest days that February weather could offer, Pastor Ludwig Kastenmayer, in a downtown storefront, specifically in the Laughing Laundress, owned by Vesta Rawls and currently managed by Mitch Hobbs, as of recent days another of St. Martin's current up-timer fiancés, confirmands-in-the-making and would-be grooms, baptized Viana Beasley, daughter of Jarvis Beasley and Hedwig Altschulerin.

In a storefront, because Hedy, the focus of a major jurisdictional controversy between the State of Thuringia-Franconia and Saxony over the validity and status of her marriage, had been strongly advised by Judge Maurice Tito not to leave the boundaries of Grantville in West Virginia County for the time being.

St. Martin's in the Fields was outside the ring, in the SoTF, but in the County of Schwarzburg-Rudolstadt. This part of the County of Schwarzburg-Rudolstadt. There was another fragment of it up north of Erfurt.

The same way that Count Ludwig Guenther's cousin, who was the head of the County of Schwarzburg-Sondershausen, had a piece of land down here, over west of the Schwarzburg castle.

The newspaper published a notice of the baptism.

Pankratz Holz, who was running his own storefront church Lutheran operation in Grantville, published a series of outraged pamphlets.

April, 1635

Mitch didn't have this stuff down anywhere near as pat as the rest of them. He was glad that they were reciting a bunch of it in unison. He mumbled. In a pinch, he looked at Walpurga, who was sitting in a pew angled sideways to most of the rest, mouthing the words.

"We believe that the Holy Spirit proceeds from the Father and the Son...."

"We do? Do I believe that? Must have gone over it pretty fast in class. God of Walpurga, if you're out there somewhere, watching this, remind me again. What's the Holy Spirit and why do I care who he proceeds from? Whom? She? It? No offense meant."

Walpurga had assured him that it would be fine. Once he got the management of Grantville MaidenFresh Laundries down pat, they could go to Teacher Muselius' catechism review classes on Saturday afternoons and he could go through it all again, more slowly.

"He could? Ye gods! What next? Oh, well. Things could probably be worse."

AND SOME ON STONY GROUND

Lew Jenkins and Sabina Ottmar April, 1632

Sabina Ottmar picked up the ten-gallon milk can easily, swinging it onto the bed of the truck. And the next, and the next. Her heavy skirts matched the rhythm of her muscular arms. The last one in, she fastened the back of the "pickup" in place with a stick rammed through the broken latch and called, "okay," to the driver. He took off for town. She went into the milk shed to clean up. If she worked fast, it would be done before lunch.

Sabina loved her new job at the dairy goat farm of Mr. and Mrs. Manning Booth. She had to remember that. Mrs. Booth. Up-time women had the name of their husbands. There was so much to remember. She pulled the kerchief off her hair, re-tied it, and started to wash and sterilize the jugs that the truck had brought back from town. The kettles of water boiling on the wood-burning stove were heavy, but she could handle them. She knew that many people laughed at her looks, but if you were Sabina Ottmar, it was good to be tall and strong. You had work to do, and no one else would do it for you.

It was good that this work was so fine. The Booths treated her as a fully qualified dairy maid and paid her accordingly. She had a room of her own. She ate at their table. It was more than she had ever hoped for.

* * *

Sabina had never heard of a totem pole and probably never would. But if there had been one in the village of Keilhau, her family would have been at the bottom of it. By the time Sabina was old enough to remember, her father had been a landless day-laborer. He had once had his share of the lease, true enough, but had lived as such a wastrel that he had been forced to sell it -back to his brother. Then he had died, when she was only five. He had been drunk, of course. He choked on his food.

Her oldest brother, Heinrich, was twenty, then. He had been a hard-enough worker—still was, for that matter. But he was in service to another farmer. He scarcely earned his own keep. Not enough to support a mother, a quite young brother who was simple, and a sister much too small to be sent to work. Her second oldest brother—carefully, she walked to the outside of the milk shed and spat, where it would not mess the "sterilization" of the jugs.

Good riddance that he had gone for a soldier. Too bad that he had taken his miserable wife and children with him. Lucky he left before their mother remarried—otherwise he would have stayed, trying to get money from her.

They had eaten, after her father died, on the charity of others. When she was twelve, she had gone into service herself. For little wages, so young, and the daughter of Martin Ottmar the drunkard. The worst of the work; the worst of the beds; the worst of the food.

The worst of the hired men.

God was merciful, however. He proved it. She was barren.

Seven years after that, her mother had made a fortunate marriage into Quittelsdorf. Old Matthias Dornheimer, twice widowed already, wanted a housekeeper. But he was a respectable man who would have no breath of scandal. He picked a woman past childbearing and married her with all the banns called. He had taken in his simple stepson (who also was his godson, and to whom, thus, he owed a duty). But he had seen no reason to take in a stepdaughter who could work.

By then, though, Sabina had reached her full growth. Scarecrow thin, but tall. Arms and shoulders formed by the hardest of work in the barns and with the cattle.

Strong enough to take care of herself.

And treated kindly by her stepsister, the well-placed daughter of a prosperous farmer. Not loved, exactly, but not scorned. That had been, perhaps, God's kindest grace of all, that Rahel did not treat her as a slut. Though she must have known the things that had happened, at least by report. In a village, everybody did, of course. Keilhau was not far from Quittelsdorf.

Sabina's meditations continued. It was good to be working for the Booths. The cleaning crew in Grantville had not been bad, but she was glad that the girl on the other farm, Staci Ann Beckworth she was called, had told her about this job. She would be quite happy to remain in service on this farm for the rest of her life.

April, 1634

Lew Jenkins had never been married; never wanted to be. He had been living with Staci Ann Beckworth, though, back when. Not that her parents were happy about it, but she'd been going through some kind of spasm about being adopted.

Then the Ring of Fire.

It seemed that people thought that he was a perfect example of the kind of able-bodied man who could be spared to enlist full-time in the army. They broke up. Well, after he went into the army, she couldn't afford to keep up the rent on the trailer, not with what she was earning as a waitress at Cora's, and moved back in with her parents. Then she got notions, finished her GED, learned German, married a German farmer. Lew was pretty sure the guy had ambitions. Arnold Pflaum, his name was. Plummy. President of the Grange, he was now. Hadn't hurt him a bit to marry an up-time girl.

Of course, he was also wearing his feet off right up to the knees, running those farms. Farming sure wasn't a life that Lew had ever wanted. The army suited him fine.

Some of the guys in the army complained about latrine duty. Hell, before the Ring of Fire, Lew had worked for O'Keefe's. Every damn day was latrine duty when your job was pumping septic tanks and catchment basins. In the army, at least, you had some days that weren't.

Today, for example. He went back to work. Whole barrels of uniforms had arrived, with no sizes on them. And, once they had opened a few, no consistent sizing within each barrel. He was holding each piece up against cardboard cutouts of three different sizes of soldiers; then folding them into three different piles. He got to decide which of the three guys they would most likely fit best.

"*Responsibility Jenkins, that's me.*" He grinned. He even refrained from deliberately mixing up the piles with one another.

His sister Bernita would be proud of him if she knew.

May, 1634

Walpurga Hercher looked at the list of possible husbands that "*die Krausin*" had drawn up for the Quittelsdorf girls. She put her finger on Lew Jenkins' name and asked, quite simply, "Why?"

Margaretha Vandiver, once upon a time "*die Krausin*," looked a little defensive and said, "His sister."

"His *sister*?"

"Yes." The older woman reached across the table and tapped the name on the slate. "Mrs. Walsh, the clerk at the post office, is his sister."

Walpurga reflected once more on the utter absurdity of this custom of a woman's giving up her own perfectly good name for that of her husband (and possibly, should she be widowed, for that of another husband, and yet another—how ridiculous). It made it practically impossible to tell how people were related. Had not God himself in the Bible said that Mary was the wife of Joseph? Not that she was Mrs. Joseph? Walpurga had no intention at all of changing her name when she married.

Margaretha was continuing. "They are good jobs, in the post office. Jobs that Germans can do. Just to read the addresses. It is easier for us to read the up-time handwriting than for the up-timers to read ours. To sort the mail, take the mail to where it goes. These can be done by people who do not have the strength for the mines or making the roads. We need to always know when there is a vacancy. Before they put up the hiring notice. To make sure that the best people are ready to apply. These are extremely fine jobs." She paused. "And he meets what Pastor Kastenmayer asked for. He is not a constant drunkard, not a brawler, not a lazy lout who will expect his wife to support him."

"He does not have a house. He does not even have a 'trailer.' He lives in the barracks for the army. He does not earn enough to support children." Walpurga wasn't even nearly finished with her litany of Lew Jenkins' defects as a potential husband.

Rahel Dornheimer looked up, motioned with her hand, and asked, "Is he handsome? Is he kind of man who attracts women? Who has seen him?"

"He is not handsome. Not hideous; not misshapen or a monster. But odd looking. His lower face is scarred—the skin, almost as if he survived smallpox." That was Maria Krause. The whole table chimed in.

"Is he young? How old?"

"Thirty years, maybe. It is hard to tell."

Rahel asked, "Would he be kind?"

"Who can tell, with a man?"

September, 1634

"They want me to make this marriage." Sabina Ottmar looked at the other woman, who was nursing a baby daughter. "I don't want to make you unhappy, my lady. I don't want to make Herr Pflaum angry that I ask you. But I think that you, perhaps, would know."

Grantville was like Keilhau in one way. People gossiped.

Staci Ann Beckworth, now very respectable and, by marriage, Lutheran, wife and mother, church member in good standing, looked down at her baby, then up.

"I was a fool when I was living with Lew, okay? I was wearing black leather mini-skirts and spiking my purple-dyed hair with mousse."

Sabina looked bewildered. Staci Ann detached the baby—she was pretty well done anyway—and handed her over to the other woman with a burp rag. "Give me a minute."

She went into the back of the house and returned with a little book. "It's my old album. I don't know why Mom kept this." She opened so Sabina could look. "Mini-skirts; that's purple dye; that's fluorescent green dye in this one. And overweight. Ye gods, I was at my low point. I'd mostly gotten rid of this by the first time I met you." She took the pictures and left the room again. To put it back, Sabina guessed.

"That was me, then." Staci Ann looked up. "I guess, to you, I looked like a little whore. But I wasn't. Lew was the only one, before Arnold." She chewed nervously on a fingernail. "Lew had me at my worst, see. And, yeah, he was kind. Not just that he didn't hit me. He didn't even yell at me, no matter what stupid thing I tried. He'd make a joke of it. Or go outdoors. There's no mean streak in him."

She sighed. "Don't get me wrong. Me being me, I'm better off with Arnold. For Mom and Dad and the farm and all that. Mom despised Lew. But if it hadn't been for the Ring of Fire—for the kind of kid I was then, I could have done a lot worse, and that's the truth."

"I am barren," Sabina said nervously. "I can't have children."

"Well," Staci Ann answered, "neither can Lew. His mom didn't believe in vaccinations, the stupid cow. Mumps. Junior year of high school. And a gossip in the doctor's office told someone, so it got out. She got fired, but by then it didn't do Lew any good. Not the way guys that age are. 'Little Lewie lost his balls.' That's why he dropped out, I think, the things they said to him. He's smart enough that he could have finished, God knows."

April, 1635

Sabina looked at the line of confirmands. In an hour, she would be a married woman. With a cottage on the Booths' farm, newly built, where she would live. Where they would live when he was on leave. She had no dreams. She was marrying this man because it had been arranged for her. He was not being confirmed because she had charmed him into it. He was being confirmed because Staci Ann Beckworth had asked Arnold Pflaum to talk to him, and his sister, about being Lutheran.

Herr Pflaum had also acted as the broker for her, in making a marriage contract, along with the Booths. It was kind of them. Of course, that was the sort of thing that a village's mayor did. Herr Pflaum had never been to Keilhau, of course; he was from Lichstedt. President of the Grange in Grantville was not *quite* the same, but Herr Pflaum was also a church elder at St. Martin's. Herr Pflaum was very young for such responsibility. But he did it well. For many more than the people from his own village, which lay a bit outside the Ring of Fire.

Sabina was not fully happy about being married to a soldier. She was aware as anyone that soldiers run the risk of being killed. Now that she finally would have a husband, which she never expected, she would rather keep him alive. But Lew had gotten used to the army during the last three years. He didn't want to change.

So be it. She would live in the much-too-big cottage by herself.

* * *

Lew's sister, Bernita Walsh, watched from the unfamiliar pew. She was so glad that Lew was getting married now—that he'd have someone. She knew that she had sort of pushed him into it, after the idea came up. And after she had met Sabina. She'd been worried sick about what would become of him, ever since Doc Adams had told her about the cancer. She only had a few more months, maybe a year at most, maybe a lot less. Sabina would take care of him, now. And David and Ashley. She wouldn't mind going so much, with Sheldon already gone for nearly two years, if it weren't for the kids.

Staci Ann knew. And Arnold Pflaum. And Manning and Myrna Booth. Those were the only ones she had told. But the new cottage that the Booths had built for Sabina and Lew had two extra rooms.

Sabina would make a place for the kids. Things could have turned out a lot worse than this.

BRIAR ROSE

Roland Worley and Rahel Rosina Dornheimer
October, 1634

"Prickly pear," Roland Worley said.

"That is?" Jonas Justinus Muselius asked.

"It's a, umm, a cactus."

"And a cactus is?" Jonas' English was probably better than that of any other down-timer in Grantville, but this topic had never come up in his many conversations with Gary Lambert.

The conversation at St. Martin's rectory was interrupted by a hike to the high school, which had the nearest library, a visit to the World Book under the topic of Cactus, and a picture of a prickly pear.

Muselius grinned. "Oh, yes. We would agree. Her name is not just Dornheimer, you know. She is our own little *Dornröschen.*"

"*Dornröschen,*" Roland asked.

"Thorny little rose." Jonas started to tell a story.

Roland picked his teeth. He thought, he said, that he had heard this one somewhere.

They headed for the librarian's desk. Between Colleen Carson and Elias Kurtz, the answer was finally, "I don't think we have a copy, here in the high school library. You ought to be able to find one at the public library. Or at the grade school. It's a fairy tale. The English title is 'Briar Rose'—that's also called a wild rose, or sometimes a bramble. They're very thorny." Roland obediently remodeled his perception. Rahel Rosina Dornheimer was a briar rose, not a prickly pear. Which didn't mean that any guy who tried to get close to her wasn't likely to get poked with something sharp.

July, 1631 - September, 1632

At the time of the Ring of Fire, Roland was divorced. His ex-wife had taken the kids and moved to Beckley in 1996. Leaving him, a guy from Denver, Colorado, in Grantville. With a job, true enough—he was a machinist, and a good one if he did say so himself. Nat Davis paid him pretty well. And a house that he could afford the payments on, given that Nat Davis paid him pretty well. And, since he'd been in, between '83 and '85, a pretty decent slot in the West Virginia USAR. All of which meant that moving would have been a real hassle, so he stayed. A perfectly healthy guy with a bank account in a town where not one of the available females really appealed to him.

Then the Ring of Fire.

Jackson hadn't activated him. He was more valuable where he was, in the machine shop. He stayed in the reserves. In a couple of months, Nat hired a regular clean-up crew. What with the apprentices to train and all the new orders coming in, it was a plain waste of his men's time to do that.

That was where Rahel had appeared, sweeping around his machine. Prickly little thing. Pointy nose like a cute Halloween witch—not the big hooked kind, but the little one like his kids had drawn, two sides of a triangle. Hostile. Not picking-a-fight hostile, but keeping to herself. The only person she ever seemed to talk to was one of the other cleaning women, older than she was and not much friendlier. Sabina, that one was called. Sabina the Scarecrow, one of the men called her; she was all gangly and awkward.

Then Sabina disappeared. That was the first time he'd actually talked to Rahel—he asked her where Sabina was.

"She got another job. Goat dairy. She is good dairy maid. Better job than this." Rahel returned to her sweeping. Rahel was protective of Sabina. When her father married Sabina's mother, any number of people had taken it upon themselves to tell the sixteen-year-old Rahel precisely what had happened to her new stepsister after she was first placed into service at age twelve. Some plain; some with embroidery. From that day onward, Rahel had never let a man touch her.

A month or two later, Rahel disappeared off the cleaning crew. By that time, Roland realized that he wanted her. The only thing that he couldn't figure out was why. He wasn't given to introspection. It never occurred to him that the fact that his ex-wife had been sugar-sweet the whole time they were dating and turned indifferent the day after she had the wedding ring on her finger had anything to do with it.

But he went looking. The new job Rahel had found was working for Irma Lawler and Edna Berry, the two elderly "plant ladies" who were no longer up to long, uninterrupted days of labor on bedding plants and seed gathering. He'd leaned on the fence. He knew better than to trespass on her turf in that garden.

It took several months of fence-leaning on his day off before he learned much about her. Her two brothers had been killed protecting the villagers fleeing from Quittelsdorf, so now she had her father, who was seventy-five, and her stepmother, who was seventy-two, to take care of. It turned out that Sabina was her stepsister. She also worried about her widowed sister-in-law, who originally came from a different village and was in Grantville with three sons to bring up and no marriage prospects.

Roland asked her out. Rahel told him plainly that if he wanted a wife who would keep house for him, he would be doing a charitable act if he married her sister-in-law Dorothea instead. She introduced him to Dorothea and encouraged them to go out. After three tries, Roland concluded that Dorothea was a weeping drip, and not someone it would be any fun at all to have for a wife. But he did find her a job as a live-in housekeeper to old Edgar McAndrew and his sick wife, which gained him a few points with Rahel.

He thought. It would take the most finely calibrated device in the shop to measure progress with Rahel.

May, 1634

Rahel didn't like the whole idea of having the Quittelsdorf girls go out and marry up-timers as a project. She also didn't like living in a big town, any more than Sabina had. But she needed the better money that she could earn in the city.

And if—*if*, mind you—she did agree to do this, she could ignore *die Krausin*'s list. There was an up-timer she could marry. A much better-off one than any of those. She'd gotten to know Roland Worley pretty well. But—as she had repeated to him many times, "I'm a farm girl. I want to marry a farmer." She even said once, as she extracted herself from a more compromising position than was customary before committing herself to something irrevocable, "This is silly. It would make much more sense for me to marry Guenther Conrath, if we had the capital to buy a lease. Or Hans Guenther Hercher." *Well, maybe Hans Guenther Hercher, if anybody knew where Walpurga and Lisbet's brother was, considering that he quarreled with his father when he was almost twenty and left home in a temper. He hadn't been seen by anyone in Quittelsdorf for the last fifteen years. But, surely, Roland would not be interested in such petty details as the shortage of suitable and available grooms.*

By that time, he had pretty well figured out what portions of her anatomy he could approach without getting pricked too hard. Advancing upon an ear, he asked, "Would they do this?"

Rahel was increasingly furious with herself. She suspected that it was unlikely that either Guenther or Hans Guenther would ever do that. Lease or no lease. Present or absent. *She was beginning to enjoy this.*

July, 1634

Rahel started piling on the objections. "You would not want to be a Lutheran." She stated it as a foregone conclusion.

"I might be willing to consider it. Depending on what it involves." Roland thought that he was seeing signs of a snowmelt, but he didn't want to ruin everything by moving too fast. Not even though, the way he was feeling at the moment, he was inclined to say, "Lady, if you would just go to bed with me, I would be happy to put on a clown suit and do somersaults in front of City Hall if that's what it takes."

"Maybe Pastor Kastenmayer won't think your wife is dead."

Roland had made up his mind to marry his prickly pear, briar rose, Rahel even if this might involve a future as a Lutheran married to a female farmer, so he went over on his next day off and did an end run by talking to the minister out at her church and the teacher who did the translations. They both agreed that it didn't matter whether his up-time wife was dead or not, since they happily ascertained that he had been legally divorced from her before the Ring of Fire—and for a reason that down-time Lutherans thought was okay. It appeared that taking the kids and moving to Beckley was "desertion," and someone named Saint Paul had said it was a good reason for divorce. They seemed to put a lot of stock in Saint Paul.

Pastor Kastenmayer was surprised to learn that Roland had never heard of Saint Paul, except for the city in Minnesota. The discussion had required a visit to the library in the high school. Pastor Kastenmayer he hadn't truly taken to heart Jonas' discovery that many of the up-timers in Grantville were heathen.

Muselius borrowed a book of children's Bible stories from Gary Lambert and gave it to Roland to read. He figured that instruction had to start someplace. That seemed as good as any other.

Roland had heard of Adam and Abraham, though not in any detail. Noah's ark. And Jesus in the manger. The rest of the stories were news to him.

October, 1634 - March, 1635

"Of course you must learn it all if you are going to be a Lutheran." That was Rahel's reaction to his protest that the *Shorter Catechism* was really a bit much to expect a guy to memorize.

"Why?"

"Because when you are a *Hausvater*, you will need to teach it to the children."

If Rahel had children on her mind, that had to be a good thing. After all, there were certain prerequisites for producing children. Roland snaked his arm around her waist. His hand angled somewhat upward and to the left. She didn't move away. He kissed the pointy nose. She moved a little closer, which meant that the hand could start to investigate the region where her bodice met her shift.

* * *

Roland spent a lot of time discussing the Lutheran canon law of both divorce (established) and time displacement (unprecedented) with Pastor Kastenmayer and Jonas Justinus Muselius. He wasn't sure entirely why. The other guys in the confirmation class just had to make the run through the *Shorter Catechism.* The question of time displacement and whether his wife would be considered dead if they hadn't been divorced seemed to fascinate Jonas and the minister. Pastor. He had to remember to call him a pastor. Lutherans didn't call them ministers or reverends or any other word he'd ever heard for it.

They even took him to Jena to meet some really big guns in the church. He didn't see quite why at first, since they'd already agreed that he was properly divorced. But they kept talking about Gary Lambert over at the Leahy Medical Center. And that it would be much better to get the principle that "left up-time" equaled "good and dead" established in a case that didn't involve Lambert.

Finally, he figured out that Lambert's wife had been left up-time. No divorce. And that the daughter of one of the big guns wanted to marry the guy. Which the big guns thought was a great idea, if it was legal.

What the hell? If he could be useful to them, it was no skin off his nose.

April, 1635

Pastor Kastenmayer was taking his confirmands through the Christian virtues of faith, hope, and love.

Roland shifted from one foot to the other and wondered where patience fit into it all.

PROMISES TO KEEP

Jim Fritz and Maria Krause April, 1634

Anna Krause leaped off the school bus and dashed into the refugee housing complex. "Maria, Maria. Maria, is Magdalena home? Tante Elisabeth? Is anybody here?"

"I'm here, Anna." Her half-sister, Maria, who worked the night crew at the bakery for the Leahy Medical Center, dragged herself up out of sleep."

Anna at fifteen. All legs and arms. Only starting to fill out in between them. Dressed in up-time clothing. Maria couldn't remember if she had ever been so young. Or what she had been like, if she was. How could seven years make so much difference?

"I don't know where Magdalena is, *Schatz*." Maria shook out her shift. "At work, I guess. If Cora's is busy, she'll stay as long as she can get overtime."

"Franz says it would be cheaper for Cora to hire another girl. Two at regular rates equals the cost of Magdalena, and she's only working one-and-one-half times the regular hours." Anna plopped herself down on a hassock.

"*We* are getting the money for one-and-one-half times the regular hours. *We* need every penny we can earn. Don't let Franz give Frau Ennis any ideas." Maria yawned. "Tante Elisabeth went to supervise the cleaning crew. *Die alte Heiderin* is sick. They took her to the doctor's office this morning."

"Godmother is sick?" Anna's face clouded up.

Maria cursed herself. She should have been gentler. Anna had lost all the bounciness that had propelled her into the apartment. "She'll be all right, *Püppchen*. I'm sure of it." *"No. I hope it,"* she added to herself. Maybe she could bring the bounce back. "What were you so excited about when you ran in?"

Anna's face suddenly glowed. She pulled out a piece of paper. "Look, Maria, I won. From all the sophomores in the school, my science project was the best. They will show it in the lobby at the hospital. With my name on it. For two weeks. Will you come see? I know that Tante Elisabeth and Magdalena won't have time. But it's not far from the bakery, and the lobby is open all day and all night. Please, Maria. Please come see it. Just for a few minutes."

* * *

Six o'clock in the morning. Time to get off work. Maria was so tired that she thought she might die, but she forced herself to make the walk to the lobby. Anna's project was there, just as she had said. With her name on it. She stood, looking.

Softly, behind her, a voice asked, "Do you understand what she did, Maria?"

She looked back. It was the nurse from the Low Countries, coming up on those silent white rubber sneakers they still wore inside the hospital, when they had them. She shook her head. "No, Nurse DeVries. I can read the words and sound them out. But I do not know what they mean. The other marks, the bars lined up, the circles divided in pieces. Those I do not understand at all."

"It's a study about children's diseases in the villages around Grantville. Which diseases come most often to which village. With this, with what she has done, walking from one village to another, making records, using her knowledge of the local dialects to ask questions and gather information that up-timers cannot, our public health nurses can try to find out why. Why does a disease spare one village but regularly return to another that isn't more than ten miles away? Franz helped her, but she did almost all of it herself. The study design, the information gathering, the analysis. She's done a wonderful job. A lot of students five or six years older couldn't equal it."

Maria turned back to the display case. She stood a few minutes more. "I can read the blue ribbon, Nurse DeVries. It says my little sister Anna is the best of all the students. Not the best of the down-time students. Not the best in the special program. The best student of all, in her class, for doing this. So she will not work in a bakery. She will not be on the cleaning crew. Not in the kitchen at Cora's. I will do whatever I need. So she can be a nurse like you or Frau McDonald. Whatever I need to do. I keep my promises."

May, 1634

In the Vandivers' kitchen, Walpurga Hercher put her finger down on the next name on the list. "Take him off."

Margaretha Vandiver shook her head.

"He is a soldier. He has no house. He has a bastard child. No way is he fit to be a husband."

"The child, yes. That would be a problem. A big cost to him, on a soldier's pay. But the mother has married, now. To Friedrich Pflaum,

Arnold's brother, that is. You know him. And Friedrich has adopted the child. A small price to pay, old Johann Pflaum figured, for the farm that Owenna Lamb will inherit. Especially since it is a girl."

They all stood there a moment, thinking about the Pflaums. More than half of the arable land of the Lichstedt, the village where they lived, had gone to wherever Grantville came from, they supposed. The Ring of Fire had done that, the way it had taken the Quitteldorf fields. But an up-time farm had landed where those fields had been. Owned as an allod by a man with only two children. So Friedrich Pflaum had married well. Old Johann, truth be told, had too much of a good thing even before the Ring of Fire. Mayor of Lichstedt. Five sons, every one of them as healthy as a horse and ambitious. The other four not quite as ambitious as Arnold, granted, but still ambitious. True, he had held two leases, his own and his wife's half-share. But it would have been hard for him to place all five boys as full-farmers somewhere. Now.... First Arnold married an up-time heiress, then Friedrich. Heinrich was soon to be betrothed to Deann Whitney. It was strange that most of the up-time men had no wish to be farmers. But lucky for Johann Pflaum. With the three oldest sons farming up-time allodial land, he would have a few years before he had to think about placing Lorenz and Georg. Time, the way things were going, for him to buy up the rest of the leases for what was left of the fields of Lichstedt. There wasn't enough land to support a whole village, now. The other families were drifting off, looking for work in the new industries. Some of the Lichstedter were here in Grantville. It looked like only the Schellenbargers, Johann's in-laws and nephew, would also stay there and farm. There was enough of Lichstedt left for two, or maybe three, full leases. With access to up-time equipment through Friedrich, Arnold, and Heinrich, three men would be able to do the work. It wouldn't take a whole village.

"All right," Walpurga said at last. "Forget the bastard child. Keep, 'he's a soldier' and 'he has no house.' How can a man with no house head a household?"

"Who are we talking about?" Else Krause tried to crane her neck around Walpurga's shoulder.

"What are you still doing in here, Else? You've already said you won't be part of it. Go away and play. Take Barbel with you." Margaretha was annoyed.

Instead of going, Barbara Conrath poked her head over Walpurga's shoulder from the other side.

"*Ach*, we can kibbitz. James Anthony Fritz. Never heard of him."

"What does 'seasonal employment' mean?"

"Part of the year, I think. The way migrants from Switzerland come at harvest time."

"Unemployed" is pretty plain.

"Where did you *get* this stuff?"

Margaretha looked very prim. "I gossip."

"How old?"

"Thirty-two. Maybe thirty-three. I don't have a baptismal record."

"Who are his family?"

"He's an only child."

"Still, he has to have parents. Are they inside the Ring of Fire."

"Yes, here." Margaretha picked up another slate. "Mother and father divorced."

"For how long?

"Nearly thirty years. Neither one remarried. Father, Duane Fritz. Presbyterian. He is a Certified Nursing Assistant at the 'assisted living' home. Mother, Garnet Szymanski. Catholic."

Maria Krause said, "Stop."

* * *

Jim Fritz had not written home the whole time he had been in the army. His mother was not surprised.

Garnet had faced it a long time ago. There was something odd about Jim. Like Duane.

She shouldn't have married Duane. But she had never been a pretty girl. Thirty or forty years ago, she had, aside from the gray in her hair, looked pretty much like she did now. Which wasn't bad, for a woman in her fifties. It was sort of—expectable. The thick waist and sturdy legs hadn't been attractive on a girl in her teens or a woman in her twenties.

Admit it, Garnet. You panicked. Twenty-five years old. No husband, no children. Certainly no religious vocation.

Duane hadn't been a passionate suitor, but he had been there. Two years younger than she was. Not objecting, really. She had done all the things right, for marrying a Protestant. Gotten him to sign the promises, been married in the rectory by the priest. Jim had been born sixteen months later. By then, she knew it was a mistake. At first, when they went to activities at her own family's, she had tried to tell herself that Duane was intimidated a little by all the noisy Szymanskis and O'Malleys. That was why he went off into a corner and watched TV the whole time. But then they went to the Fritz picnic, up at the fairgrounds. His own people. He took a folding lawn chair and sat at the very edge the whole time. Drumming his fingers on the aluminum tubing until they could leave.

Duane wasn't crazy. Not the way most people around Grantville meant it. He did a good job working at the assisted living center. He followed orders and memorized routines. He had an apartment. No one had ever called the police to complain about either noise or trash. He didn't wander around shouting in the streets. He didn't see visions or go through emotional cycles from high to low. He wasn't even depressed, in any clinical sense. But he wasn't normal. Not interacting-with-other-people normal.

Neither was Jim.

If she hadn't faced up to the truth and divorced Duane before there were any more children, she would have condemned herself as the world's worst mother when Jim grew up to be the way he was. Stand-offish. Touch-me-not. The older he got, the worse it got—he dropped out of school because having so many people, loud and rambunctious, in halls and classrooms, abraded him more than he could stand. He had gone to First Communion. He hadn't been confirmed. Maybe she should have tried harder, but right then, working full time and everything, getting him through school had been all that she could deal with. Not CCD on top of it. He hadn't been to mass in, well, years. More years than she wanted to think about. Fifteen, at least.

She had sort of wondered how he ever got close enough to Owenna Lamb to get her pregnant. At least, little Andie seemed to have been spared it. She was a cute kid. The down-timers seemed to be realistic about these things. Friedrich Pflaum had invited her to the adoption ceremony at City Hall. And to dinner afterwards. She hadn't been forced to give up Andie altogether. Probably the only grandchild she would ever have.

Pflaum had invited Duane, too, but he didn't come. Jim sent back the consent form, signed, witnessed, and notarized. No letter wishing them well. That wouldn't have been Jim, to send a letter or a note. Or even a card. It wasn't the sort of thing that occurred to him. He did what needed to be done. The little flourishes and trimmings that put the grease in the works of human relations were completely beyond him.

Thirty-one years now, as a divorced Catholic, toeing the line. With no letters from your son. It gave you a lot of time to concentrate on your career.

Garnet picked up another pile of papers to grade. Classes in health care at the VoTech Center were crammed to capacity. Life went on. She really wondered how Jim managed to endure army life.

* * *

Jim Fritz liked the army. Things were reliable. You knew from one day to the next what would be going on. Basic training had been unpleasant, a hassle—too many people around, almost like school. But the sergeants told you exactly what to do, and if you did it, you were okay.

Then, after basic, they put him here, at the supply base in Erfurt. It was a really good job. If it hadn't been for the PT part of it, it would have been great. For that, and for shooting, he had to get out with the other guys. Mostly, though, he spent almost every day in this little side room off the main warehouse by himself, putting things on shelves, taking things off shelves, sorting things into bins and making lists of how many of them there were. They all had numbers, so he didn't have to worry about what they were, as long as they were alike. Then he packed them up to send out. He had lists of how many to put in each keg or crate. Old Man Stull told him where to send them.

Dennis Stull, the civilian procurement head in Erfurt for the army of what had been the New United States, considered Jim Fritz one of the best finds of his life. The man had absolutely no curiosity. He didn't care what he sorted or what the parts might be for, where they came from, or where they went. Plus, he never went out with the guys and got drunk or consorted with prostitutes who might pump him. Or, if he did consort with them, he wasn't likely to be chatty about it.

For R&D projects, Jim Fritz was the fulfillment of a security officer's dreams. Jim Fritz had a lifetime career in this man's army, if he wanted it, as far as Dennis Stull was concerned.

July, 1634

First, she had to find him. Finally, Maria went to the army headquarters and asked. The young man, boy really, at the desk gave her the address. He smirked. She guessed what he was thinking—the man already had one bastard and was about to have another.

Let him think.

She asked for two days off from the Leahy Medical Center bakery. She was surprised to discover that she had been accumulating something called "leave time" for three years. Her English hadn't been very good, back when she was hired. Since then, she had never had reason to ask for more than her Sundays, so she never had.

She walked to the base where he was, all the way to Erfurt. She had gotten Ursel to use the telegraph ahead ahead of time. He knew she was coming.

He didn't know why. Some things, she thought, were better explained face-to-face.

At least, she thought so until she was speaking with him.

He sat there. Perhaps he listened to her. But there was no face-to-face.

Until she said, "Look at me."

After that, he looked at her.

* * *

Garnet was surprised to hear that Jim would be marrying a German girl. Well, perhaps not all that surprised. A marriage without a lot of verbal communication required might suit him.

April, 1635

Jonas Justinus Muselius had found an English-speaking chaplain at one of the many Lutheran churches in Erfurt who was willing to undertake the man's instruction.

Jim had seen no reason to come to Grantville for the confirmation and wedding. Maria had spoken to Herr Stull, who ordered him to. Orders were orders.

Garnet had been surprised to receive the nicely-written invitation (Margaretha had finally found a use for Else and Barbel in this project). She had been even more surprised to discover that Jim was joining a church. Any church. Jim was not a joiner.

She came by herself. She was the only one of Jim's relatives who did. She was a bit uneasy about it—the rules for Catholics taking part in the services of Protestant churches had eased a lot since she was a girl, but she still had a nervous feeling that watching your son join one was stretching the limits. She got there early, in spite of being nervous. Or, perhaps, because of it.

The teacher introduced her to her future daughter-in-law, Maria Krause. Who had a teenaged girl firmly by the arm. And spoke English—fairly good, actually. "Frau Szymanski. This is my half-sister Anna. She won the prize for the best science project last year. Maybe you saw it. It was at the hospital lobby then. She has won the prize again this year. It is in the lobby now. You can go see it."

From Grantville, then—not some girl Jim had picked up at the base.

"She is to be a nurse. I need for her to live in your house, not in the refugee housing. In refugee housing, there are too many chances for Anna to do what she should not." Maria turned and pointed. "Her other half-sister. Other side of the family."

The girl appeared to be nine months and two days pregnant. She was sitting with Perry and Dayna Baker.

Maria said firmly. "I marry your son. You are our family now. Anna can live with you. It will be much better. Don't worry, I earn the money. Pay you. Rent, food, all. I work hard."

"Ah." It was clear that Maria had no doubts. Did Garnet want a teenaged house mate? Even one who won two science fair prizes? It appeared that she had been relieved of the decision. "We can talk about it. When? Next week?"

"Tomorrow." Maria was firm. "He goes back to Erfurt. In the morning. I go back to work at the bakery. In the evening. In between, I bring Anna to you. Not waste time."

Garnet had a relieved feeling. This, she thought, was a girl who could cope with being married to Jim. Having a Lutheran son was a small price to pay for that.

* * *

Maria watched as the confirmation liturgy ran its course. Somewhere in her mind, carefully covered over so that she didn't have to look at it directly, was the thought that in wars, soldiers on active duty get shot at, and sometimes they get killed. Then their wives are widows.

But as long as he was alive, she fully intended to do her marital duty honestly. Each month, she would take her "leave time" and visit him in Erfurt.

Things had been worse in the past. They might get worse in the future. Maria kept her promises. The rest was in God's hands.

* * *

Confirmations completed, the congregation adjourned to the porch for the weddings. And to the school courtyard for an event that would probably rank as the party of the year in Grantville.

But, as Pastor Kastenmayer watched the beer flow, it wasn't enough. *I want*, he thought, *Andrea's husband.*

THE WOMAN SHALL NOT WEAR THAT

Summer 1634

No. Pastor Ludwig Kastenmayer put it out of his mind. His eyes must have deluded him. The cleaning woman at Countess Katharina the Heroic Lutheran Elementary School, here on the outskirts of Grantville, could not have been wearing...that.

He put it out of his mind until, while walking along the road to Rudolstadt, he observed some others of his female parishioners among a street-sweeping crew, among a gutter-cleaning service, and a window-washing crew. In each case, some of them seemed to be wearing what? He tried his best to pretend that he had seen no such thing.

Until the day that he entered his own home and observed the nether garment that Salome—Salome? his wife Salome???—was wearing as she bent over to clean the hearth.

He sat in his study and checked the appropriate references contained in Martin Luther's Table Talk—comments on whether or not it was worth a pastor's while to preach in regard to female modesty. They brought him no joy. Luther's thesis had been that it was not usually worthwhile to preach on such topics because, as a result of the German climate, one's female parishioners were ordinarily wearing multiple layers of skirts and petticoats that covered them from head to toe, a head scarf or hat, and not uncommonly a cloak, wool socks, lined boots, and mittens, with a hot brick under their feet.

This, the venerable Luther had pointed out, relieved German pastors of worrying about the topic of modesty, which had preoccupied so many of the early church fathers. They, living in a Mediterranean climate, had naturally been more concerned with the impact upon morals and mores of skimpy coverage, flimsy fabric, and revealing that which was better concealed. If a pastor had an affluent parish, an occasional sermon on the topic of luxury in dress might not be amiss, but that applied at least as much to men as it did to women. Usually more. For the average rural village church, even that was scarcely a problem, though.

The German climate had not changed significantly. Most of the time, at least in winter, the up-time women went around dressed in items such as "sweat shirts" which provided full coverage and did little to emphasize those female attributes which many men found tempting. The garments were, in fact, Pastor Kastenmayer thought, quite literally as ugly as sin. The up-time men wore "sweat shirts" also, but surely only the devil himself, Kastenmayer thought with some humor, could persuade a female to put one on.

In the summer, however.... Pastor Kastenmayer sighed. Although the up-timers were not his direct concern, their impact upon Grantville's Lutheran women was. It looked like it was going to be "back to patristics" for the themes of some of his sermons this year.

Plus, there was a more serious theological concern.

Only a few of the younger down-time women and almost none of the respectable married women in St. Martin's in the Fields parish had been tempted to try "jeans." Pastor Kastenmayer -suspected that more and more of the girls attending the up-time high school wore them on weekdays, when they did not expect to be under his eye. Little Anna Krausin, Maria's sister, came immediately to mind. He occasionally had a depressing feeling that he really should try to do something about that. Although what he could do other than preach a sermon was something of a quandary.

Even Anna Krausin came to church wearing skirts of a respectable length. If not, precisely, of a respectable width, and almost certainly lacking petticoats beneath them. He referred this concern back to the topic of modesty, which appeared earlier in his notes.

If "jeans" were a peripheral matter because they had not made great inroads in his congregation—he added a mental "yet" to this analysis—those...things...that Salome had been wearing were not.

Upon inquiry, he found that the offending garments were sometimes referred to as "divided skirts" or "culottes," but the most common variant was called "skorts." Apparently these disguised trousers had become widely accepted among his parishioners.

He had refrained from reproaching her directly because...Salome, although an excellent wife in most ways, did not always accept reproaches as meekly as theory indicated that she should.

His first wife hadn't, either.

Hardly any wives did.

This was unquestionably one of the more lasting effects of original sin.

Except, of course, that if one read the narratives quite literally, which one certainly should do, Eve had not been inclined to obey either Adam or God Himself even before the Fall of Man. Which was most perplexing, no matter how various theologians attempted to explain it, since supposedly things had been perfect in the Garden of Eden. Did this imply that God regarded a woman with an independent mind as a proper component of paradise? Surely not. But, then....

Nevertheless. He pulled his thoughts together and focused them.

It was his clear duty to do something. In the Bible, more precisely in the Old Testament, more precisely at Old Testament, Deuteronomy 22:5, there was to be found the statement, in Luther's German translation: "Ein weib sol nicht mans gerete tragen/vnd ein man sol nicht weiber kleider an thun/Denn wer solchs thut/der ist dem Herrn deinem Gott ein grewel."

The English language Bible that Gary Lambert had loaned him agreed. "The woman shall not wear that which pertaineth unto a man, neither shall a man put on a woman's garment: for all that do so are abomination unto the Lord thy God." King James Version.

Anxiously, he checked it in the Greek translation of the *Septuagint*. He followed this by reference to the original Hebrew. Why waste all those years of education in the biblical languages that had been forced down his throat, after all?

His obligation was clear. He must enter the confines of Grantville proper to discover the exact cultural status of skorts and such related items as divided skirts. Did they, or did they not, pertain to a man?

Feeling vaguely morose, he wandered into an otherwise empty classroom at Countess Katharina the Heroic Lutheran Elementary School, next door to the church. Where he observed his daughter Maria Blandina teetering on the top of a too-short step stool, trying to tack up a new set of alphabet letters. Experiencing a panicked concern that she was going to fall off, carefully avoiding startling her, he suggested that she come down. She did manage to make her way down safely, surrounded by his anxious admonitions to "find someone taller to do that." In the process, alas, he observed that she was wearing what? Yes. That. Under her full skirt, but wearing it.

Of course, he had to admit, worn as an undergarment that did contribute a great deal to the preservation of appropriate feminine modesty. Far more than petticoats did. Hmmmn.

* * *

"I do feel obliged to do it," the pastor said to Jonas Justinus Muselius and Gary Lambert a few days later. "To determine the status of these 'culottes' and 'skorts.' " After a few moments of further contemplation, he added, " 'Jeans,' on the other hand. They are obviously male clothing."

"Actually," Gary said, "they're sort of both. They come in two kinds. Sometimes girls do wear guys' jeans, but not usually. Not if the girl has a shape. If she does, guys' jeans are, ah, mostly the wrong shape, if you get me." He gestured with his hands. "Since Sheila was left up-time, I gave her clothes to the Ecumenical Emergency Refugee Relief Committee early on, so I can't show you. Unless we could borrow a pair from someone else."

Kastenmayer looked a little daunted by the prospect of a demonstration.

"Maybe Ronella Koch would lend us a pair, if we asked her," Gary continued.

August 1634

"There you go," Ronella said. She had almost finished mounting Maria Blandina's new alphabet cards. She was only four inches taller than her friend, which didn't make a lot of difference, but had arrived from the trolley carrying the Kochs' eight-rung aluminum stepladder, which did.

She would start her adult career, teaching at Grantville high school, in a couple of days. Mathematics department. Advanced algebra and trigonometry. Her mother's determined tutoring had paid off. Combined, of course, with the incredible turnover that the high school faculty had experienced in the past three years as experienced teachers were yanked out for other work in government or industry, replaced at first by retirees and teachers called up from the lower levels. Then the retirees, getting no younger themselves, were often unable to maintain the pace of full-time teaching and grading indefinitely.

Up-time, these plum courses would have gone to a teacher with more seniority. Here and now, down-time, Victor Saluzzo, himself the third principal in four years following Ed Piazza's move into government and Len Trout's death, counted himself lucky to get her. Even without anything resembling a teaching certification.

Her mother, Carol Koch, most widely known among down-timers for her role as an up-time delegate to the Rudolstadt Colloquy more than a year before, had steadfastly refused to sell the stepladder for its aluminum content, no matter how many anxious buyers appeared at her doorstep. In fact, after receiving several urgent appeals, she had removed the stepladder from the tool shed in the yard and now kept it under her bed in the house. As she said with perfect logic to a would-be purchaser who was pressing her strongly, "It doesn't matter how much more money I would have in the bank. If I sell you that, we won't have a tall stepladder that's light enough for Ronella and me to carry around when we need it. And we probably never would again. So there."

"Stick your head in next door, will you, and ask Jonas if he needs anything put up, taken down, or changed around while I have the ladder here?" Ronella started to tack the last few letters to the molding.

"Will do." Maria Blandina ducked out the door.

* * *

In the next classroom, Jonas Justinus Muselius was looking glumly at his friend Gary Lambert. "I don't see why not?" he said. "It would be suitable."

"I don't want to marry Ronella," Gary answered. "Any more than you wanted to marry Maria Blandina when the pastor asked you. Even aside from the fact that she's ELCA rather than LCMS, I don't want to marry her. I like her, but I don't see her as wife material. At least not wife material for me. I haven't met anyone I've seen as wife material since Sheila was left up-time." He paused. "There's nothing wrong with Ronella. I'm sure she'd make a perfectly nice wife for someone else," he added charitably.

Jonas looked glum. "She's old enough that she's bound to be getting married pretty soon. We can't expect her to stay unmarried much longer. Somebody needs to make sure that she has a husband who appreciates her and will be kind to her. We ought to find her the right kind of husband. Someone with a sense of humor. Otherwise, since I'm sure that her parents will want it to be someone with a university degree, she'll end up stuck with someone like Johann Georg Hardegg, who never laughs at all. Simply because he's a lawyer and suitable."

Gary would never have described himself as an intuitive type. Nevertheless, he looked at Jonas, suspicion dawning.

Jonas was thirty-two. Five years older than Gary. Jonas would never consider himself suitable for Ronella Koch, daughter of a prosperous up-time mining engineer. Not for Ronella, newly turned twenty-three and already with a faculty appointment at the prestigious Grantville high school. Not with only one good arm. Not on the salary of a down-time elementary school teacher. Not.

So he was trying for what he considered the next best solution. A suitable husband. One who would make Ronella happy in the long run, even if it left him utterly miserable himself.

Jonas was that kind of person.

Gary was still thinking about this when Maria Blandina stuck her head in the door asking about any possible stepladder needs.

Jonas hated not being able to do things that required two hands. He was also realistic about not being able to do things that required two hands. He had a list of a half dozen little classroom chores that could benefit from the attention of Ronella and a stepladder.

Maria Blandina went back to her own domain. Ronella appeared with the stepladder.

Ronella didn't make concessions to Pastor Kastenmayer's flinch reactions. She was definitely wearing jeans. And a tee shirt. She scurried busily up and down, Gary moving the ladder from place to place for her.

Jonas sat there, watching the passing scenery a little wistfully. He saw no objection to jeans at all. Especially not on Ronella. There was nothing at all about jeans on Ronella that would delude anyone in the world into thinking that they pertained to a man. As an attempt at cross-dressing went, they were a total dud. When she wore them, it was perfectly clear that she was female.

Of course, that was always perfectly clear to Jonas. Meaningfully clear. Crystal clear. Increasingly clear. More transparently clear with every day that passed.

* * *

"Do you suppose," Ronella asked Maria Blandina rather wistfully, "that Jonas is ever going to make a move?"

Maria Blandina's life thus far had left her with few illusions. She had managed to hold onto a few dreams. Illusions, no. Approximately eighty children, first and second graders, day in and day out, did that to a young woman. Although she, like Ronella, was twenty-three, she had been teaching full-time for five years already. Part-time since she was sixteen.

"Probably not," she answered.

Early in the spring, Ronella had decided, "That one!" after she heard Jonas leading the prayer before the upper grade girls' softball game between Countess Kate, as the Lutheran elementary school was known almost universally among the up-timers, and the middle school in Grantville. He chose the first verse of Psalm 26. In the King James Version, since Countess Kate was playing an English-speaking school.

"Judge me, O LORD; for I have walked in mine integrity: I have trusted also in the LORD; therefore I shall not slide."

"That one!" she had said to herself. "The one with a wicked sense of humor. The one with a *bilingual* wicked sense of humor."

Now she asked, "Is there anything I can do about it?"

"Would your father be willing to propose to him for you?"

Ronella jumped.

"Well, you know," Maria Blandina said in a reasonable tone of voice, "Papa asked him if he would be willing to marry me and he just said no. So we know that he'll say no if he isn't interested. How much worse off would you be if your father asked him and he said no?"

"None, I guess," Ronella admitted. "But at least the way things are I can sort of hope. It would really sort of put the kibosh on everything if he refused."

"But it would be a lot less embarrassing than if you just flat kissed him and he ran away," Maria Blandina pointed out. "Which I sort of suspect you're on the verge of doing any day now. Kissing him, I mean. It gives you a lot more room to save face to have your father do it."

* * *

"Maybe," Salome Piscatora suggested tentatively, "you could make your inquiries to the Interdenominational Ministerial Alliance in Grantville. The association that quite a few of the different pastors belong to. They might have an answer."

Pastor Kastenmayer regarded his wife with scandalized horror.

"They use the same Bible," she pointed out. "Even if it's translated into a different language."

He delivered an abbreviated version of his standard sermon on the hideous consequences of consorting with heretics.

Salome had heard it all before. Her father had been a pastor, too, and both of her grandfathers had been school teachers.

After long enough exposure, a sensible person got sort of inured to sermons and lectures.

Not that she wasn't fond of Ludwig, of course.

But she had no intention of giving up her divided skirts, culottes they were called, now that she had obtained them. They were such a convenience. She had the tailor cut them full enough and long enough that Ludwig would never even have noticed if he hadn't come in unexpectedly and seen her bending over.

Which only went to show. If they had pertained to a woman well enough before he noticed, it made no sense at all to argue that they didn't after he had noticed.

She would have to talk to Carol Koch about it. Carol was pragmatic and sensible, even for a woman. Much less a man.

Ludwig went off to his study to prepare his next sermon. Salome sat down heavily on the bench under the window in the main room of the parsonage.

Salome knew that she herself was pragmatic and sensible, even for a seventeenth-century German Lutheran pastor's wife, which was saying something.

She hoped that Ludwig would talk to Jonas before he did anything rash. Jonas was the son of her much older half-brother. Her mother's first husband had been named Jonas Musch; Muselius was one of those fanciful Latinizations to which academics were prone.

She herself was the next to the youngest child of her mother's second marriage. Another Latinization, this time from Fischer to Piscator. So she was called Piscatora rather than by the sensible German name of Fischerin. She had been four when her mother died in Ohrdruf. That was in the county of Gleichen, which did not exist anymore. Her father, for a wonder, had not married again, even though he had small children. His widowed sister, whose second husband died the same year as Mama, brought her own five children from two marriages and came to take care of them all. Tante Margaretha had been a good and conscientious woman who did not accept her third husband, a Flemish merchant then residing in Nürnberg and now gone to his final rest these two years past, until after Papa died and no longer needed her. She still was good and conscientious, for that matter. At the age of eighty-one, she lived with her oldest son in Weimar these days—Lutz Reimarus was an outstanding organist and she would think so even if he wasn't her cousin. And to think that his father had been a simple village boy from Quittelsdorf, singled out by the pastor for his talents and sent to school to become a teacher himself!

Papa had become a pastor in Erfurt shortly after Mama died. Not a prestigious pastor in that great city. He had spent all the rest of his life as an auxiliary appointee, caring for parishioners in one of the poorest sections of the city to the best of his ability and maintaining his large household on a small stipend. This meant that aside from schools and books, their lives were in no way more luxurious than those of their neighbors. The schooling had to be reserved for the boys, who needed it to make their way in life. Papa had not died prematurely. He had been seventy-three, but it certainly had not helped that her two older brothers, Reichard and Thomas, had both died unmarried, a couple of years before he did. He had not lived to see his youngest son marry so well, to the daughter of a Wittenberg professor no less, and begin to make a great success of himself.

She had no learning but what Papa had time to teach her after fourth grade. He didn't have the money to send her to a city school for girls. No accomplishments suitable to a fine young lady other than how to play the lute, which he played himself. He had taught her and her older sister Anna what he knew himself. Latin and a little Greek. The ancient classics. Theology. Dull things, not likely to attract suitors. Otherwise, she worked in the house, helping Tante Margaretha. The four years after Anna married and moved back to Ohrdruf, she had worked hard. Five grown men in the house to be clothed and fed, with Tante Margaretha so sad those first years after her only daughter died.

The letter from Anna had come as an absolute shock. Their pastor had been widowed, she wrote, with five small children to care for. He needed to remarry as soon as possible. She had suggested Salome and the pastor had said, 'If you think she is suitable, which you must, then ask your father.' Papa had considered it an excellent opportunity to place her in a household of her own. He had been afraid that Tante Margaretha would keep her home too long and she was not likely to have many chances. So, at the age of twenty, she had traveled to Ohrdruf, to Anna. Three weeks later, as soon as the banns had been read, she married a man she had never met before she got there. Ludwig was almost twenty-five years older than she was, three months a widower. A widower who had loved his first wife deeply.

Overall, it was as well that she hadn't expected more out of marriage than she got. In fact, she got more than she had expected. Kindness, absolute reliability, and no expectations that she should achieve more in the way of food and domestic comfort than was possible within the limitations of a pastor's salary. And, over the years, eight sons. By the will of divine providence, seven of them still alive and still to be educated. Joseph, the oldest, was nineteen, in his second year at the university in Jena. The youngest, Thomas, only three.

Plus, they were to be blessed again. In October, if all went well. Two more months to go. She was forty-one years old now. In the heat of this summer, she occasionally had a little trouble persuading herself that the creator was entirely reasonable in the way he distributed his blessings. She could not help but think that here were many childless women in the world who would have welcomed this particular blessing a lot more than she did. Ludwig was sixty-five and could not be expected to live forever. At some point, probably not too far distant, she was going to be a widow with no income and a large family of sons to finish bringing up.

And precious little help, probably, from her stepchildren. Matthaeus was a junior pastor now; Martin an assistant city clerk. Self-supporting, but in no position to assist anyone else. Johann Conrad still at Jena, soon to be a lawyer, which also meant several years before he had any significant income. Maria Blandina, dowryless, teaching for no salary at the school here.

And Andrea. Andrea, the selfish little snip who in April had clouded Ludwig's life by showing so little gratitude for a lifetime of paternal care that she eloped with a Roman Catholic up-timer, a representative of the anti-Christ on earth.

Salome knew that in this matter, at least, she was a failure and would be judged for it before God when the time came to separate the sheep from the goats. In spite of all her efforts, she had not managed to imbue her stepdaughters with sufficient common sense and pragmatism. Maria Blandina more than Andrea, but neither of them fully.

They were both, especially Andrea, much like their mother, from all she had been able to learn. So there was probably little she could do about it. Ludwig was inclined to indulge them because they were so like Blandina Selfisch had been.

And she had been sitting long enough. She pulled herself up and went into the kitchen to see what the girl was doing. Thecla wasn't much of a servant. But she was fourteen and an orphan. By the time Salome was finished training her, she would be a competent housewife in a few years' time. Competent enough, it was to be hoped, that some sensible man would overlook her lack of family and funds when he came to pick a wife. Or, if not, fitted to earn her living as housekeeper to a prosperous family.

Somehow, their servants were always like that.

* * *

"If Papa thinks that he absolutely must," Maria Blandina said to Jonas, "then I guess that he absolutely must go walking into Grantville interviewing men as to whether or not these various up-time garments pertain to men. Though I have a terrible feeling that he's going to get himself into trouble.

"How does he intend to do it?" Jonas asked, looking at his step-cousin. Now that her father had formally sounded him out about the possibility of a marriage between them and he had politely declined the honor, they had reverted to their normal ease with one another.

Maria Blandina had been terrifically relieved that Jonas wasn't willing to marry her. As far as she was concerned, it would have been sort of, well, like marrying one of her brothers. In age, Jonas was right between Matthaeus and Martin, and he had been in and out of the house ever since Papa married his aunt when he was eleven and she was two. She knew Jonas awfully well. Although she would have made the best of it if that had been her fate. She didn't expect to duplicate her older sister Andrea's dramatic elopement with an up-timer, but if she ever did find a husband.... She paused and sent up a silent prayer. "Dear Father in heaven, if you ever give me a husband, I would like to have one who is a little different, if you don't mind. Someone I -haven't known almost since the day I was born. That would be nice, all by itself."

She hadn't known the up-timer Gary Lambert since the day she was born, so she had thought about him occasionally. The thought, though, was that she didn't want to marry him, either. She might as well have known him since the day she was born. There must have been a lot of what Jonas now called "cultural continuity" among the German Lutherans who moved to America in that other world. Gary, even if he came from 350 years away, was much like her brothers. A recognizable type. Even aside from the fact that he wasn't interested in marrying her any more than Jonas was. She sighed. Who would be?

"Papa can't carry a huge suitcase with him as he walks around town. Not at his age. So I borrowed things from Walpurga Hercher. Things that came into MaidenFresh Laundries. Temporarily, of course. She found a child-size version of each of the various styles for him to take with him on his researches. As examples." She opened the box on her desk to display her trophies.

Jonas looked at the contents and shook his head. There was a divided skirt that would be knee-length on a small child, something called "capri pants," and jeans. The culottes were lavender, the capri pants were yellow and white checked gingham printed with daisies, and the jeans were embroidered. But the *piece de resistance* was an up-time shorts/overskirt combination, the style which the pastor so nervously thought of as "That." Maria Blandina called it a skort. Both pieces were sewed to the same waistband, buttoning on the left side. In a floral print of white, lavender, light blue, and a darker pink, with dainty green vines tying the individual blossoms together. With a pale pink background. Trimmed with pink rickrack on the pockets and around the hems of both the shorts and skirt. And pink plastic buttons molded to match one of the kinds of flowers in the print.

Poor Papa, Maria Blandina thought as she handed the box over to her father the next morning. With a certain amount of malice aforethought, she admitted to herself a little guiltily. However, as Jonas said, he would have to learn sometime.

Magdeburg, August 1634

Mary Simpson's normal school committee got everything organized and sent off to Duke Ernst in the Upper Palatinate. It would open in the Jesuit *Collegium* in Amberg in September and start training elementary school teachers for the villages of the USE.

They had managed to get it all done on time. Except for one crucial thing.

The new institution still did not have a permanent administrator.

For the moment, Duke Ernst's personal secretary would add it to his workload. That was obviously not a feasible solution for the long term.

September 1634

"You know," Walpurga Hercher said, "the pastor could get into a lot of trouble doing this. Especially if he went into some of the rougher places, like the 250 Club." She looked at her sister Lisbet consideringly. "I think we ought to get the boyfriend collection to steer him a bit. You and Jonas can ask Errol to sort of fall in walking with him the morning he sets out, can't you? Once Errol is finished playing for the children's music class at the school in the morning. Make sure that he doesn't go to the wrong spots."

"What do you call this?" Lisbet asked suspiciously.

"Reasonable prudence," Walpurga answered. "Pastor Kastenmayer isn't such a bad sort. Maybe Errol could take him to the Freedom Arches to talk to Derek Blount and those guys. If he wants to ask young guys. If he wants to talk to up-time women about it, he could go to Cora's. Ryan could take him there, since Magdalena works in the kitchen."

"I don't see why he couldn't talk to Errol and the others out at St. Martin's," Lisbet said. "After all, they come to church with us now."

"The pastor's a man," Walpurga answered. "That would be far too simple a solution to the puzzle."

"You want me to what?" Ron Koch asked in horror.

"I just told you," Ronella answered.

"But."

"Look, Dad," Ronella said. "I want to marry him. We're at a standstill. You don't have anything against him, do you?"

"Well, no. But it's...err, *primitive*...for me to arrange a marriage for you. Or try to." Ron had, after all, proposed to his beloved Carol on the basis of ten minutes' acquaintance. This project was distinctly alien to every one of his sensibilities.

"Please, Daddy," Ronella said. "Pretty please, with sugar on it." She clasped her hands, rested her chin on them, and batted her eyelashes.

That was not fighting fair. She knew it and so did her father.

"Jonas is a fine young man," Carol Koch said. "I got to know him pretty well during the Rudolstadt Colloquy, and I really like him."

They both looked at her.

"If you won't ask him for her," Carol said, "I will. It's not as if he's going to find anyone nicer than Ronella."

Both of the elder Kochs looked at their daughter with considerable parental satisfaction and pride, pleased with their achievement and mutually agreed that no one would ever find a girl nicer than Ronella.

Ron Koch groaned. Outmaneuvered again. He wasn't good at talking to people. Not persuasive. He knew that. He preferred to let the facts speak for themselves when he made a presentation. He hadn't been trying to persuade Carol of anything when he proposed as soon as he saw her. The fact that they absolutely would never be happy again unless they got married to each other as soon as it could be achieved had been perfectly plain to both of them.

It was hard to think of any facts that he could lay out in such a manner as to demonstrate that Jonas would be the best of all possible husbands for Ronella. For himself, the facts that she wanted the guy and Carol approved of him were enough.

Lots of young couples started out on a shoestring. He and Carol would be content with that for Ronella.

He had a suspicion that down-timers didn't look at it that way. He'd have to ask one of them how a father was supposed to go about this.

Maybe he could ask Pastor Kastenmayer, he thought.

Pastor Kastenmayer subsequently confirmed that Jonas was not the product of a world that believed in trying to live on love.

* * *

Pastor Kastenmayer transferred the samples that Maria Blandina had collected for him from the box into a small satchel with a handle and set forth on his journey of exploration.

Errol Mercer joined him before he had even gotten out of the courtyard that lay between the church and the school. Mentally shaking his head about the stuff that a guy would do when Lisbet asked him to.

He set out to do a little steering. Luckily, walking into town from St. Martin's, a person passed the Freedom Arches before getting to the downtown part itself.

The pastor politely greeted Derek Blount, who was eating his breakfast. Ursel Krause kept peeking from behind the counter, trying to see what was going on.

"Morning, Pastor Kastenmayer," Derek said. "Meet my brother Donnie."

He hadn't prepped Donnie. But he was, after all, Donnie's brother. The two of them had lived in the same house all their lives. He knew him pretty well. He had complete confidence in Donnie. At least as far as solving this little problem went.

Kastenmayer smiled. Derek's brother. An up-timer who was not scheduled to become one of the grooms for the girls of Quittelsdorf. Thus, an impartial witness.

He explained his mission.

He reached into his satchel.

He came out with the pink floral print skort.

"Would I wear that?" Donnie jerked back in spontaneous horror. "Hell, no. What do you think I am?" he asked. "Some kind of girly man?"

Although, in the interest of thoroughness, Pastor Kastenmayer pursued his inquiries for the remainder of the morning, through such venues—pre-selected by Walpurga—as the office of the "home economics" teacher at the middle school and Karen Reading's bridal shop, he knew that he had his answer. He returned home with a considerable feeling of relief. This was certainly going to simplify life.

After all, the pertinent passage in Deuteronomy did not say a word describing the prohibited garments. It did not state that they were any variety of trousers or indicate what they looked like. It merely forbade, "that which pertaineth unto a man."

October 1634

"Okay," Gary Lambert said. "I'll come to Jena with you all and tell them what I know about the whole "spouse left up-time" marriage thing. They need to come to some kind of a final resolution. Roland Worley seems a nice enough guy, so we ought to clear the decks if he wants to marry Rahel Dornheimer. I can kill two birds with one stone. Beulah McDonald has been nagging me to come and meet some of the faculty members there outside of the school of medicine. Dean Gerhard is planning a dinner party. I'll have her invite Pastor Kastenmayer and you, too, Jonas. Since you're going to be there anyway."

* * *

"Daddy," Ronella Koch said. "Do you mean to tell me that you haven't said a word to Jonas *yet*?"

Ron Koch looked miserably uncomfortable. "Honey," he said. "Uh. That is. Don't you think that if Jonas wanted to marry you, he would do something about it himself?"

"To be perfectly honest, no. I think that left to himself he'll be noble and self-sacrificing until the end of time."

"I really don't want to do this."

Ronella knew that already.

"Please, Daddy. Please. Maybe you could say something to Pastor Kastenmayer and then he could say something to Jonas?"

That was a little ray of sunshine. Thin, watery, and wavering. But at least not his own personal rain cloud following him around.

Ronella looked at him. If Daddy hadn't done something by Christmas.... Well, she would think of something. Right now, she had papers to grade. Stacks and stacks of papers to grade. Oodles and gobs and mountains of papers to grade. One of the few things that could be said for the first year of teaching was that it sure took your mind off your other troubles.

Jena, October 1634

Johann Gerhard, dean of the faculty of theology at the university of Jena, looked at his dinner party.

Overall, he was satisfied. Basically, the handling of the case of Roland Worley's up-time marriage in the briefs submitted by expert advisers from both law and theology schools throughout much of Lutheran Germany indicated that a spouse left behind in such a way should be considered deceased. Without requiring an extended waiting period or an individual decree in each case. The Saxe-Weimar consistorial court had ruled accordingly this morning, concurring with that of Schwarzburg-Rudolstadt.

This meant that in addition to the now basically Philippist consistory in Schwarzburg-Rudolstadt, they had a ruling from the basically Flacian consistory in Saxe-Weimar. Flacian Lutherans basically thought that Philippists were suspiciously lax with tendencies toward crypto-Calvinism. Philippist Lutherans frequently thought that Flacians tended to be uptight, overly orthodox, ultra-rigid pains. They rarely agreed on any point of doctrine.

Gerhard was orthodox himself, of course. Though suspected of pietist sentimentalism by even stricter Flacians. All of the Jena faculty was Flacian.

That the two consistories agreed on the marriage issue was a relief, since the alternative would have been the need for the party now in the seventeenth century to apply for divorce on the grounds of abandonment and that would have proven impossible. Abandonment, as everyone knew, had to be willful. It would be impossible to interpret the parting of spouses caused by the Ring of Fire as having been deliberate on the part of either one. That would have been a dilemma. A serious dilemma when it came to finding a wife for Gary Lambert. Now...he had representatives of both contending schools of Lutheran thought at the same dinner party. Which might possibly turn out to be touchy.

Gerhard's wife Maria smiled at him from across the room. She was talking with Beulah McDonald. Since her father had been a well-known physician in Coburg, the two had common interests. Standing with them were Catharina Barthin, the wife of Friedrich Hortleder, and her daughter. The Hortleders had come from Weimar specifically to attend this dinner.

Ludwig Kastenmayer was talking to Hortleder himself, introducing Gary Lambert.

Hortleder as a historian was delighted to be meeting another up-timer.

Hortleder as a lawyer was as happy as Gerhard to have one more issue surrounding the up-timers pretty well settled. A settlement to which his own brief had contributed as much as Kastenmayer's tact.

Hortleder as a bureaucrat, the former tutor of the young dukes of Saxe-Weimar and the chancellor of the duchy at the time the Ring of Fire occurred, always felt a need to be cautious around the up-timers. It had been, after all, on his watch that Grantville "slid" Saxe-Weimar out of the grasp of its rightful rulers while they were away fighting on behalf of Emperor Gustavus Adolphus. Logically, since the dukes appeared to bear the up-timers no major grudge, they should bear Hortleder no major grudge, either. But human beings were not always logical, so Hortleder remained careful, even though the nature of his position as chancellor, which he still held, required him to work closely with the up-timers.

Hortleder had been a bit startled when he first discovered that Herr Michael Stearns was, if anything, a Calvinist, while Herr Edward Piazza was a Catholic. But he had borne up well, under the circumstances. He had also provided them with the loan of many young, well-trained administrators and bureaucrats—a commodity of which they were acutely in need.

When humans were being logical, Gerhard thought, Hortleder was the kind of man who logically ought to appeal to the up-timers. Not a nobleman. Not even close. He came from modest circumstances. His father had been a farmer and local administrator at Ampfurth bei Wanzleben. He had studied law at Helmstedt, then at the universities, Wittenberg and Jena, as a scholarship student and gotten his doctorate in 1606. He spent some time as a private tutor. Two years later he had become tutor to the young dukes of Saxe-Weimar. Wilhelm Wettin, as he was now, Bernhard, Ernst, Albrecht, and the others so sadly deceased. A year later, he received an additional post as lecturer at the university of Jena. In 1617, they appointed him court historian, in recognition of the publication of his history of the League of Schmalkalden. And, as so often was the fate of scholars, moved him into administration. He became a member of the ducal council and was placed in charge of the duchy's archives.

Catharina, his wife, was the daughter of the chancellor of Brandenburg's Neumark. They had married while he was still a student, which was most unusual. It was even more unusual that Chancellor Barth had permitted it. There had certainly been no guarantee back then that Hortleder would have an outstanding career.

The joy and sorrow of their life was their daughter Anna Catharina. Joy because now, at twenty, she was a lovely girl. Sorrow because she was their only child.

Gerhard's gaze continued around the room. Zacharias Prüschenk von Lindenhofen had accompanied the Hortleders. He had come to the university of Jena four years ago to get his law degree. He now wanted to marry Anna Catharina. More precisely, he wanted to marry the only child of the chancellor of Saxe-Weimar, who happened to be Anna Catharina. Gerhard feared that in Prüschenk‘s view, she could as well have been anyone else.

From Sulzbach in the Upper Palatinate, he was twenty-four and ambitious. The Ring of Fire had destroyed his prospects of an advantageous betrothal to Gertrud Romanus, the daughter of the mayor of Naumburg, when the political constellations changed. Although he was of the lower nobility, or at least claimed to be, he was now willing to condescend to marry the only daughter of the commoner who was chancellor of Saxe-Weimar for the connections she would bring him.

Prüschenk was...Gerhard looked around...over there, talking to young Muselius, his back turned to Kastenmayer, Hortleder, and Lambert.

That was good, because Beulah McDonald was clearly about to introduce Hortleder's wife and daughter to Gary Lambert, whose role at the Rudolstadt Colloquy made him of such piquant interest to many of Thuringia's Lutherans. Gary was a wonderfully orthodox Lutheran, Gerhard thought with satisfaction. The up-time LCMS to which he belonged was nearly equivalent to being a Flacian. Whereas the ELCA to which families such as that of Herr Ronaldus Koch and his wife belonged was essentially Philippist. Gerhard found it comforting to discover that the eternal verities had continued so far into the future.

Though it was a little startling that Gary continued to be personal friends with the Kochs and Muselius—even with Kastenmayer—in spite of their theological differences.

Gary clearly piqued Anna Catharina Hortleder's interest a great deal. She seemed to be in no way disillusioned by the reality of the slightly stocky build, prematurely receding hairline, and thick spectacles of the first real up-timer she had ever met.

Gerhard sighed. He and Maria had hoped to find some nice, suitable girl in whom Gary might take an interest once his matrimonial status was cleared up.

But not that one.

Friedrich Hortleder was looking at his daughter and Gary with one of those "What the hell have I done?" expressions on his face.

It was too late to change the list of guests Maria had invited to dinner and back Chancellor Hortleder and his family out of the room.

Prüschenk would not be pleased to have a second prospective fiancée slip out of his grasp.

* * *

Pastor Kastenmayer had not wanted to stay in Jena to attend this dinner. He would have preferred to return home at noon, as soon as the court had issued its ruling. Salome was very near her time. He didn't care for the idea of leaving her alone with the children longer than absolutely necessary. However, since he was here, he would do his duty. His telling of the story of his adventures among the up-timers in pursuit of enlightenment in regard to Deuteronomy 22:5 was the hit of the evening.

Zacharias Prüschenk von Lindenhofen did not find it funny.

He was also dissatisfied with the matrimonial ruling that had been issued that morning. After all, no matter what had been concluded by the consistory of Saxe-Weimar, on the basis of the majority of the expert opinions it had gathered, it had failed to take into consideration advice from the saner portion of German Lutheranism. The more prestigious university of Wittenberg, in Electoral Saxony, under the patronage of Duke John George, had not yet ruled in the matter of presumption of death for spouses left up-time. Nor had the Saxon consistory. In Prüschenk's view, the Jena faculty and Saxe-Weimar had acted prematurely.

Prüschenk frowned at Anna Catharina Hortleder, making his disapproval of her obvious interest in the up-timer Lambert clear. She ignored him.

Perhaps it was not too late to change his allegiance. If he could obtain an appointment in Saxony, then the possibility of his marrying Gertrud Romanus from Naumburg might be revived. She wasn't betrothed yet.

He could probably start by writing a pamphlet denouncing Kastenmayer's methodology and conclusions in regard to Deuteronomy

22:5. A pamphlet with woodcuts. Citation to legal precedents. Something involving heresy and the whore of Babylon as well as skorts and culottes. Prüschenk's mind drifted as the guests moved into the dining room.

Weimar, October 1634

Gary Lambert was finding a lot of reasons to go back and forth to Weimar these days.

The staff at Leahy Medical Center extended its indulgence to its business manager. Beulah had clued them in. There was a general consensus that if anyone deserved a few rays of sunshine in his existence, it was Gary.

So he was talking to Friedrich Hortleder. And his wife. And his daughter. About the problems of his friend Jonas, whom Hortleder had met at Dean Gerhard's dinner.

"So, I thought," he asked a little hesitantly. "They haven't hired anyone for the job yet. It's the kind of thing he would be really good at. It would pay enough that he could marry Ronella. And since you were their tutor, maybe Duke Ernst would pay attention to a letter of recommendation from you?"

Hortleder considered.

"I believe," he said, "that I should know more of the situation before writing Duke Ernst. Not that I doubt your assessment of the situation. But, perhaps, I should come to Grantville for a week or two. Observe Muselius for myself, beyond what one can learn at a dinner party. Meet the young woman and her family. Talk to Pastor Kastenmayer in more detail."

He looked briefly at his wife and daughter. "Bring my family with me, so that I may also -benefit from their assessments."

Anna Catharina jumped up, yelled "Papa" at the top of her lungs, and hugged him.

Hortleder continued to speak with undisturbed solemnity. "In the meantime, I will write Duke Ernst only to the effect that I have identified a suitable candidate for the position of administrator of the new normal school and beg him to make no other appointment until he hears from me again. In fact, I will request you to send a radio message to him from me. A message to that effect."

October 1634

Salome Piscatora was extremely indignant at the pamphlet that arrived in the mail. It came out of Saxony. It portrayed her in a set of divided skirts in a style she had certainly never worn.

Never would have worn.

Abominable thing. Salacious.

The pamphlet said awful things about Ludwig, who had gone to Rudolstadt today to meet with the consistorial court. Things going all the way back to before he had transferred from Saxony to Ohrdruf in Gleichen. Long before he had come to Schwarzburg-Rudolstadt. Whoever wrote it must have connections in Saxony.

Then it said things which accused him of misinterpreting the scriptures in regard to Deuteronomy 22:5.

She looked at it, sputtering.

Stood up. Sat down. Realized that the baby was coming.

St. Martin's in the Fields parsonage had not yet been equipped with a telephone.

Jonas had one installed in the school, though.

Carefully, she crossed the courtyard to the school.

"It's not right," she said to Maria Blandina. "I've had enough children to know. It isn't coming right. There's something wrong."

Jonas called for an ambulance and put the older children on the honor system until he returned.

The pastor's wife had expected to be delivered at home by a midwife, of course. But it was clear that there would not be time.

It was also clear, Jonas thought, that there was nothing an ordinary midwife would be able to do to help her.

"So you see," Ludwig Kastenmayer said to the visiting Friedrich Hortleder the next morning, "I was wrong. I refused to pay for a 'telephone' with parish funds. I thought it was a frivolity. We had lived without one for all of our lives, so why should we need one now.

"Jonas paid for it himself. For emergencies, he said. Without it, I would have lost both Salome and the child. Three physicians were called to assist. One revived the child. 'Resuscitation' they call it. The other two performed surgery.

"I don't know what I would do without Salome. I have come to rely on her so much, in every way. We are naming the baby 'Jonas Justinus,' of course. I will hate to lose him if the up-timers find him a different job. He is a wonderful teacher."

Hortleder nodded. He sent a follow-up letter of recommendation to Duke Ernst that evening. One considerably warmer than the first, which he had mailed as a courtesy to Gary.

At the hospital, Ronella Koch stood on her toes, trying to peek over Gary's shoulder into the nursery.

Gary didn't move out of the way. If he had moved, Ronella would have had no reason to grab onto Jonas' good arm to help her stay balanced on her toes. There were all sorts of ways to be a friend.

She got a good look at the baby. Her fingers tightened on Jonas' arm, so hard that he flinched and stepped forward even with Gary, bringing her with him. She sank back down on her heels, looking at Gary.

"Yeah," he said. "We revived him, of course. That's what we do with babies who can live. Whether they'll thank us for it in the long run is another question. But that's what we do."

Maria Blandina, standing on the other side of Jonas, was frowning. "Papa has baptized other such infants," she said. "They do not often live long. That is in the hands of God. At least my stepmother did not die. Papa would have missed her very much."

The Hortleders had let Anna Catharina come with Gary to see the baby and then go to a student concert at the high school on condition that the two of them remained with Jonas, Ronella, and Maria Blandina. Carol Koch had bribed Herr Hortleder, in his role as historian, to permit this excursion with the promise of an exclusive interview concerning her perspective on the Rudolstadt Colloquy.

Anna Catharina was frowning in turn. "What is wrong?" she asked Gary.

The group adjourned to one of Leahy's many cubicles to discuss Down's Syndrome. At the end of that conversation, Jonas claimed that he ought to excuse himself from the remainder of the evening in order to be available to assist Pastor Kastenmayer and his wife if he was needed. At least, that was what he said. In fact, he found proximity to Ronella increasingly uncomfortable.

"You can't," Gary said firmly. "You can't duck out on the rest of the evening, because having you here was one reason the Hortleders let Anna Catharina come to the high school play with us." He managed to make it Jonas' duty to remain. Jonas had a strong sense of duty. Unfortunately, the only way Gary could think of to persuade him that he had a duty to marry Ronella—wouldn't work. Not given his conscientious avoidance of proximity.

Jonas was going to be as proximate to Ronella as Gary and Maria Blandina could maneuver him all evening. No having Ronella on one end, the other three of them in the center, and Jonas on the far end. Which he would try to manage if nobody watched him carefully.

"Conspirators 'R' Us," Gary had said to Anna Catharina. Then he had to explain the context. It had taken quite a while, but neither of them minded. She said that she was quite willing to help with the maneuvers.

November 1634

Ron Koch was feeling acutely uncomfortable.

Not that Pastor Kastenmayer didn't understand the problem.

"What Jonas needs, if this is to occur," Ludwig Kastenmayer said, "is a better job. Not that I wouldn't hate to lose him at the school here. He is an excellent teacher. But the fact is, he is in no position to support your daughter. He's perfectly right about that. He would have been an acceptable match for Maria Blandina, since she is used to being as poor as he is. But...."

"I was afraid of something of the sort."

"He left his studies at Jena after two years to take the job teaching at Quittelsdorf because he was out of money. If he should return to the university now, it would be at least five years before he would be in a position to marry," Pastor Kastenmayer continued. "Even if he received a plum job offer immediately upon completing his degree. There is no family to provide him with a subsidy. Consider the proverb 'poor as church mice' and apply it to his case."

"Should we factor in that Ronella would be perfectly willing to wait?" Ron asked. "Not happy, but willing. She has a bad case of wanting to marry Jonas and no other."

Pastor Kastenmayer fingered his goatee.

"The other possibility might be for Grantville or the State of Thuringia-Franconia to hire him in some sort of an administrative capacity. Someone such as Herr Adducci. Or, perhaps, Herr Chehab in the Department of the Interior. Many of your leaders do not have university degrees. Jonas is capable. He would make an excellent chief of staff or personal assistant. He would be a loss to our school, of course. A great loss. He is an excellent teacher. A truly outstanding teacher. And because of his friendship with Gary Lambert, he has learned more about working with you up-timers, perhaps, than anyone else among us."

"What the USE doesn't need right now," Ron Koch said, "is to lose any more of its good teachers."

"Daddy," Ronella asked a couple of days later, "have you talked to Jonas?"

"Ah," Ron Koch said. "Well, I've talked to Pastor Kastenmayer. We're trying another tactic. Trying to find Jonas a job that pays more. I'll talk to the SoTF personnel office to see what they have for openings. Or a scholarship from Count Ludwig Guenther, so he can finish his degree and get a job that pays more later on. Your mother is going to talk to Count Ludwig Guenther about scholarships. If he has that, maybe he'll, ah, take care of the rest of the project himself."

"You really don't want to talk to him about it for me, do you?"

"Honestly," her father said. "Not one little bit."

"If you don't do *something* pretty soon...." she wailed. "Daddy, you're going to have to adapt."

"What still bothers me," Carol said afterwards, "is that we don't really know whether or not he wants to marry her. Noble renunciation doesn't usually last this long. Maybe he's just not interested."

"According to Gary, he's interested," Ron said.

"Well, that's a relief."

"It's a relief, but it doesn't seem to simplify matters any. The general consensus among the sensible and pragmatic members of down-time society seems to be that he can't even afford to court her, much less marry her."

The other courtship was easier. Friedrich Hortleder was finding more reasons to travel to Grantville to consult with other members of the administration of the State of Thuringia-Franconia these days. Frequently, he brought his family.

"I'll show you the outside of the 'trailer' where Gary lives," Pastor Kastenmayer said to him. "I've gotten to know quite a few of the people who live in this 'trailer court' now. More and more of the 'units' are occupied by Germans. It is not by any means a fine house, but what more does a bachelor need? I feel sure that he is in a position to afford better now, should he chose to marry again."

"I," Hortleder's wife said, "would much appreciate seeing this 'small electric organ' that he is said to own. "Can you arrange for me to view it? I have trouble visualizing the concept."

They were not surprised when Gary invited them to dinner.

They were surprised that he cooked it.

"I've gotten better at it," he said cheerfully. "When you have to eat your own cooking, you either get better at it or get indigestion. I eat at the hospital cafeteria sometimes, especially breakfast. Or pick up some carry-out, if I'm in a hurry. But most of the time, I cook."

After dinner, Gary and Hortleder dived into the contents of Gary's grandfather's footlocker. Hortleder discovered many things of interest.

"You're welcome to come and look again any time," Gary said. "I'm glad I've found someone who really appreciates the stuff. Now if you look at this...." He picked up a red book. "It's the *Concordance to the Lutheran Hymnal.* It doesn't just have the words in both the original language and the English translation, but also short biographies of the composers and lyricists."

Hortleder thumbed through. Biographies of composers now well known. And those of boys now young children. Giving, frequently, their birth places and the names of their parents. Boys whose careers could be furthered, whose development could be enhanced by scholarships or appointments to cathedral choirs.... Through the patronage of the dukes of Saxe-Weimar, who could thus continue to be of great importance in the duchy that the up-timers had slid out from under them on his own watch, while they were away.

"Could I borrow this?" he asked.

"Sure," Gary said. "I hardly ever use it. It's not the kind of thing the state library has any need for, either."

Amberg, Upper Palatinate, December 1634

"Because it appeals to my sense of humor," Duke Ernst said to his secretary. "A Christmas present for him."

"One for me, too, Your Grace," Johann Heinrich Böcler said. "Doing another full-time job has not been fun. When?"

"After the end of the school year, I'm afraid. In the spring."

"Better than never. What does Mrs. Simpson think of the decision?"

"She doesn't know him, but she doesn't object. Moreover, since I'm paying his salary, it is my decision."

Duke Ernst had a firm grasp on the reality of patronage. Namely that the person who controlled the purse strings controlled the project, no matter how courteously.

"I will employ this Muselius, and I will notify him by radio. Making sure that the full package of paperwork is there in advance, of course."

Jena, December 1634

Dean Gerhard and his wife invited Gary Lambert to Jena for Christmas. Gary accepted. It provided him with a graceful excuse to avoid the issue of taking communion at St. Martin's in the Fields. Pastor Kastenmayer was, basically, of the Philippist persuasion.

It would also be nice that the Hortleders were permitting Anna Catharina to visit the Gerhards over the holidays.

Very nice, really.

Grantville, December 1634

"Why now?" Jonas asked wearily. The last thing that he needed on the late afternoon of Christmas Eve, the day when he would need to direct the children's play in the evening, was a summons to the Department of International Affairs to receive a radio message. "Can't someone transcribe it and send it out here?"

Maria Blandina's eighty, more or less, first and second graders were singing loudly. Not melodically, but loudly.

Errol Mercer had introduced some new melodies for them. Jonas had written more theologically suitable lyrics. "A host of heaven'ly angels" now stood in for "Rudolph the red-nosed reindeer." Combined with the traditional "Vom Himmel hoch da komm' ich her," every child would get to sing a solo line.

That was important to the parents of the littlest ones.

For the older children, of course, the program was more ambitious. A pageant for the third and fourth graders. They were setting that up in the courtyard. It was convenient for a director that heavenly angels appeared in hosts. It gave a person something to do with the children whose voices did not carry well outdoors.

Then his own upper grades.

He was grateful that Ronella had offered to help with the program.

He really was.

It was kind of her. Especially on top of her own heavy teaching obligations. He kept assuring himself that she was doing this out of kindness.

If it only hadn't caused her to be right here in his classroom so much of the time after school for the past two weeks. So visibly, physically, present.

Right here and right now, she was waving the telephone receiver at him. "You can come and talk to them yourself. They want you there when the 'radio window' opens up."

He stood up. "I'll go."

"Catch the trolley both ways," she said. "It's faster. That's an idea. I'll get Daddy to add some money into our special Christmas contribution to cover trolley fares for the Countess Kate staff when they need to go downtown or to Rudolstadt. I'll run the kids through one more rehearsal for you."

Jonas winced. Special contribution. Casually add enough money to cover a year of carfares for the staff. One more reminder of how far she was beyond his reach.

But he took the trolley.

"God damn and blast," Ronella muttered under her breath. She couldn't seem to spend an hour with Jonas without saying something that rolled back against her.

* * *

Jonas looked disbelievingly at the radio message as it came in from Amberg.

It had to be a joke.

But it wasn't. The final line was a statement that the paperwork was in Herr Jenkins' office, and he should pick it up before he returned to the school. Reply requested within one week.

He went into Wes Jenkins' office. Consular Affairs. The packet was there.

He put it in his cottage when he got back to the school and turned his attention to last-minute rehearsals.

Maria Blandina and the ladies of the congregation were feeding the children supper here. It took too long for them to go home from rehearsals and return again for the evening. St. Martin's in the Fields parish covered too large a geographical area for comfort. Not like a village church, nestled snugly in the middle of the houses, or a town church, drawing parishioners from one district of the city or one suburb outside the walls.

Adapting, always adapting.

If he left, who would do his work here?

If he left, he would miss the friends he had made since the day he brought the remains of Quittelsdorf among these strangers.

If he left, he wouldn't have to be here when Ronella married someone else. As she must do, some day.

At Chancellor Hortleder's personal recommendation to Duke Ernst. But how come?

Gary. Yes, Gary, of course. If he left, he would miss the friends he had made here.

A normal school. To administer a normal school, to shape it in accordance with his vision of up-timers and down-timers working together.

He had done these programs so often. He moved through it as though he were aware of what he was doing.

Then the midnight service.

Finally, back in his own rooms, he lit a candle and opened the packet to find out what the exact terms of employment would be.

* * *

Ron Koch said good-night to Pastor Kastenmayer and his wife. He looked around. Carol was standing behind him, a determined gleam in her eye.

"That way," she said. "That's Jonas' place, at the back of the courtyard. The cottage with a candle lit. This is your last chance, my dearest darling. Either you go talk to him or I do. You have all your talking points in your pocket if you need them. We've talked to Count Ludwig Guenther. There's a scholarship for Jonas if he wants to take it. Ronella would like to know if there's any light at the end of the tunnel. If there is, she's willing to wait. If not—well, then, not. You know. Just go do it."

Feeling remarkably like a lamb sent to the slaughter, Ron went off to perform his paternal duty.

Pastor Kastenmayer headed for the parsonage, muttering under his breath about the fact that an up-time girl named Denise Beasley, who had come to the service—she called it a "play"—with Gerry Stone, who was now studying in Rudolstadt with the intent of becoming a Lutheran pastor, had been wearing jeans at the Christmas Eve service. Her best jeans. With a coat over them. But still, jeans.

He was beginning to suspect that the more up-timers became Lutheran, the more women wearing jeans there would be in his parish. Theology was one thing. Trousers on women might be adiaphoral, but he would still prefer to see women wearing skirts. Even divided ones.

Carol wiped the slush and snow off the church steps with an old piece of paper and sat down. The stone was cold, but this was likely to take a while.

What was an old newspaper doing here on the church steps? She looked at it, as well as she could, in the light reflecting off the snow. Not a newspaper. It was another of those horrid pamphlets about Deuteronomy 22:5.

Looking more carefully, it was a new horrid pamphlet about Deuteronomy 22:5. There were stacks of them at each end of the church steps, waiting to be picked up by parishioners coming out of Christmas Eve services and coming in for Christmas morning services. Merry Christmas from Santa Claus. Who in hell in Saxony would care enough about St. Martin's in the Fields to keep them coming? And why? One more irritant out of Saxony. Why did the Saxons care?

The stone was really cold. She grabbed a stack of the pamphlets and sat on them. Someone might as well get some good from the things, even though she realized that she might end up with printers' ink on the back of her skirt, which would be a real pain to get out.

"Carol," Salome said softly behind her. "What is the matter? Don't you want to go inside? Ronella went over to the parsonage with Maria Blandina to stay warm until you are ready to leave."

Carol looked around. Salome was cuddling baby Jonas in a blanket and trying to lock the church doors at the same time.

"I thought you went home when Pastor Kastenmayer did."

Salome shook her head. "I wanted to show little Jonas the manger once more. Before I took him home. I'm so glad he lived to see Christmas. I don't think he will live much longer. Each time we take him to the hospital with breathing problems, he comes home weaker. But now, by the faith his baptism worked in him, he knows that he will get to go to heaven and play with the baby Jesus there."

Carol hopped up off the steps, took the huge key, and turned it, using both hands. "How does that work, since Jesus grew up and was crucified?"

"Oh," Salome said. "Eternity isn't time that goes on forever. It is a place without time, where everything *is* all at once. Everyone knows that. It's the main reason that purgatory was such a stupid idea, theologically. You can't have souls doing penance for certain amounts of time in eternity."

Carol blinked.

" 'He the alpha and omega, He the source, the ending, He.' It would be nice if the baby could see Easter, but at least he has seen Christmas. Now," Salome said briskly. "What's the matter? Why were you sitting on the steps?"

"Nothing's the matter. I'm waiting for Ron. Who is, I hope, telling Jonas that Ronella wants to marry him. Or something of the sort. If we're lucky, he'll manage to get the idea across."

"Well, then," Salome said practically, "it's as well that they have found Jonas this new job. Chancellor Hortleder told Ludwig that he would receive the formal offer today. He would never have been able to afford her, teaching here."

"What new job?" Carol asked.

OR THE HORSE MAY LEARN TO SING

Christmas Vacation, 1634

The Reverend Al Green opened the back door into the rectory kitchen, stomped the snow off his boots, shook it off his hat, kissed his wife Claudette, looked around, spotted their adopted children Clemens and Emilia helping the maid accomplish various food-associated chores, and asked, "Where's Anthony? Isn't he going to be home for supper?"

Allen, the Greens' older son, looked up from the book he was reading and called through from the once-upon-a-time television room off the kitchen that was now his bedroom since they'd adopted Emilia, "Hi, Dad. Gone with some of his friends to look at the outdoor manger scene at the Lutheran Church. Back later."

Grantville's Baptist minister laughed. "That seems harmless enough."

* * *

"We really shouldn't be doing this," Anthony Green said. "Not here."

Carly Baumgardner giggled. "Why not? It's fun. Not as handy as Mrs. Genucci's gazebo was when the weather was warmer, but it's been pretty hard to find any place we can get together this winter. Over Thanksgiving, we didn't have a chance at all. And we never do when school's in session full time. Because you're either doing homework on weekday evenings or at church with your folks on the weekends."

"Even so." Anthony looked anxious. "Carly, it's a *manger* scene. Right here between St. Martin in the Fields church and Countess Kate school. It's *religious.*"

She reached over and tickled him. "But it's still fun. Or...isn't it still fun, for you?"

"I worry about what could happen."

"We've lucked out so far.

* * *

Jonas Justinus Muselius locked the door to the upper-grades schoolroom at Countess Kate and looked across toward the church, thinking he had heard something. What? A girl's voice? From the manger scene?

Then there were footsteps. "Jonas," someone called. "I was hoping we could catch you before you left."

"Oh," he smiled.

Gerry Stone came around the corner of the church, his friends Denise Beasley and Minnie Hugelmair with him.

"We were wondering.... "

The four of them moved away, down the slight incline toward the trolley stop.

Ohrdruf, State of Thuringia-Franconia, February 1635

The household worship in the small section of Schloss Ehrenstein, which the will of the late and last count of Gleichen had assigned to his widow as a residence, came to a close. The countess withdrew to her private chambers, accompanied by her lady-in-waiting. Two maids, sent in the by steward, began to remove the chairs they had gathered in the center of the room to their usual locations, neatly against the walls.

"Her faith is greater than mine," Ezechiel Meth said to his mother.

Die Stiefelin looked after their patroness. "Her faith is remarkable indeed. Perhaps even greater than that of my brother Esaias. She still lives in hope that since God brought about such a miracle for Sarah, he will bring about such a miracle for her. Not merely that God can, because of course he can. But that he in fact will."

* * *

"I hereby declare that Countess Erdmuthe Juliana of Honstein..." The voice behind the bullhorn continued to boom.

The woman looked out the window of her residence which was, effectively, a townhouse fronting directly upon the street. If she had been living at one of her late husband's castles, out in the countryside, the demonstrators could never have come so near.

"...Dowager Countess of Gleichen..."

She laughed, a little bitterly. "Make that 'widow of the late Count Johann Ludwig of Gleichen,' why don't you? she said to the window pane. "You need a lesson in heraldry, you insolent little man. It's impossible to be a dowager when there is no new count. When the county itself has become extinct, and the lands have fallen to distant cousins such as Hohenlohe."

"...once again harboring in her household Ezechiel Meth, *chymicus*, relapsed from his solemn vow to return to the practice of orthodox Lutheranism...."

"Does our steward know who is speaking?" The countess addressed these words, more or less, in the direction of an elderly man standing by the other window.

"Pankratz Holz, I believe, My Lady. A Silesian. For several years now, he has been an errand boy for Superintendent Melchior Tilesius in Langensalza. Most recently he has been in Grantville, I understand. I am somewhat surprised to see him here."

"Not if there is trouble to foment." A lady-in-waiting, at least as old as the steward, moved away from the fireplace to join him in looking out the window. "Neither of them has any jurisdiction here. Not even if the Erfurt city council gave them permission, as they claim."

"Who would have jurisdiction?" the countess asked.

The steward shook his head. "I have no idea. First the New United States and now the government of the State of Thuringia-Franconia have refused to accept any responsibility for supervising the Lutheran churches of the county of Gleichen as it formerly existed. The peculiar entity that chooses to call itself Vasa County, Thuringia, which embodies all the parts of the former county of Gleichen that West Virginia County—that's the new name for the Ring of Fire, Grantville and its surroundings—had not already annexed, will, I suppose, set up a superintendency. When it gets sufficiently organized. Until then, the pastors and congregations in the cities are being supervised by the city councils. The villages are appealing to the various neighboring superintendencies for aid and assistance when they encounter any problem above the strictly parish level. Without any kind of authorization, I must add, which is probably why Count Ludwig Guenther has been so reluctant to become involved in the problem, even though he, in Rudolstadt, is as close to Ohrdruf as Tilesius."

"And why Tilesius has not been reluctant at all." The countess pressed her face against the window again. "He has been looking to destroy the followers of my prophet for thirty years now. He must see this as an unequaled opportunity."

A man standing behind Holz—behind the man who was probably Holz—bent over, picked up a stone, and threw it at the window where the countess was standing.

She flinched back. The stone cracked one of the panes several feet above her head and then rattled down the window before it bounced off the sill and landed on the ground next to the front steps.

The elderly lady-in-waiting moved across the room and grasped her shoulder. "My Lady, come away."

The countess shook her head. "Why won't the SoTF government take charge of this? Deal with this kind of thing?"

"It's in their Constitution," the steward said. "Separation of church and state, it's called. That the government has no authority over matters of faith. The up-timers are said to be utter fanatics on the topic, which is why, so far, they have forbidden the city council to arrest us because of our beliefs."

The countess turned. "So the SoTF will not persecute. Will it protect? That might be too much to expect. But I am sure that this 'hands off policy' shouldn't extend to permitting actual violence by one religious group against another. Does it? Do we know?" She looked toward the rear of the townhouse. "Has anyone summoned the watch?"

"Ezechiel said that he would send one of the stableboys. But I'm sure that whatever the SoTF believes, the city council of Ohrdruf has no interest in protecting us." The older woman sighed. "Rather, they are probably looking for a member of Your Ladyship's household to commit some kind of violence in return. Hoping for it, rather—which would give them an excuse to arrest us. Like the Erfurt city council arrested us when we were in Gispersleben, at St. Kilian's. In Solomonsborn. So long ago."

"Arrest us, when we are the ones being attacked?"

"Who is there to testify to that? Other than we ourselves? Whose testimony the city council will refuse to accept."

There hadn't been any more stones. The countess returned to the window.

The man with the bullhorn continued to declaim.

* * *

"You can't let it keep going on. Somebody's going to get hurt." Fred Jordan, right at the moment, dealing with the city council of Ohrdruf, was not appreciating his job as liaison between West Virginia County and outside-the-Ring of Fire law enforcement agencies. Which had led him into being, right at the moment, Ed Piazza's personal emissary to Ohrdruf.

"I don't believe you quite understand," the deputy mayor of Ohrdruf answered.

Fred realized that it was a status thing. They—being the deputy mayor and two other guys—were communicating that he wasn't important enough to deserve a face-to-face with the mayor himself.

"The countess has been residing in Ohrdruf quite voluntarily. She is under no obligation to remain here. Not the slightest. She could always go live somewhere else on the income she receives from her dower lands. Erfurt, for example. There are nice townhouses in Erfurt. Also, I understand, a significant number of your up-timers now live in Erfurt.

Perhaps they would wish to take her and her household of extremists under their protection."

"The point," Fred said patiently, "is that she and her folks, whatever they believe and no matter how peculiar it is, have a perfect right to live anywhere in the State of Thuringia-Franconia. Undisturbed."

One of the other guys—the lawyer type, Fred rememberes—rustled through a folder of papers. "According to the false prophet Esaias Stiefel," he said solemnly, "the countess was to be the designated mother of the Messiah at his second coming."

Fred swallowed. His parents weren't church members, and he'd never gone himself, back when he was growing up. He'd had to take a kind of short course after he proposed to Bitsy. She was Presbyterian and wanted to get married in church. Old Enoch Wiley wouldn't do the ceremony unless he went through with that. Then, after the kids came along, he'd joined up, because Bitsy said it would be less confusing for them.

Not that he ever actually went, except for the kids' programs and such. But he was pretty sure that some lady giving birth to the baby Jesus again was not in the curriculum.

Even so. He looked at the lawyer. "If that's what she wants to think, she's got a right to. Weird isn't a prosecutable offense, Mister."

"I beg to disagree," the lawyer type answered. "I have right here—my researcher found it at the state library—a discussion of the limits on freedom of speech under the Constitution of the United States of America. One of the justices of your up-time Supreme Court wrote that the right of free speech did not extend 'to yelling *fire* in a crowded theater.' The beliefs of the countess and her household are the religious equivalent of that kind of provocation."

"I expect," Fred answered, "that you're going to need to talk to one of Ed Piazza's legal staff to iron this out. I was just a deputy sheriff. But I don't mind saying that I'm here to tell you that you've got to keep a handle on the demonstrations. Holz and his guys can picket and proclaim all they want, but if there are any more rocks, somebody's going to arrest them. If it isn't you and your watch, it will be the SoTF. We don't have a state police yet, but we do have the Mounted Constabulary, and he'll send them in if he has to."

Grantville

There was a flash of light. April Lafferty put her hands on her hips, looked at the overhead fixture, and said, "Oh shit."

"April." A reproachful voice came from the next room.

"The bulb blew out."

"That doesn't excuse unladylike language."

"Sorry, Mildred."

For the five hundredth time, she wished that her mother's house had a basement, where she could work in peace. But the rock around Grantville didn't lend itself to basements. She looked at her work bench again. She'd have to sweet talk Mildred out of another one.

She could predict it now. At least one more apology for the bad language. Up to three more apologies. Two serious conversations about keeping a closer eye on Carly. A couple of extra turns at doing the dishes, since Mildred thought Carly was sloppy about them. At least one trip to the Senior Citizens' Center to play games with the old folks. Mildred didn't approve of either cards or bingo, so a weekend wouldn't work. It would mean giving up a Thursday, which was their board games night. Mildred would play Clue or Chinese Checkers or Uno. Scrabble. That sort of thing. Scrabble was her favorite.

Mildred was really stingy with her light bulbs. After it had hit her what the Ring of Fire meant, she'd gone through her and old Horace's house and taken all but one bulb out of every lamp in every room. Wrapped them up carefully in wadded newspaper and stored them. Brought them along when she moved over to Mom's.

Which did mean, at least, that they were among the comparatively few families in Grantville that still had a stash of light bulbs.

* * *

"What do you think, Claudette," Al Green asked. He relied heavily on his wife. On her common sense. On her good heart. He told her so often. "It's what Mildred Baumgardner wants. She's a faithful member of the church. So was Horace, before he died. But her grandson has never testified to his faith...."

Claudette frowned. What she *wanted* to say was that the Baumgardners had been so estranged from their son Zane, and so hostile to the woman he had, eventually, married, several years after Ronnie was born, that they hadn't made any real effort to give the boy a Christian upbringing back when it might have done some good. But she had to live up to the "good heart" bit, even if sometimes, in private, she thought that her husband was a more than a bit unworldly and needed a keeper about as much as he needed a spouse. Or maybe more than he needed a spouse. Still...she supposed she had to talk him through it, to the point that his own good heart would override all the scruples that seminary had instilled in him.

"They don't want to make a big fuss about the wedding, do they? No gigantic production with white satin and the trimmings? Not so soon after the mine disaster."

"They couldn't afford it, even if they did want to. Megan and Mariah both—I have to give credit where it's due, even if they aren't from a churchgoing family—have been supporting themselves and pitching right in to help their grandparents ever since the Ring of Fire. Not by themselves, of course. Della Frost and Jennie Lou Burston help with Glenette's expenses, and Gayleen, Robyn, and Samantha with Sandra's, ever since John's been gone. Except for Della, their aunts all have children of their own who have to be fed and clothed and housed. I'm pretty sure the girls don't do more than get by."

"Megan's not pregnant, is she?" Claudette thought that if she was, that might be what had Al worried. Part of the marriage counseling materials they used advised strongly against "have to" marriages as not being a good basis for an enduring commitment—too likely to lead to divorce.

"Not as far as I know. It's not a 'short notice' marriage. They've been engaged quite a while. Several months, at least. She's not very feminine, though. Is she likely to make a good wife? A heavy equipment operator for the Streets and Roads Department?"

"So's Crystal Blocker—Dorrman, now—and you married her to Walt here in the church."

"Crystal's a member. So's Walt Dorrman. Megan Collins isn't. Neither is Ronnie Baumgardner."

"It doesn't seem very...welcoming...to tell them to go to city hall and get it over with."

"They want Ronnie's brother and Megan's sister as the attendants—witnesses. Garrett's still in high school. Allen says he's planning to join the army as soon as he graduates. It's all right legally as far as being a witness is concerned; he's over eighteen now. As a member of the wedding party, though.... Neither of them is a member of the church. And Mariah went off to be an actress last summer. My father always thought...."

"That actresses are immoral. And I'm sure that some of them are. Anyone who ever stood in a grocery store line reading the tabloid headlines could figure that much out." Claudette paused. "But that doesn't mean that Mariah Collins is. I've never heard anything against her. Not that she's wild, I mean."

"What do you think, then?"

"Does Mildred insist on having it in the church sanctuary? Or would she be satisfied with the fellowship hall? Especially since they won't be having a lot of guests. Thirty or so people, maybe, including all the kids? That way...." Claudette paused. "You could think of yourself as being an officiant, not a minister. After all, it's the state that licenses you to perform marriages, not the church. Well, it's West Virginia County now, but it will probably be the state again once they get new legislation covering matrimony in place. So...."

"Closer to fifty, probably," he said, picking up on the number of guests expected. "They don't plan to have a reception, so they won't need the fellowship hall to set one up."

"Even fifty people will look a little isolated up in the church. So suggest the fellowship hall. We—the Ladies Aid, I mean—can decorate it for them. Tell them that it will be a friendlier atmosphere downstairs, considering the number of guests they're inviting. After all, we want 'friendly.' Maybe they'll come back and actually start attending church if they see 'friendly.' -I'll talk to Mildred—explain your reasoning."

"Soft-soap her, you mean." Al Green smiled. "That will work. We can do it that way."

It all worked out.

"I feel really strange being here," Carly whispered. "In a church, I mean. Thanks for sitting next to me, or I'd have freaked out by now." She hoped that the piano would drown out anything she said.

"Good grief, Carly. It's your brother's wedding. You're not in the church, anyway. This is just the basement."

"Even so, Anthony. I don't think I've ever been in a church before. I'm glad we're not upstairs. I'd feel even worse. I guess it never sunk in, quite, before, that your father really is a preacher."

Mildred Baumgardner turned around in her chair. "Hush, you two. Here come Garrett and Mariah. Ronnie and Megan will come in right after them."

The ceremony was fine.

"Thanks for everything," April Lafferty said. The rest of the family had gone. She'd stayed behind to gather up anything that needed to be carried back home. A couple of vases with bittersweet and cattail arrangements in them. A pine cone wreath that she'd put colored candles in. She looked around. She'd done her best, but she hadn't been able to find a lot of festive stuff in the middle of winter. "I'll write a note to your Ladies Aid thanking them for bringing the rest of the decorations. Ah, just in case...." She didn't want to say just in case that Ronnie and Megan didn't. It wasn't the sort of thing that was likely to occur to either of them.

"It's too bad that the rest Ronnie's family couldn't be here." Claudette Green switched the subject of the conversation tactfully.

"Ray's in Wismar; so's Mom. Vance is with the army in Erfurt and couldn't get away. That's what he said, at least, and it would have been three days, I guess. One to get here, one for the wedding, and one to go back. Right in the middle of the week. Uh. I meant thanks for everything, Mr. and Mrs. Green. Not just for doing the wedding. For back in January and all. With the mine."

"You did very well," Al Green said. "Kept your head. Did everything you could have. Several people said how well you kept your cool."

"That was on the outside. Not the inside."

"If you ever feel like you need to talk about it," Claudette offered, "come and talk to me. Any time you need an ear."

April looked a little guilty. "I'd hate to use up your ear when I don't belong here at your church. You know, the three of us Lafferty kids are on the rolls at the Church of Christ. At least, Grandpa Dave put us there when we were little. Maybe Ray got himself taken off—Christina's a Lutheran and I'm pretty sure he joined that church up there in Wismar so they could get married. But I've not been to church since Grandpa Dave died, and that's when I was two years old. Ray was ten, then; Vance was four."

"Come anyway," Claudette said. "I don't care where you're officially enrolled, so to speak."

"I might then." April took a deep breath. "Sometimes, living with Mildred—sometimes I could bend your ear right off, I bet."

* * *

Zane Baumgardner opened one eye. "I'm not drunk, y'know," he said. "Just lazy. Haven't been drunk for months."

The down-timer standing next to his bed looked down at him. "Probably because you can't afford to be. You left your door unlocked again."

"Oh, damn. Somebody would probably rob me blind if I had anything worth stealing." He opened the other eye. "You're back. You're not going away, are you?"

"Not yet."

"Who the hell are you? I know, you told me the last time you showed up, but I managed to forget it. Tried real hard. Took a lot of doing, but I managed it."

"My name is Ludwig Kastenmayer."

"Don't mean a fucking thing to me."

"I am the Lutheran pastor at Saint Martin's in the Fields."

"Still don't mean a fucking thing to me."

"When did your ancestors cease to be Lutheran?"

Zane groaned, sat up, and threw his legs over the edge of the mattress.

"I don't know if they ever were. Why ask me? Ask my righteous dad. No, wait, he's dead." He rubbed a hand over the stubble on his chin. "Let me shave, will you?"

"Gladly. Shall I heat some water for you? I'm afraid that your electricity has been turned off for non-payment, but the gas stove appears to still function."

"Natural gas. Direct hookup. No point in paying for bottled gas if you don't need it." Zane stood up. "Ask the genealogy club."

"About what?"

"When my ancestors stopped being Lutheran. If they ever were."

"I did. They don't know."

"Oh hell. Yeah. My grandpa was from up in Pennsylvania somewhere. Pennsylvania Dutch, they call them. Germans, though."

"That is obvious from your name."

"Then go look it up at the library. They probably stopped being Lutheran somewhere between when the Pennsylvania Dutch got to Pennsylvania and when my grandpa came down to West Virginia to work in the mines. And that's the best I can do for you." He grabbed for a shaving mug, brush, strop, and straight razor. "I have a safety razor, but I can't afford the new blades they're making down-time. This, I can sharpen. He died when I was three—my grandpa. This is all I have that was his. We weren't exactly in the family heirloom category."

Zane got rid of the down-timer, but it didn't last. The next time....

"I brought cheese sandwiches."

"You don't give up, do you? Pastor Klicketyklack or whatever you're called."

"Rarely."

"Why the hell do you care? Talk to Dad's sisters. Kit Fisher and Ila May Thornton. Maybe they remember something. They'll remember more than my mom. Ila May married one of those Mormons. She'll be your best bet. But her husband will try to convert you."

"I am prepared to do the same to him."

"Hell. Wish I could see it." Zane choked and laid his sandwich down. "That's the first time I've laughed for longer than I can remember."

"Why are you living without electricity? I have become fond of it. Of the telephone, as well. Which you also no longer have because no one has paid the bill. Would you be interested in selling the telephone set? Or the remaining light bulbs? There are customers for such items, you know."

"I'm living without electricity and the telephone because Cheryl Ann isn't around any more to pay the bills. And to tell the truth, no, I don't really mind doing without them. I've rigged up a cistern on the roof, so unless we have a real drought, I'll still be able to flush. Now, that I *would* miss. Does that shock you, Pastor Klusterfucker or whatever you call yourself?"

"Not really."

"About those bills. I'm not going back into the mine. I'd rather live without than go back into the mine."

"I understand that you have other skills. Another trade."

"Because of the last few years—hell, it's getting closer to fifteen years than ten—nobody's likely to hire me. Chad Jenkins sure won't, and he's pretty much got the small appliance business here in town cornered. Once he gets the idea that a guy's unreliable, it's in his head for good. I've been doing some stuff for Ted Moritz—reconditioning, repairing, when he manages to get hold of used stuff to put into his new construction."

In the middle of all his other parish duties, Pastor Kastenmayer spent some time thinking.

"If you're willing to try to convert old Harold Thornton from being a Mormon, not that you're having any luck, why aren't you trying to convert me?" Zane asked at his next visit.

Ludwig Kastenmayer smiled. "I am a patient man. Also, I was informed before my first visit that you are not the religious type."

The recently acquired daughter-in-law whom Zane hadn't really met wasn't the religious type, either, as Pastor Green had known perfectly well when he was worrying about the wedding.

"Aren't you *glad* that Pastor Kastenmayer is trying to help Ronnie's dad?" Hans-Fritz Zuehlke asked.

Megan and her sister Mariah both looked a little doubtful. But Hans-Fritz was family now, sort of. The step-son by his first marriage of the current husband of Ronnie's mom.

"Our family doesn't really do church," Mariah explained. "Um, I know you go to Pastor Kastenmayer's. The one out on the Rudolstadt road. Like Eddie Junker does. April said so. I, uh, well, I asked her. It's not that I have anything against it, you understand."

"Zane needed help," Megan offered. Tentatively. "It's not like Ronnie didn't know that. Everybody in town knew that. He's needed it for a long time. It's just...."

"We're not church ladies," Mariah said again. "Maybe Megan can explain it better than I can."

"On our mom's side, the Baxters, our aunts and uncle got converted at some point, at a big revival meeting at the Church of Christ that Aunt Della's husband went to. Still goes to."

"Yes."

"After that, they hassled our mom to get converted, too. Mom didn't take well to being hassled. So after that, we didn't see much of them. I was actually surprised that they came to the wedding when we invited them. And the Collinses don't go to church at all, except for Samantha. She joined Steve Jennings' church when they got married. That's Presbyterian, but not the Reverend Wiley's church. They went to someplace in Fairmont before the Ring of Fire." Megan giggled. "Actually, there were probably more Collinses in the basement of the Baptist church for our wedding than had been in any church in the last ten years, all put together."

"So," Mariah said a little anxiously. "It's not that we aren't grateful to Pastor Kastenmayer. I know that Ronnie is—isn't he, Megan?"

Megan nodded.

"It's just that it's all a little strange to us."

"I'm not really sure that I am courting Mariah," Hans-Fritz said to Jonas Justinus Muselius over a beer. "I am escorting her. Which is a fascinating word play in English—escorting, courting. How are they connected? Linguistically, I mean. Perhaps not at all. But if I were courting her. No, that is in the present tense subjunctive. She deserves to be escorted by a man who treats her with respect. If I were to be courting her, at some time in the future...." His voice trailed off.

"Saint Martin's is delighted to welcome new members. As with the weddings we are preparing to celebrate in April."

"*Ja, richtig*. But. As far as I know, from what I've heard around town, none of those guys actually resisted being turned into Lutherans."

"No. They proved to be quite cooperative. Of course, they were all heathen to start with."

"So is Mariah Collins. But I am not sure that she would be that compliant. That is, I'm not sure that conversion-by-matrimony would work with her."

"Then, perhaps, she is not the wife you are looking for. If you are just considering that it is time that you get married, which it probably is, it would be simpler for you to fix your attentions on someone who is already a Lutheran. With your advantages, government position, salary—you shouldn't have any difficulty in attracting an appropriate wife."

Hans-Fritz picked a pen out of his shirt pocket and started playing with it. Looked down and noticed what he was doing.

"I like many up-time things," he said abruptly. "Shirt pockets, among them. And a world in which one can keep the things one needs openly available, on the outside of one's shirt, in view of others, rather than hidden inside one's doublet."

Jonas nodded.

"You're marrying Ronella Koch, aren't you? An up-timer?"

"Yes."

"If she hadn't been a Lutheran already—didn't want to be one—would you have given up the idea that easily?"

Jonas frowned. "It wasn't an issue, of course, so I hadn't really thought about it."

Hans-Fritz waited.

"I don't know." Jonas paused. "That isn't the truth. No, I would not have been dissuaded. This new world in which we are living can be complex."

"So?"

"The first thing, I suppose—you will need to ascertain if Mariah would object to having your children baptized."

"That's not the easiest topic to bring up when a man's not even sure if he's courting a woman."

Jonas smiled. "You're not dumb. You'll figure something out, if it's important enough to you. Or when it becomes important enough to you."

Ohrdruf, early March 1635

"Damn, but these roofs have a steep pitch." Harley Thomas switched his grip from one rope to another. "I'm too old to be climbing around up here."

"Snow load." Fred Jordan shook his head. "You should have seen this place during the winter. It's a little basin, right at the foot of the *Thüringerwald.* The weather comes over the mountains and dumps on it."

"Who's the guy with the bullhorn today? I thought Pankratz Holz was gone."

"He is. Back to his little storefront church in Grantville. He came over here, stirred the pot for a bit, and went back to making his other mischief."

"Then why isn't this tapering off?" Harley looked down from his perch on the roof of Countess Erdmuthe Juliana's section of Schloss Ehrenstein, peering around the false gables.

"Sometimes, once something starts, it keeps its own momentum." Fred Jordan looked around. "We've got everyone in place. The countess and her ladies are on deposit in the mayor's house, and I've made pretty clear to him that any harm that he lets come to them there.... Well, the guards I have on duty will let it come to the women in his own family, too. Okay, that's harsh, but I didn't see any other way, short of getting them out of town, and I don't have enough men to manage that. Meth and his men are out in back, in the courtyard. Even the old man, Joachim Rosenbusch, the steward, insisted on staying. I've got to say that they're loyal to her. Fanatical. The windows are boarded up. The building is as secure as we can make it."

Harley beckoned. "Corporal Rempel, do you have the walkie-talkie?"

"Yes."

"Then you take my place. Benisch, you take Jordan's."

They started creeping across the steep roof with its slick slate shingles toward the ladder. One of Harley's feet skidded. "This blasted mist isn't helping."

Fred crawled. "Do you suppose that 'secure' is the operative word?" A wind gust blew the next rope he was supposed to catch barely out of his reach. "Damn."

"What do you mean?"

"These guys..." Fred grabbed onto a slightly projecting shingle with one hand and waved the other in the general direction the mob gathered in the street. "They've had a lot of changes to deal with the past few years. Their job security is all broken down, a lot of them. Tailors, shoemakers, people like that. People talk about all the new opportunities, but how many are there, really, for a man up in his fifties with a family to support and the only job he knows is the trade he learned when he was a teenager. What's he supposed to do? Go be an unskilled laborer? These are the people who survived the war, weren't killed off by mercenaries, didn't die of disease. Now we're digging the foundations right out from under a lot of them."

"Which doesn't mean they can come in here and riot against people because they don't like their religious ideas. It's not as if the freaking countess and her oddballs have anything to do with economic changes."

"They're familiar," Fred said. "They're a familiar enemy. And they're here. Ohrdruf's not exactly on the frontier of economic progress. If there was a shoe factory here, they could riot against that. But the factory shoes are coming in from somewhere else. If there was a clothing factory here, they could riot against that. But the sewing machines are in Badenburg and Arnstadt and Rudolstadt. It's the finished clothes that are coming in here. Mostly through the Wish Book. How can you riot against a mail order catalog?" He pushed himself up on his knees to look down at the street again, groping for the rope. "Oh, hell."

That was when the shingle he was using as his handhold came loose.

Grantville, early March 1635

Harley got to the police station with the news before the wagon arrived with the body.

"I hate doing this," Preston Richards said. "I really, really, hate it. I did it for Ralph and the others last week. Not that either of the Hansens had anyone to notify. Now I'm doing it again."

Bitsy Jordan opened the door. Saw that there were two of them. In uniform. "Press? Harley?"

"Can we come in?"

"Sure. We're back in the music room."

They followed her. Daniel and Leah were both sprawled on the floor, doing homework. A man was seated at the piano.

"You know Signor Carissimi. He..."

"...wrote the song about Hans Richter's death." Press reached out his hand. "I haven't had the pleasure, before. Pleased to meet you. Um...." He looked at the children.

"Whatever it is," Bitsy said, "they'll need to know. Bad or the worst?"

"The worst," Press admitted. "They're bringing him back."

She sat down on the end of the piano bench. "What goes around, comes around, I guess. Last week.... Last week I was actually feeling—sort of good, maybe even a little bit smug—that Fred was over there in Ohrdruf. Safely away from what happened at the hospital and the synagogue. As safe as a man could ever be, in his line of work."

She gestured vaguely with her hand. "I'll need to call Jenny Maddox at the funeral home, I guess. To be expecting him. I don't know who else, really, since Reverend Wiley is dead."

Carissimi stood up. "Orval McIntire," he said. "The man who preached the state funeral. Admirable eulogies—the ones he delivered for the mayor and your minister. Stay with Daniel and Leah. I will call them both. That much of the burden, Elizabeth, I can take from your shoulders."

Ohrdruf, March 1635

"I have decided," Countess Erdmuthe Juliana said.

"The household is leaving Ohrdruf?"

"Yes."

"Perhaps the countess should reconsider. The rural castles are even less safe from attack than we are in town. Think of what the farmers did in Thuringia last year, even to strongholds that were in good repair, and defended. Most of the old Gleichen castles are decaying, in poor repair. For decades, there has been no maintenance at all except to the bailiffs' quarters. No staff except one bailiff in each to collect the dues." The steward paused.

"We are moving inside the Ring of Fire. To West Virginia County, where the authorities feel obliged to protect our religious rights. As they have now proved to us. Amply, more than amply, by sacrificing one of their own men."

"Into Grantville?"

"Not into the town itself. Some distance outside of it. The real estate broker to whom their chief of police sent me described it as a 'big, huge, ugly house, out off the highway.' The owners did not reside there permanently. They were from a nearby imperial city, I understand, called 'Washington D.C.' It escheated to the government after the Ring of Fire. There have been different tenants several times in the last few years but it has not been truly convenient for any of the residents." She looked at the paper in her hands. "This Mr. Colburn has assurances from one of the officials, a Mrs. Trout, that they will be delighted to sell it. To 'get it back on the tax rolls,' he said. Hohenlohe will be delighted to have us out of my share of Schloss Ehrenstein. We're ruining the value of his real estate with all these unpleasant events. He's paying me enough to vacate that I can afford to buy the house outright."

"Is it suitable for Your Ladyship?" her elderly lady-in-waiting asked anxiously.

The countess smiled ironically. "For a time, Frau Canzler, there was consideration of locating Princess Kristina's household there if she came to live in Grantville permanently, so I believe it should be adequate for the needs of a widow and her small retinue."

"Yes."

"It needs repairs, however. Not the repairs that it would need after decades of neglect, like the *Drei Gleichen* castles. A few years, only. There will be new requirements. I do not want to rely upon outsiders who are not of my household." She looked at the man in the room. "Let our steward find and employ a man who knows how to repair and maintain the up-time 'appliances' as the real estate broker calls them."

April 1635

"The man we need bargained," the old steward said. "Bargained very well. Very shrewdly. He has a great deal to offer us and knows it. Not just the necessary training and experience. Also several of these 'light bulbs' that are necessary for the lamps. The former tenants stole all the ones that were originally in the house, it appears, if they had not 'burned out.' I need to ascertain the meaning of that term. Also, a telephone set that can be fastened into this 'jack.' " He walked across the room, bent over, and pointed to a small box affixed to the wall near the baseboard.

"So the household has a new majordomo?"

"Assistant steward. I will not live forever. Perhaps, not even for long. Long enough, I hope, to train this Zane Baumgardner in the necessary duties." The old man paused. "There should be a certain...prestige...for the countess in having an up-timer in her employ."

"If he does not start drinking to excess again," Margaretha Canzler said. "Once he is receiving sufficient wages for him to pay for it."

"Where did you hear that?"

The elderly lady-in-waiting smiled. "From a friend of a friend who has a cook who knows a cook who works in the household of the pastor of a heterodox church in Grantville." The old woman smiled. "As heterodox as we are, I am sure, from the perspective of Superintendent Tilesius or Pastor Holz. But much more securely placed."

"As we hope to be."

"Baptists," they call themselves.

"This man, though. He is not one of us. Not a believer. I ascertained that."

"No," the lady-in-waiting said. "But his parents were among these 'Baptists.' His mother still is; she is still living. So perhaps he will have some understanding of our problems. Or can learn, if he cares to." She paused. "What is he like? In person? What does he look like? Short, tall, fat, thin?"

The steward paused. "Tall, like most of the up-timers. Thin. Otherwise? Weathered. Not unattractive, but well-worn."

Zane hadn't expected his duties to include a lot of listening.

"The great mistake of Martin Luther," Ezechiel Meth said, "was his attachment to the literal word of the written scriptures."

Zane Baumgardner raised an eyebrow. "You folks don't believe in the Bible? I can sort of see how that would get you in trouble."

"Not, um, exactly. To some extent, the concepts go back to Karlstadt. *De spiritu et littera.* Christ lives in everyone—or, at least, in everyone who accepts him. And in the created world, immanently. It is this living spirit of God, not the dead letter of a book that is the true faith. Not any written down scripture. Not even the Bible. Although, of course, there are many useful precepts to be found in it. But those precepts cannot be made into a law. That contradicts the notion of Christian freedom."

"Which you define how?"

Al Green looked at Zane Baumgardner. Talk about an unexpected visitor.

"I'm feeling a little stupid, Reverend. I think I need to read a book. And I haven't learned to read German, so asking that busybody Pastor Kastorbean out at Saint Martin's isn't going to be any help."

"Well from what you say.... " He got up and started looking up and down the bookshelves in his study.

"The guy Meth calls himself a *chymicus*. I don't think that's 'alchemist' at all. I think it's an apothecary. The countess' personal pill peddler, which she takes too many of, if you ask me, not that I'm in a position to criticize. His father was a doctor. Uh, these people aren't a batch of snake handlers from up in the hollows. His uncle, this Stiefel guy, was a merchant. Fish. Woad, that blue dye stuff. It's big business up around Erfurt. Wine. They had property. Money. He was supposed to be immortal. You'd think that when he died it would have sort of undermined the whole project, but...."

Green was muttering to himself, pulling various books of the shelf and then putting them back. "Anabaptist origins, of course. Probably, here in Thuringia, some early connection with Thomas Müntzer. Um, rebirth from the spirit. From what you say, their teachings seem to have some things in common with the Quakers."

"That I've heard of. William Penn, right? Pennsylvania."

"But the Quakers don't exist yet. Not in the sixteen-thirties. I'm bound to have something here that should help, if only I can find it." Green shoved another book back into its place. "Maybe the Schwenkfelders," he muttered.

"The *who*?"

* * *

"I'm going to have a baby, Anthony." Carly buried her face in her hands. "I guess the Christmas spirit got to us in that manger. I wasn't ever morning sick or anything, so I tried to tell myself it wasn't happening. I didn't want it to be happening. Oh, god, I'm so sorry."

"It's not exactly just your fault. It's not as if I didn't notice what we were doing. What we've been doing."

"We can't tell anybody." She grabbed his arm. "You understand that, don't you? April's really still upset because of—everything, really. The mine explosion, still. What happened last month. And Mildred will put the blame on her, which she doesn't deserve. Dietrich and Hans-Fritz will preach at me. And Mildred will try to make Mom come home from

Wismar and 'deal with it,' when she's actually happy, I think. Not just coping with what life threw at her. Maybe happy for the first time in her life. For the first time since I'm old enough to remember—that much I'm sure of. I won't let Mildred ruin it for her."

"It's not your fault. You're really still a kid."

"I'm old enough to know what I'm doing.

"You're fifteen. That's not exactly ancient."

"Well, you're sixteen. It's not that much older."

They looked at each other.

"We've got to tell somebody. Whether you want us to or not. Like you said, it has to be from Christmas vacation."

She nodded.

"Then pretty soon, people will notice. I know that much."

Carly shook her head. "We can't tell anybody." She grabbed his other arm and started to shake him. "I mean it, Anthony. Your dad will skin you alive."

"Uh, no. He won't. He'll be 'deeply and gravely disappointed' in me. Which is a lot worse, sometimes. But he's that most of the time. Did you know that when they adopted Clemens and Emilia, they let Allen move downstairs and have the room off the kitchen, but they made me stay upstairs, sharing my old room with Clemens."

"You've mentioned it a time or two."

"Allen's just a year and a half older than I am. Clemens is six whole years younger. Which pretty much shows you where they classify me. Still a kid. A kid who's not reliable enough to trust to sleep in a downstairs bedroom. Still has to stay right under their parental eyes. What do you bet that when Allen moves out, they'll keep it for him? Not let me get out from under the kid's toys."

"That makes it even more important for us not to tell them. Your dad won't let you go to the university if he finds out, I bet. I won't do that to you."

"Do what?"

"Make it so you can't go to the university. Jena. Like Allen's going to do as soon as he graduates this spring. And you're planning to do, after next year. I'm not going to muck that up for you."

"I could quit school, I guess. Get a job."

"No." This time Carly screeched. "Your dad went to college. So did your mom. Your brother's going to. And you, too." She socked his shoulder with her fist. "Nobody in my family's ever gone to college, did you know that? Never at all. Your folks will go ballistic if they find out. You're not even allowed to *date* yet."

"Uh, yeah."

"And if you were, your dad wouldn't want you to date someone like me. Not even if Mildred belongs to his church. Do you think I couldn't tell how sort of...chilly...the atmosphere was when Ronnie and Megan got married? Maybe I'm white trash, but I'm not stupid."

"You're not...." he started to say. "What about your dad? Will he skin you alive? Your mom's up in Wismar, but he's around here, isn't he?"

"I don't have the vaguest idea. He walked out when I was three years old—about that, anyway. I hardly know him at all. But he's not likely to take enough interest to skin me, no."

"That's a relief. Would your grandpa have?"

"What?"

"Skinned you?"

"Well, Mom's father died when she was a baby, so I don't have the vaguest about him either. Horace would have disapproved just as much as Mildred. He was pretty rigid, from what Mom says, but he wasn't into skinning, as far as I know. Or beating people up."

"Why do you call your grandparents by their first names?"

"Well, until Mildred moved in with us, I'd hardly ever seen her."

"Even though you all lived right here in the same town?"

"Yeah."

"That's really odd. Dad's parents lived in Shinnston. We saw them all the time. Mom's folks were in Kentucky, but we visited a couple of times a year. They were all left up-time. I've missed them a lot."

"If Mildred finds out, she'll probably throw me out."

"How could she? It's your mom's house. Mrs. Baumgardner's the one who moved in. She was in assisted living until your mom came up with that idea."

"How'd you know that?"

"Mom makes nursing home visits to church members. It's just, sort of, one of the things that she does. And takes us kids along, sometimes. And the dogs. Not the cat—she's too cranky." He stood up and started down the path. "We've got to tell somebody."

Carly followed him, grabbing the back of his jacket. "Hell, no."

They stared at each other.

"What's the matter with Anthony," Al Green asked. "He's seemed sort of distracted the last few days."

"End of the school year syndrome, I suppose," Claudette answered. "Some kind of teen-aged angst, maybe. He could be upset about Allen's going off to college next spring." She moved a stack of Red Cross handouts off the table. "I'll try to talk to him one of these days, if I can find the time."

* * *

Denise Beasley braked her bike. Minnie Hugelmair, following closely, did the same.

"Boy, if the two of you don't look like a little puddle of misery."

Carly looked up, her face smeared with tears and—upon a closer look—little bits of charcoal gray acrylic fuzz from Anthony's sweater.

"What the hell is going on?"

Carly sniffled. Anthony said they had to tell somebody. Denise and Minnie were somebody.

"Go home, you two," Denise admonished. "I have to think about this a bit. At least school's out for Easter break, so...."

"I ought to be thinking clearer," Denise said. "You know I ought to."

"You've got an excuse. You're still sort of reeling from your dad getting killed last month. Which isn't an excuse that Carly and Anthony have." Gerry Stone shook his head.

"They've got to do something. It's not going to go away. Maybe it could have earlier, if Carly hadn't been too chicken to go to Doc Adams. But she's left it too long, now. Somebody's going to have to cope. Why didn't Anthony have the sense to use something?"

"I'd be surprised if he'd had the birds and bees talk, beyond what we get in health class in school. His dad's not as practical as mine. Sort of disconnected from the real world."

"We've still got to come up with something. I wish to hell they'd told someone else."

"We could talk to Dad and Magda. If they were here."

"Yeah. To Dad, too, if that goon hadn't axed him." Denise stared morosely at her toes. " 'If wishes were horses, then beggars would ride.' Dad used to say that. I don't think Mom would have any sympathy for them, right now. She's taking things pretty hard, down underneath."

"The first thing we've got to do is figure some way to get Carly out of sight as soon as school's out. It's still fairly cool. She can wear sweatshirts up till then. She's got that tall and skinny build, like her mom."

"Let me think a bit," Gerry said. "Maybe Pastor Kastenmayer will have an idea."

He did.

"It's a temporary fix," Minnie said. "Sending Carly out to spend the summer in the country with her dad where he's working now. She says that April's suspicious that something's going on."

"If you ask me, April will be so glad she doesn't have to spend her whole summer babysitting a teenager that she'll let it go."

"What about when she has to start school again in the fall?"

"It's better than nothing," Denise said. "My dad used to tell this story." She stopped.

"Story," Gerry prodded. "Your Dad."

"About a guy, a stable hand, I think, back in the middle ages who offended some high muck-a-muck, who was going to chop his head off. Not clean, but with all sorts of fancy and painful tortures associated with the process. But the man said that if they gave him a year, he could teach the caliph's horse to sing. That was what the muck-a-muck was called, the caliph."

"Arabian Nights," Gerry said. "Probably."

"Dunno. Never heard of them."

"Probably."

"Doesn't make any difference. Anyway, another stable hand asked him what the point was. The guy answered that a year could make a lot of difference. The caliph might die. He might die. 'Or, who knows, the horse may learn to sing.' That was Dad's point. There are times when a temporary fix is a lot better than no fix at all."

June 1635

Salome Piscatora bent over and kissed the bald spot on the top of her husband's head. "Now, Ludwig," she said. "It is not so bad. The man has stopped drinking excessively. He has a responsible job. Admittedly, that is because the countess of Gleichen thought that it would be an ornament to her household to have an up-timer in the position of majordomo. He has even accepted responsibility for assisting his daughter. It isn't as if your efforts have accomplished nothing."

"But for the wrong reasons." Pastor Ludwig Kastenmayer continued to stare gloomily into his beer.

"What have you done for the wrong reasons?"

"Nothing. *Herr* Baumgardner has agreed to be, as Gary Lambert calls it, 'rehabbed' for the wrong reasons. Not because he has come to recognize that his body is a temple of the Holy Spirit which should not be abused. He mainly listened to my exhortations to reform, I think, because he otherwise could no longer find a consort to pay his bills and his bar tab."

At the new residence of the countess of Gleichen, Carly, on the way from the kitchen to the cottage with a handful of early plums, stopped in the middle of the driveway. In mid-dash. Looked at her stepbrother. Horrified. "What are you doing here?"

Hans-Fritz Zuehlke looked back. At her face, her stomach, then her face again. "The state government is moving to Bamberg.

"Everyone knows that."

"Including the personnel office, where I was working. I didn't want to go. For various reasons. So I transferred to the West Virginia County tax office." He waved a clipboard. "Which sent me out to reassess the Countess of Gleichen's new property."

"You'll tell, won't you? Mildred and April and Dietrich and...everybody."

He looked at her again. "Not until I have spoken with your father. Who, clearly, since you are with him, already knows about the problem. It's his responsibility, after all." *Also*, he thought to himself, *not until I have consulted the pastor.*

"It is Zane Baumgardner's responsibility," Pastor Kastenmayer said. "He has accepted it. Which, I must admit, is more than I expected of the man, given his past history." He steepled his fingers together. "The rest of her family know that she is with him. They aren't worrying about her."

"Oh, sure. They were pretty surprised when he invited her. Mildred and April, that is. Ronnie and Megan too, I guess. Surprised, but sort of relieved. She's not been the easiest person to live with, the past few months."

Kastenmayer nodded decisively. "It's her father's responsibility. Unquestionably. You don't have any obligation to tell her grandmother anything more than that you saw her and spoke with her."

Hans-Fritz was considerably relieved. "I'll find a chance to head out to the countess' new estate again to break the news."

"Take Gerry Stone with you," the pastor advised.

So the three of them were leaning against the new fence behind the countess' stables.

"You teach them to make rail fence?" Gerry asked.

"Naw." Zane stubbed out his cigarette on one of the posts. "I guess guys from around here brought rail fence making to the good old USA when they came over."

"Pretty nice-looking horses," Hans-Fritz said.

"Yep. Ezechiel came along with me to help pick them out. He may be the countess' personal apothecary, but he's also a fair horse-doctor.

Good at spotting the things that a used-horse salesman would rather you didn't notice."

"Meth? The enthusiast? Spiritualist?" Hans-Fritz raised his eyebrows.

"You think that this Meth guy is a religous nut?" Zane asked. "Come to think of it, someone did say that's why the countess separated from her husband. That would have been about four or five years before the Ring of Fire. Because he went back to being a Lutheran after Ezechiel's uncle died, but she still had faith in him."

Gerry Stone frowned. "Meth's a whole religious fruitcake, all by himself, according to Jonas. And so was his uncle."

"Heretics," Hans-Fritz Zuehlke said. "Even heretics think they are heretics. Jakob Böhme has written several pamphlets designed to confute Stiefel's teachings. Refute them."

"Böhme? Who's he?"

"I'm sure that either Pastor Kastenmayer or Paster Rothenmaler over at Rudolstadt would be happy to explain it in a lot more detail than I can. He's from Silesia. Or was. A shoemaker at Görlitz. He's been dead ten years or so, but he has sons who keep his ideas going. A few years before he died he looked into a reflection in a pewter pitcher and started to see mystical visions."

Gerry blinked.

"Oh, hell. That's too oversimplified. These little sects pop up all over the place, all the time. I picked up some of this information while I was over at Danzig. Böhme started out as a Lutheran, like Stiefel and Meth did. There was a Lutheran preacher at Görlitz who said that religion should be the development of the whole spiritual person rather than what he called 'blind obedience to empty Church law.' He started a little semi-secret society called the "Conventicle of God's Real Servants.' I guess you up-timers would call it a discussion group. It involved quite a few people, not limited to tradesmen. Members of the local nobility. Gentlemen of the leisure class who had some academic training. Böhme was part of it. The minister made a lot of enemies on several university theology faculties. When he died, the authorities replaced him with a 'by the book' kind of Lutheran pastor who tried to wipe out the discussion group and its ideas. Böhme started to write down his visions a few years later, and the other guys from the group backed him up. Some of his stuff is still circulating in manuscript form, but a lot of it's been printed."

"Visions," Zane snorted. "Don't these people come with crap-detectors?"

"How do you mean that?" Gerry asked.

"Like the countess. She's not bad to work for. But talk about gullible. You could use her to define the word, if you ask me. She got involved with Meth and his uncle, this Stiefel that even Hans-Fritz' Silesian thinks was out of it, maybe ten or a dozen years ago. About the time she realized that the one thing that a noble's wife was really supposed to do—have babies—she hadn't managed to do and wasn't ever likely to do. So the counts of Gleichen, who had been around for centuries, were going to go extinct with her husband. Which they did, a few months before the Ring of Fire happened. Because none of the women married to his brothers or cousins managed to have kids, either. Not boys, at least." He leaned down and picked up a piece of straw to chew on.

"How old was she?"

"Back then? About thirty-five, I guess. She's forty-eight, now."

"A woman of thirty-five is still of child-bearing age," Hans-Fritz said.

"Yeah, but she'd been married for years and nothing had happened." Zane leaned back against the fence. "She talks to me a lot, so I spend a lot of my time just listening. She's as lonely as hell. Her mom died when she was three and her dad when she was six. She had four brothers and sisters, but they all died as kids. Her stepmother got married again and had another family. She married a man more than twenty years older than she was and, like I said, didn't have any kids. And wasn't likely to. I gather that he wasn't getting it up any more. For that matter, before she got involved with the fruitcake, just about everyone else died."

"What do you mean by that?"

"Her husband had half-sisters and she'd made friends with them, but they both died. Her mother's sister died, and so did her son, the countess' cousin. He'd been married twice. The first wife was dead—the second one's still alive, but they don't visit, because she lives somewhere over on the other side of Brandenburg. Her only female cousin on her mom's side died. Her dad's sister died. No uncles. One of her stepsisters died—no, not even that close, her stepmother's stepdaughter by another marriage. Her husband's younger brother and his wife died. All of them between 1615 and 1622. All she has left are a couple of male cousins. They're married and have children, but they live over to the west of Hesse. Nowhere around here."

"Bleak," Gerry said. "I mean, I'm worried about the way things are going in Italy and I haven't seen any of them except Ron since last fall, but at least my dad and brothers are still around."

"I guess it is." Zane tossed the now-well-chewed straw down. "Used to drive me nuts, having my mom and dad and sisters and then Tina Marie, Cheryl Ann after her, all nagging me. Maybe I shouldn't have complained." He picked up another straw. "Now. The reason I wanted you two to come talk to me is, really—what's this Green kid like? The one who knocked Carly up?"

* * *

Preston Richards found the guest chair in the office of First Baptist Church uncomfortable. He uncrossed his legs; then crossed them in the other direction. "Okay. So this Tilesius guy who manipulated all the trouble in Ohrdruf by way of Holz—and now Fred Jordan's dead because of it and I had to notify Bitsy—is trying to make trouble right here in town. We've got Holz'little storefront organization, fussing because Kastenmayer baptized Jarvis Beasley's baby, yelling about the Countess of Gleichen harboring dangerous Anabaptists. Getting the Erfurt city council to send letters to all and sundry. So I figured that I needed to know, and you'd be the most likely reliable source. Are Anabaptists dangerous?"

"It depends on how you define the word 'Anabaptist,' " Al Green answered.

Grantville's police chief sighed. "I am not following you, Brother Green. I'm a member of your church. So's Melanie. We come on Sundays—almost every Sunday, not just holidays. We both went to Sunday School. We send our kids to Sunday School. But I'm not a theology student, and I'm never likely to be one." He paused. "Could you dumb it down, please? At least a little bit."

"Okay." Green stood up and started pacing. "Maybe I'm too much of a historian to be able to put this to you in black and white terms. Have you ever heard that poem about the six blind men who went to see the elephant? 'And each was partly in the right, but all were in the wrong.' Joe Jenkins is partly right. Pankratz Holz is partly right, too. Neither one of them's seeing the whole picture, and I'm not sure, given how prejudiced they are, that either one is capable of seeing the whole picture."

"Are Anabaptists a threat to the public order?"

"To fix on what you're probably worrying about, Press—Joe Jenkins' batch aren't. Neither are the Mennonites who've settled inside the Ring. Their movement evolved out of Anabaptism, too."

"So far, so good."

"Then, may I please define the word 'Anabaptist' for you?"

"I have a feeling that you're going to, whether I really want to know or not."

"What sets our church—modern Baptists—off from most of the rest of the churches, both up-time and down-time?"

Press thought a minute. "Believers' baptism. We don't baptize babies, for whatever reason. I'm a little vague on the 'whatever.' "

Green stopped pacing for a moment, leaned over his desk, and made a note in regard to a clearly necessary sermon, upcoming shortly. "Keep going."

"So we baptize adults. Or, at least, people the church council thinks have reached the age of reason and know what they're doing. Sometimes we stretch it a bit, for young teenagers, if their families are good members, and we think they'll keep them pointed in the right direction while they finish growing up."

Green nodded. "These, our ordinary candidates for baptism, are people who have never been baptized before."

"So?"

"So, ordinarily, we Baptists are not Anabaptists. The word 'Anabaptist' means 're-baptizer.' Tell me what happens if an outside adult wants to join our church—someone who was already baptized as a baby, Catholic, Lutheran, Methodist, Presbyterian, whatever."

"Well, he—she if it's a woman—they have to be baptized as an adult. That's a requirement."

"Which is the point at which, technically, Baptists become 'Anabaptist' too. When the movement started, a century or so ago, everyone who joined up had already been baptized as a baby. Theologically, the early proponents of adult baptism denied the validity of about every existing baptism in the world, excepting only a few adult converts from heathendom. Since the

Bible states, 'He that believeth and is baptized shall be saved,' they implicitly denied the salvation of everyone who had been baptized as an infant for a thousand years and more."

"Uh, oh. That can't have been good."

"It didn't have the most favorable impact, no." Green started pacing again. "You do realize that we still teach the same thing?"

Richards dropped his mouth open. "You mean, we think that, uh, Father Mazzare, or, um, Pastor Kastenmayer, is going to hell?"

"We do normally try to phrase it a little more tactfully. But when push comes to shove —yes."

"I don't think anybody ever told me that. Not, at least, quite that flat-out."

"Possibly nobody did."

"Now that I come to think about it, definitely nobody did." Richards changed position. A loose spring poked him. He stood up. "You need a new chair. But we've got to get back to the question I came in with. Forget about who's going to hell. As long as they're nice people otherwise, that's really not the police department's problem. If Anabaptists aren't a threat to the public order, why does Holz think that they are?"

"To go back to the beginning again, or at least to a century or so ago and ignoring various claims to apostolic tradition for the various Baptist churches...."

"Dumb it down, please."

"Should I start with communism or polygamy?"

"Baptists!" Richards sat there, his mouth open.

"And, of course, there's always eschatology."

"Dumb it down."

Green thrust a fist toward the ceiling of his study and proclaimed in a deep, dire, voice, "The end of the world will be here any minute, so prepare."

"You mean that cult stuff? Sitting out in an open field wearing white robes and staring at the sky."

"More or less."

"Baptists!"

Green nodded. "Yes. Which doesn't even start to get us into mysticism, visionaries, and the like. Joe Jenkins would like to forget those parts of the Anabaptist heritage. They're all that Pankratz Holz remembers. Which doesn't make it easier for those of us who know perfectly well that, historically, it was 'both/and' rather than 'either/or.' They didn't get things sorted out, about what was going to be 'mainstream' and what wasn't, until a lot later than the year we're living in."

July 1635

"I mean it," Gerry said. "It's not a romantic tragedy. Not like they were Romeo and Juliet or something. They're not crazy in love with each other."

"What is it, then?" Mariah asked. "Carly's pregnant, after all."

"Proximity," Hans-Fritz suggested. "Propinquity."

"Not that, either. Some, I expect, but not quite. They really are friends. They worry about each other. Don't want to hurt each other. Actually, they try to protect each other. They're not in love with each other, but... It's more like...." Gerry stopped, floundering for words.

"Look, Anthony's okay—not like the Partow kid, with a different girl every week and notches on his belt. It's more like Carly was a stray kitten someone had left out by the side of the road. Anthony's the kind of person who'll always pick up a stray. Feed it. Pet it. Tame it. Eventually make sure that he's found a good home for it. And if the kitten's actually a girl. Purring, cuddling up, rubbing against that kind hand. For months. And he's a guy. Oh, I don't know how to explain it."

"I think you just did," Mariah said.

Out on the road crew, Megan snapped her lunch box closed. "So that's where things are, Crystal. Carly's out there in the country with her and Ronnie's dad. Which is, I guess, okay, at least for the summer—he really does seem to have straightened up. But—don't you think that we ought to tell Anthony's parents?"

Crystal Blocker, now Dorrman, laid her container of cottage cheese down.

"No. Honestly, Megan. No, I don't think so. It's not because I don't think the world of the Reverend and Mrs. Green, because I do. But."

"But what?"

"They don't really *see* Anthony, either of them."

"What do you mean—don't *see* him."

"It's hard to explain. Those boys were, oh, maybe ten and eight when the Greens came to pastor at First Baptist. They're a lot alike, you know, Allen and Anthony. Not just looking alike, even though they both have that same straight light brown hair and gray eyes. Two stair steps. Faces alike, body build pretty much the same. Perfect for handing clothes down, don't you know?"

"Uh-huh."

"I'm not a psychologist. But I've been reading some of the stuff that Walt's dad uses when he does peer counseling. I think...well, the boys are so close in age. Both about equally smart. A lot of the same interests.

But...everything that Anthony ever did, Allen had already done it, a little bit before. Joined the Scouts. Made the team. The whole routine of growing up. They'd been excited when Allen did anything. They're always busy at the church, of course. By the time Anthony did the same thing, well, ho-hum. Even if he did it as well."

She picked the cottage cheese up again and made a face. "I hate this stuff, but I guess I'd better eat it. Whether I want to or not. Calcium, you know. They make it out of milk that's already gone sour, so it's not like taking fresh milk away from little kids, or anything."

"Yeah, me too. Go on."

"You too?" Crystal giggled. "Back then, I bet, in the nineteen-eighties, the Greens were thinking, two kids. A boy and a girl. They already had the boy. Then Anthony was another boy. So he's sort of bobbed along in Allen's wake, like a kind of ditto mark. Or reflection in a mirror. The only thing Anthony's really ever done that Allen didn't was take drama class in high school. Which didn't sit too well with his dad. Pastor Green has his doubts about actors and actresses. So. Well, I don't think that this is the best way for them to really focus on him for the first time—because he's gotten a girl pregnant."

"Maybe I see how you're thinking. You know the family a lot better than we do." Megan dug the toe of her work shoe into the grass.

"I'd leave it be." Crystal nodded her head decisively. "As long as Carly's okay, and you say that she is, I'd really leave it be, as far as the Greens are concerned."

Late August 1635

"I'm really glad the two of you are back," Gerry said.

Denise pulled off her helmet. "Don Francisco's a nice guy. He knew how we felt about leaving for Prague. Going is fine, but it would have been bad not to come home first. We brought Benny back to stay. He enjoyed doing the folklife festival, but he's too feeble to go to Prague with Minnie and me. He'll stay with Louise and her husband. And I didn't want to go away for who knows how long without seeing my mom again."

"Carly had her baby two days ago."

"Boy or girl?" Minnie asked.

"Boy."

Denise frowned. "Isn't it early?"

"About a month." Gerry plopped down on an old bench in the storage yard. "She was still all stressed out, worrying about Anthony—maybe that had something to do with it. He's fine, though. The baby, I mean. A midwife delivered him, out at her dad's cottage on the countess' estate. Down-timer. The midwife, I mean. They didn't have to go to the hospital. Anthony's fine, too. He made it out there yesterday afternoon, all worried to pieces, and looked at the kid. He'll go again today, I expect. His folks are moving his brother into a boarding house in Jena and took the two little kids along. He stayed home on the excuse of feeding the pets—as if they couldn't have gotten someone else to do it."

"So why are you so glad we're back."

"We've got to come up with another fix. And I'm totally out of ideas."

Denise eyed him. "Out on that hippie commune when you were a kid—did your dad ever read *The Cat in the Hat* to you?"

"Not that I can recall."

"Have you ever read it?"

"Don't think so."

"Well, goddamn." Denise ran into her mother's trailer and came back a few minutes later with a book. "Now listen." She started reading.

"What's the point?" he asked after she'd finished.

Denise smiled. "Like that cat.... Listen, Gerry. I have a doozy of a 'wonderful, awful, idea.' " She explained.

"We'll have to talk to Zane. Get him to set it up. He's Carly's fucking father," Denise said. "He ought to take some responsibility for her beyond housing her for three months in an emergency, which we had to talk him into doing. Dads are supposed to be...more than that. A lot more than that."

"I know what you mean. Buster was. Mine is."

"Benny is, too," Minnie said. "Even if he's not exactly my dad."

"Then let's go."

Zane looked at them for quite a while and then said, "Ooookaaaay. Nothing ventured, nothing gained."

"If your uncle could come up with divine inspirations, you can too." Zane Baumgardner looked at Ezechiel Meth. "Look, we—Grantville that is—are covering your ass. Covering the countess' rear end too, for that matter. Making sure that Holz and his people leave you in peace. So pay a little back. Look, you've been wandering around Germany and Switzerland for the past twenty years or more proclaiming that you're the Archangel Michael on earth. The least you can do is come up with a little revelation when we need one."

"But."

"This is a damned good revelation. I've spent days and days riding around these fields two steps behind the countess while she exercises her horse, listening to her talk. She believes it, damn you. She really believes that she's going to have a miracle child in her old age. Your uncle told her that. Got her to believe it. All you've got to do is modify it a bit. She's lonesome enough that she'll bite."

"So I'm supposed to tell her that...."

"He was a bit off. She's not supposed to be the Messiah's natural mother. She's supposed to be his foster mother. Hell, if she could keep believing that your uncle was an immortal prophet after he kicked the bucket, she can believe anything."

"The advantage is clearly to you, since the child is your grandson."

"You want her to die without a kid to love? It's not as if there's an inheritance involved, or anything like that. Once she dies, all of her dower income escheats to the state anyway."

Meth looked down the hill.

"By the creek," he said.

"Yeah. Got to be."

In Grantville, Denise begged rather than extorted. "Mariah, please do it. We need one more person. Minnie can't. She's too recognizable. With her scar and the glass eye and stuff. You were actually an actress for a while, so we figure you can memorize." She looked at Hans-Fritz. "Tell her to do it, will you. Please. We need her, Gerry and me."

"I'm not a teenager," Mariah protested. "Ten years ago, yeah, this sort of thing would have made a kind of crooked sense to me. But my mind's outgrown that. It doesn't work that way, any more."

"*Please.*"

"How the hell do I get myself into these messes? Who am I supposed to be, again?"

"Moses' mother. The baby's mother, anyway, who gets called in to be a nurse. I'm going to be Miriam. Gerry'll be Aaron."

"I'm not a nanny. I do silo site surveys."

"You don't have to be a nanny. Agree to be the godmother or something. I'm not sure they have godmothers in that peculiar religion of theirs, but 'or something' should do it. Whatever she says. I'd have asked Megan, maybe, since she's Carly's sister-in-law, except that she's already starting to show, so the countess might not believe that she was the mother of a newborn, too. Plus, you went with Master Massinger's troop last summer. *Please*, Mariah. *Please.*"

"Oh damn. All right. What are you using for the basket?"

"I don't know."

"It has to be waterproof. Just a minute." Mariah disappeared into the back room of her grandmother Nash's house and came back with a light blue plastic picnic cooler. Which had been molded to look like a fake basket. "This'll do. What are you doing for bulrushes?"

"There are cattails in the creek. Carly's dad found a good spot. A little pool. Right below it, the water runs over gravel, shallow enough that the basket with the baby in it can't get away from us. Here are your lines. Anthony wrote them, so they're pretty much straight out of the Bible story. The countess ought to pick up on how the script goes in a hurry. We hope."

Denise pushed a piece of paper into Mariah's hands, grabbed the basket, and hurried out the door, afraid that if she waited any longer, Mariah might change her mind.

Mariah, though, buried her face in Hans-Fritz' shoulder. "Tell me," she wailed. "What am I doing here and why am I doing it with these nuts?"

Show time.

"Meth's going to distract Frau Canzler," Zane said. "Keep her and Rosenbusch occupied with something up in the house. Carly's promised to stay inside, at the cottage. Can't risk her going off half-cocked right in the middle of things. The Green kid is with her, holding her hand."

Gerry took a deep breath. "Denise has the baby and the basket. Okay. Mariah's behind the willow trees. Go get the countess. I'll start the screen credits rolling. Or something."

"I've got to give Meth credit," Zane said afterwards. "The man has a golden tongue. By the time the countess got up to the house carrying the baby, he had the steward and lady-in-waiting all primed to make delighted cooing noises. Nobody in the whole household asked, 'What the hell?' " He looked at Mariah. "Uh, they kept the picnic basket. For a bassinet. And then someday a religious relic, I guess."

"Okay."

"I can't believe it worked," Anthony said.

"I hope he's all right. He was so little."

"The baby's going to be fine, Carly," Denise said. "The countess is going to take real good care of him. Herr Rosenbusch is out beating the bushes for a wet nurse this very minute, before he even has a chance to get hungry again. She picked out a really pretty name. Immanuel Renatus."

"Sort of fancy," Carly said. "Real down-timey."

Anthony, who by now had three years of Latin under his belt, looked dumbstruck.

"She'll cherish him," Gerry put in. "Adore him. He's going to be better taken care of than any kid since Jesus Christ was born, probably."

Carly nodded.

"Having him early was actually a good thing. You can go back to school next week, when the new semester starts after Labor Day, with the rest of the kids none the wiser. That's what you wanted for Anthony's sake, isn't it? You'll still be a little sore, maybe, but if you're creaking around the halls, you can tell people you fell off a horse or something while you were staying out in the country with your dad."

"I guess."

"Hell," Denise said. "We're going to be around town for another week or so, before we take off for Prague. If you need backup, I'll even embarrass myself by saying that I skidded and tipped you off my bike."

"If Dean Gerhard ever finds out about this," Gerry said. "Or Superintendent Rothenmaler. Or any other Lutheran pastor. Griep. Or Holz. Or anyone at Jena, I am going to be so totally screwed. My career plans will be totally derailed."

Minnie Hugelmair patted his shoulder. "Then be glad that Jonas and Ronella got married and moved away before we finagled it, as Benny would say. That's a big consolation. He'd have been a lot more likely to catch on than any of the rest of the grown-ups outside of Carly's family. Except for Denise's dad, but Buster never would have finked. Hans-Fritz doesn't really count. He's family, sort of. Even if he wasn't, he'd keep his mouth shut because of Mariah. He didn't even tell his brother Dietrich."

When Pastor Kastenmayer heard by way of parish gossip that the countess of Gleichen had adopted an infant, he merely commented to the scandalized informant that it was regrettable that the baby would be reared as a heretic.

Gerry stopped by the estate on his way back to school. Leaning on the fence, he watched Zane Baumgardner roll a cigarette. With a worried expression.

"Yeah, kid," Zane said. "I know that they're saving up-time newspapers like they were worth their weight in gold. But, I figured, who was going to miss the classified ads? So I kept enough out from the old ones Cheryl Ann left behind when she moved out that I can keep on rolling my own until some bright guy in Badenburg reinvents cigarette papers. They've done okay on toilet paper, after all."

"Ah, okay."

"I keep thinking," Hans-Fritz Zuehlke said, "that being a promised Messiah could be hard on the child."

"That won't happen for a long time," Gerry said. "Jesus Christ did not start his earthly ministry until he was thirty years old."

"But—isn't the countess going to have awfully high expectations while he's growing up?" Hans-Fritz protested. "It's hard enough for a child to live up to the expectations of an earthly parent. Dietrich and I sort of felt that way about Lucas, and he's just our stepfather and no saint, either. Or look at how Anthony feels about his folks."

Zane shook his head. "She'll spoil him sure. But look on the bright side. Maybe the countess will die before he's old enough for it to bother him. She's no spring chicken, and she was awfully sick a year or so ago—everybody pretty much thought she was going to die right then and there. Hell, given how many kids die young in this day and age, maybe the boy will die before he's old enough for it to bother him."

He raised his head and looked through a break in the hills to the still-shiny wall created by the Ring of Fire as it reflected the evening sunlight. "And who knows? Given everything that's gone on the last few years. The stuff these people talk about." He looked back at Gerry. "Can you give me an absolute one-hundred-percent guarantee that Carly's kid isn't the second coming of the Messiah?"

THE TRUTH ABOUT THAT CAT AND PUP

PART I
Grantville, January 1635

"...start planning for Jonas and Ronella's wedding," Carol finished. "I can hardly believe that we got them officially engaged. Finally. They sit around staring at each other. Jonas, as if he can't really believe his luck. Ronella, as if she can't really believe that she's actually managed to snag the man. Even with her father's assistance, no matter how reluctant. Talk about painfully honorable."

"Well, yes. He is rather...." Salome Piscatora, the wife of Pastor Kastenmayer of St. Martin's in the Fields Evangelical Lutheran Church, admitted. "I guess the first question is whether Ronella wants an up-time-style wedding. This will be the first one Ludwig has performed at St. Martin's where the bride is an up-timer. All the brides have been down-timers, so far. So are the big batch we have coming up in April. So...that's first. Will Ronella be content with a wedding on the porch with the pastor serving as the official witness to their vows, or does she hope for a walk down the aisle to the altar?"

"The aisle and altar, I'm afraid. White gown and all. Wedding march from *Lohengrin.* With bridesmaids. Have you seen one...?"

"Oh, yes. We were invited to several weddings at the Methodist church last summer. I went to the ones I thought were..." -She stopped, floundering.

"...important for maintaining cordial relations with the local community," Carol supplied.

Salome beamed. "Exactly. That was what Jonas said. Ludwig didn't feel that he could attend, of course. Heretics in the first place, and with a woman for a pastor. He's a Philippist, of course. But even for a Philippist, that's far beyond the permissible. If he had gone and any of the Flacians had heard about it, I don't think that even Count Ludwig Guenther would have been able to save him from the hellhounds."

"Flacians!" The tone of Carol's voice implied something between "dregs of the universe" and "sewer slime."

"With another one of them coming, now that Saint Thomas the Apostle is opening over on the Badenburg Road. That was the agreement that came out of the Rudolstadt Colloquy, of course, so we have to put up with it. As if Pankratz Holz isn't a sufficient cross for poor Ludwig to bear!" Salome sighed and handed Carol Unruh, wife of Ron Koch and mother of the bride, a cup of hot cider. Hard cider. A liquid which was rapidly loosening the usually discreet and tightly-reined-in tongues of both women.

"Well, it wouldn't have been so much of a problem if Count Ludwig Guenther and his wife hadn't been away for a lot of last year. Oh, I know that the pan-Lutheran colloquy in Magdeburg was important for the USE as a whole. Then when they did get back, he was worried about the election, of course. And Emelie's pregnancy. It must come as a bit of a shock to him, being a father for the first time at his age."

"It's not as if he has to change diapers. He gets to admire his son when he's all clean, fed, and happy."

Carol blinked. "There's a saying: 'The rich are different. They have more money.' "

They sat for a moment, contemplating the place of dirty diapers in the universe.

"It's one of the places the theologians go wrong," Salome said. "Focusing on the pain of childbearing itself as Eve's punishment. It goes to show that they don't stop to think about everything else involved. Laundry in the winter, for example."

This time, Carol laughed. "Laundry in the winter probably wasn't such a problem in the Holy Land, considering the climate."

"It's nothing to laugh about. They'll turn it around," Salome predicted darkly. "Sound all pious and annoyed. Claim that Ludwig has not been supervised closely enough because the count and his consistory were distracted by the colloquy. When, in fact, Holz is the one who came into Grantville last month without any permission from the Schwarzburg-Rudolstadt consistory at all." She put her cup down. "He's a spy for Tilesius. I'm sure of it."

"For, uh, whom?"

"Melchior Tilesius, of course. The superintendent in Langensalza. He was born in Mühlhausen–the imperial city up in the northern part of the SoTF, not the one in Alsace."

"What makes you think so?"

"Well, for one thing, Holz was born in Silesia, which is where the Tilesius family came from, originally. He's about forty-five years old, I think. He'd already left Silesia for Saxony in 1617. I remember that well, because he was in Saxony for the centennial of the Ninety-Five Theses. I met him at one of the celebrations." She paused. "That was quite a party—it went on for three days."

"Punctuated by sermons, I presume?"

"Oh, of course. Sermons were the 'feature attraction' as they write on the board at the Higgins Hotel for the Friday evening movies. Ludwig and I had only been married four years, then. I had never, except for the years Papa was in Erfurt, been out of the county of Gleichen. Hardly ever out of Ohrdruf. He took me to Wittenberg, and I had the most wonderful time. I got to see the actual church door where Luther posted the Theses. It was a real thrill. And I was introduced to the reformer's grandson, Johann Ernst Luther. He's still alive, you know—he was born right down the road in Weimar and lives over in Saxony, at Zeitz. He's an old man now—he must be about seventy-five. I hope he doesn't get hurt, or killed, or turned out of his home this coming spring."

Her face clouded. "In fact, I hope that the soldiers don't ruin Wittenberg when Gustavus Adolphus invades Saxony. Everyone says that he's going to, and we have to remember what happened to the Wartburg."

"I'm sure that the emperor will protect the town," Carol said. "He's very pious."

"I know. Things happen, in wartime, though, whether the commanders want them to or not. But in regard to Holz. They threw him out of Silesia after he entered into a series of controversial pamphlet exchanges in which he accused the Lutheran district superintendent of laxness in supervising the theological orthodoxy of the clergy."

"That happens," Carol said. "It still happened, up-time."

"He wasn't any easier to get along with while he was in Saxony. The year before the Ring of Fire, he was deprived of his living by the Dresden consistory. Leipzig wouldn't accept him, so he came into Thuringia and went over to Langensalza, where he's been ever since as one of Tilesius' hangers-on."

"Errand boy." Carol nodded.

"Leipzig," Salome said absentmindedly. "On that trip, in 1617, we stopped in Leipzig, too. Ludwig introduced me to all of his first wife's relatives. There were a lot."

"As a *treat*?"

"I think...." Salome paused. "I think he meant it to be." She sighed. "But Holz. The 'errand boy.' Tilesius sent him to the Rudolstadt Colloquy two years ago, as an observer. By last spring, he was professing to be horrified by Ludwig's views and actions. Pamphlets again. Not, I think, connected with the pamphlets that you found on the steps of St. Martin's on Christmas Eve, when Jonas and Ronella got betrothed. They're quite different, but still they are pamphlets."

"So he took advantage of the way the Grantville authorities do not control religion...I suppose that it does seem a rather *laissez-faire* approach to you."

Salome shook her head. "I don't speak French, Carol. I never had a chance to learn it."

"Oh, sorry. We use that phrase almost as if it had become English." They digressed for a few minutes.

"Fine," Salome said. "Yes. *Laissez-faire* does describe it well. So he came into this town, with no official sanction from the consistory at all, and established a little 'ultra-orthodox Lutheran' movement, to gather together, before the opening of St. Thomas the Apostle, as many as he could of those who are not happy at St. Martin's. He's not married, so he doesn't have the burden of a family to support. He's managed to finance this by taking on some part-time jobs, such as tutoring. In my heart, I am sure that when the new pastor arrives at St. Thomas', Holz will be sitting on his doorstep with a list of grievances against Ludwig. If he isn't over in Rudolstadt, waving them around right now."

"Tilesius' 'gofer.' "

Which led to another digression on vocabulary, until Carol said she had to go. "I get tired of these internal squabbles." She picked up her coat. "I got tired of them up-time. Do you know what they remind me of? *The Gingham Dog and the Calico Cat.*"

"Which is?"

"A child's poem, by Eugene Field. We have an illustrated copy of it at home, I'm sure, in a box of old children's books that Ronella and Jake had when they were little. I'll drop it off for you to look at, the next time I come over."

Salome stood up, too. "Do you suppose it would do any good to talk to Aegidius Hunnius down in Altenburg?"

"About what? And why him?"

"About protecting old Herr Luther. And Wittenberg. Things like that. He's the superintendent there. Maybe he could get Duke Johann Philipp to talk to the emperor. He's probably the closest I come to knowing anybody influential. And he was born in Wittenberg, so he ought to care. Maybe. I hope. It's not a very good chance."

February 1635

"It's pronounced 'greep.' " Ronella Koch thumped her coffee mug down on the table.

"Are you sure? Seems like it should be 'gripe.' " Anne Penzey, who was waitressing this frosty Saturday morning, was totally unashamed about eavesdropping. Especially, of course, since her mother helped run the Geology Survey, and anything that involved Saxony tended to impact mining.

So Ronella grinned instead of glaring.

"At least, I hear an awful lot of people are griping about the appointment." Anne grinned back.

"According to Orrine Sterling, who's teaching English over in Rudolstadt, that griping includes most of the members of Count Ludwig Guenther's consistory." Natalie Bellamy, being the wife of Arnold in the Department of International Affairs, had a definite "in" when it came to collecting regional political gossip.

"It's still pronounced 'greep.' The name is Oswald Griep." Ronella nodded firmly. "That's Oswald with a 'v' sound: 'Ossvalt'. I've met him already. Georgie Hardegg is rhyming it with 'creep' as a mnemonic device. Mary Kat Riddle thought that up."

Her friend Maria Blandina Kastenmayer, generally called Dina, blinked at the thought of anyone being on close enough terms with the rather pompous young attorney Johann Georg Hardegg to address him as "Georgie."

Ronella kept going. "Georgie's sister Christiana is married to a printer in Leipzig. He's another Krapp. There are dozens of them, and not all of them are lawyers, no matter how it seems sometimes. He says that Elector John George's Saxon officials have been pulling all sorts of political strings to get this guy appointed to the second Lutheran church right outside the Ring of Fire. They think that Pastor Kastenmayer is subversive."

"*Ja*," Dina contributed with a sigh. "Papa is a Philippist. Pastor Griep is a Flacian."

Natalie Bellamy started to stand up, but then sat down again. "Of course, the man's related to a bunch of people connected with Waffler, Wiesel, and Finck, too. Mrs. Griep is Rahel Waffler. Her younger brother Friedrich is a junior partner in the Weimar office. Her even-younger-than-that brother David is an associate in the Jena office. They're the main competition with Hardegg, Selfisch, and Krapp for down-timer legal business inside the Ring of Fire, so no one could expect Herr Hardegg to be enthusiastic."

"You do all know that Mama was Blandina Selfisch, don't you?" Dina's expression radiated the thought *that is a given—everybody knows that.*

Nobody at the table knew it. Speculation about the maiden name of Pastor Kastenmayer's first wife wasn't a staple of dinner-table conversation among Grantville's up-timers. Most of them didn't even realize that he had been married twice.

Her next contribution brought the conversation to a temporary halt. "Herr Selfisch in Hardegg, Selfisch, and Krapp is Mama's younger half-brother."

"Y'know, Mrs. Bellamy." Anne, who was supposed to be refilling coffee cups, butted happily into the conversation. "You'd better ask Dina to go over and talk to your husband. This could be complicated."

Ronella chewed thoughtfully on her lower lip. "Dina, you and Mrs. Kastenmayer have enough to do getting things ready for your own wedding, on top of everything else." She frowned. "Isn't there someone else Mr. Bellamy could ask?"

Natalie Bellamy started to fish around in the bottom of her purse, looking for change for a tip. "Have you set a date, yet?"

"We've narrowed it down to 'after Easter and before school gets out.' So, sometime in May, I guess. Mom and Mrs. Kastenmayer are still negotiating. It has to be after the huge group wedding that Pastor has scheduled for April. And at least a week before Dina's, so she can be my bridesmaid, because she and Phillip are moving to Jena right after theirs, but Jonas and I will be in town until after graduation, so she can't be my maid of honor after her wedding, but I can be her matron of honor after mine."

The audience, being female, had no trouble at all following this convoluted explanation.

Ronella went back to thinking about the preceding question. "Especially with those scurrilous pamphlets about Pastor Kastenmayer and his wife coming out of Saxony."

"My sister," Dina said. "Ask Andrea. She started everything by eloping with Tony Chabert. They're in Erfurt and he works for the government. Well, he's an army officer, and that counts as working for the government, doesn't it? A person could almost say that it's part of her job to tell Mr. Bellamy about it. She's not helping with my wedding because Papa hasn't forgiven her for marrying a Catholic. Yet."

"Yet?" Natalie raised an eyebrow.

"She's expecting a baby in July. Papa's snit doesn't have any hope of surviving the arrival of his first grandchild. I don't think, at least."

"Pastor Kastenmayer's going to be a grandpa? That's cool." Anne was prepared to join in this discussion for the indefinite future, but Cora Ennis looked over the counter and yelled, "Table Ten," so she had to go. Not without a regretful glance over her shoulder. Table Ten wasn't offering any good prospects for current and future news.

* * *

"It came to me in a dream, how we can try to protect the door where Luther posted the Ninety-Five Theses so it doesn't get burned up like the Wartburg," Salome said. "Like dreams came to people in biblical times."

Carol Koch laughed. "I have to quote my son Jake. 'Awesome, man. Truly awesome.' "

"We don't know any influential men. But we do know the Countess Emelie. And her sister-in-law. Who is the president of the *Tugendhafte Gesellschaft.* Who founded it, way before the Ring of Fire happened. Almost all of the influential Lutheran ladies in the upper nobility are members."

Carol's mind was spinning. "I know Ronnie Dreeson. Not well, but I know her. She knows the Abbess of Quedlinburg, who knows everyone in every Lutheran *Stift* in northern Germany. Ronnie's Catholic now, but she was a Lutheran once upon a time. Before she was a Calvinist, I think, but maybe after."

"And Bitty Matowski has met William Wettin's wife," Salome added. "She is Catholic, too, I know—Bitty, not Duchess Eleonore. However, she's an up-timer, so she might be willing to help...."

"What about the League of Women Voters?" Carol frowned. "I know it's a church door, but it's a worthy cause. Also, the church is in a castle. Up-time, I read something in the paper once. The government wanted to give a historic preservation grant to a church—in Boston or Philadelphia, maybe, someplace important because of the American Revolution—but the ACLU objected because it still held religious services. But maybe.... I can talk to Veleda Riddle, at least."

Magdeburg

"It's important, Caroline," Bitty Matowski said. "I really need to talk to the princess. I have a great big favor to ask her."

"A lot of people would like favors from the princess." Caroline Platzer smiled. "Few of them come out and say it quite that forthrightly."

"It's not a huge gigantic one," Bitty said. "And it won't cost any money. I have a couple of letters that need to go to the emperor and King Christian of Denmark. She's in a better position to see that they actually read them than anyone else, I guess. I thought, seeing how much she likes the Brillo ballet...."

The first week, only a few letters arrived in Magdeburg. The week after that....

"Before you go, Lennart," Colonel Nils Ekstrom said, "I have something I want to show you."

General Lennart Torstensson obligingly followed him down the corridor of the imperial palace.

The colonel opened a door upon a harried secretary surrounded by overflowing bins of paper.

"Colonel, Sir. We received three hundred and two more letters this morning. That makes a total of nine thousand, five hundred twenty-six. If you can possibly spare me a couple more clerks to send the acknowledgments...."

"What on earth?"

"Tell me, Lennart. Have you been planning to attack the door of the castle church in Wittenberg? The one that Martin Luther posted the Ninety-Five Theses on?"

"It hadn't featured in my strategic options, no."

"I'm delighted to hear it. Let's just say—don't."

Ekstrom's recommendation was well-advised.

Princess Kristina put a slightly grubby hand into the pocket under her skirt. "Papi Christian, I have a letter for you. It's important. About not shooting cannon at the door of the castle church in Wittenberg when the USE attacks Saxony, because John George has been so awful to Papa."

The king of Denmark read it solemnly. "It's good to know that so many people are concerned."

Kristina nodded. "What Martin Luther did was important."

The king of Denmark regarded his future daughter-in-law. Lessons should not be limited to stuffy classrooms. Take advantage of all opportunities. What would the lovely Caroline Platzer with the superb teeth call this? Ah, yes. A "teachable moment."

He shuddered at what he had learned of that other world, in which this child, grown to a woman, never married, converted to Catholicism, and abdicated her throne. Abdicated and converted, in reverse order, but that was the gist of it.

In this world, a disaster waited for them all if anything of the sort should happen.

"Yes," he said. "Very important. You were right to bring this letter straight to me. In the politics of the Union of Kalmar, even more than the USE, it's going to be important to protect the position of Lutheranism. No matter what we think, personally."

He looked at the pilot in the front seat. "Let the plane circle the city a couple more times."

The plane began to circle again.

Then he looked at his future daughter-in-law. "Now even though, personally, I may think that many of the doctrinal positions of the Calvinists make more sense, I would never be so imprudent as to leave the Lutheran church, the way your uncle, the Elector of Brandenburg, has done."

A half-hour later, he was certain she understood why. Her mind was superb.

"And as for the door of the castle church in Wittenberg...I will speak to your papa myself. You should come with me. We will speak to him together."

Kristina nodded.

He looked ahead at the pilot again. "Let the plane come to a landing."

Dresden

Hans Georg von Arnim, commander of the forces of John George of Saxony and, in his own mind, the probable upcoming scapegoat in an inevitable, unavoidable, disaster, looked out the window, his hands crossed behind his back.

Holk, again. When everything needed to be focused on the west, he once more would have to send a regiment at least to the southeast to control Holk's depredations among their own people. Which would probably make things worse, since that regiment, too, would need to forage.

He moved back to the table, picked up the latest intelligence report from the USE, and moved back to the window.

At the moment, the best option for the army of Saxony would appear to be to remove the door of the castle church in Wittenberg from its hinges and carry it along with them into battle, as the ancient Israelites had done with the Ark of the Covenant. At a minimum, that tactic should make Gustav's artillery non-functional in Saxony. Maybe he'd send those regiments against Brandenburg.

And as for the elector's safety?

Arnim smiled, as whimsically as he ever did.

His personal preference at the moment would be to send John George to Zeitz, to move in as roommate with an elderly clergyman named Johann Ernst Luther.

Back to serious options. He returned to the table.

Grantville

"Ronella really does want the wedding march from *Lohengrin*," Carol said.

Jonas Justinus Muselius opened his mouth to say something about the limited performance capabilities of the limited number of musicians who provided the accompaniment at St. Martin's services with the limited array of instruments at their disposal.

Carol thought she knew what he was going to say. "Oh, yes. I know. Even up-time, a lot of Lutheran pastors didn't approve its use for weddings. Because it's from Wagner's *Ring Cycle*."

He opened his mouth again.

"Pagan. Norse gods and all that. Thor, Odin. So if you don't think that Pastor Kastenmayer will let her have it, then we could always go with Beethoven's *Ode to Joy*. That would probably be the best option, if...."

Jonas eventually got a word in edgewise. "Let me investigate a little, please, Carol. Perhaps something can be arranged."

"Yeah," I've heard it," Errol Mercer said. Now one of St. Martin's musicians, he was also one of the pack of seven up-time fiancés whom Pastor Kastenmayer would confirm and marry off to their chosen, and Lutheran, brides in April, a week before Easter.

"I've heard it, and I expect one of the organists has the music, not that St. Martin's has an organ yet, but I don't know the words. Or, at least, the only words I ever heard weren't the real ones. A sort of—joke, supposed to be funny."

"A parody." Jonas nodded his head. "A well-known literary form."

"If you say so. Whatever you say. But Ronella won't want to march down the aisle to somebody singing,

---

Here comes the bride,
Fair, fat and wide.

"You're going to have to do something about the words," Errol said. "Something different. Not pagan."

Muselius nodded.

Somewhere.... There was that sermon Martin Luther had given at his niece's wedding, in praise of the sanctity of Christian marriage.

Someone in Jena was bound to have it. He'd go up and see Dean Gerhard. Turn it into verses that fit the meter of this "Wedding March."

As appalling as the music was, from what Errol had hummed to him.

If Ronella wanted it, she should have it. Anything for his bride. The bride he had, so contrary to all rational expectations, attained.

If, in the process, he could Christianize some pagan paean, so much the better. Luther himself said there was no reason that the devil should have all the good tunes. Or, given the musical quality of this wedding march, all people's favorite tunes, at least. He couldn't call it "good."

"Capuccino?" Anne Penzey asked on Saturday morning. "I've figured out a way to froth milk."

"Honestly?" Ronella grinned.

"As frothy as the mouth of a rabid dog." Anne stopped. Her mother was a science teacher, after all. "Maybe that's not the best comparison, here in a restaurant. It involves attaching a wire hand whisk to my curling iron. As frothy as the mouth of Pastor Holz when he gets going about something. Not that there's a lot to choose from, between him and a mad dog."

"I'll try one," Dina said. "You?"

"Me, too. Where's the best man? We've got strategy to coordinate."

"Oversleeping, probably. He got back really late, last night. But he got off the trolley and stopped at the rectory to say that he officially asked Herr Hortleder for Anna Catharina's hand and was accepted."

"Your dad's going to be presiding over a wedding epidemic."

"Not this one. They'll get married in Weimar. That's where she lives. In August, he said. It's too soon to get it in before this summer's war in Saxony, and considering that she's an only child, her mother wants to make a big fuss over it, so they'll wait. Wedding banquets and things. The SoTF doesn't have statewide sumptuary laws, but a lot of local jurisdictions like Weimar still have their own. Duke Albrecht's chancellor has to be a good example for other people, so they have to figure that into the planning. As big as possible, but not *too* big. The campaign should have quieted down by then." She paused. "Topic change. Jonas is coming, too. He went up to Jena with Gary, and he's gotten your music worked out. So that's one thing you can check off the list that your mom doesn't have to worry about any more."

When Jonas came, it was to report that he had achieved acceptable words for the desired wedding march. "That's marvelous," Carol said. "That means we can use *Ode to Joy* for the recessional, then. You'd better have someone arrange it for the instruments we have, so the musicians can start learning it.

"If I'd known," Ronella said, "If I'd really known what planning a wedding involves, before we got started, I think I'd have gone to city hall and let Mayor Dreeson do it."

"At least it will be in May. You won't need to make artificial flowers."

Carol looked at Dina with dawning horror and pulled out The List. "Flowers!"

"Flowers," Dina said. "And scheduling weddings around the king of Sweden's wars."

"Another spate of pamphlets." Salome picked them up. "Some are from Holz. I recognize his style by now. But some of them aren't."

"Griep?" Carol asked.

"No. Ludwig has known Oswald Griep for years. They don't agree about anything, which means that I've read a lot of incoming correspondence and annotated it for Ludwig, to make it easier for him to draw up his replies. These are nothing like his writing style, which is pretty pompous. The new ones"—she waved several of them, as if she were fanning herself—"aren't quite like the ones that showed up on Christmas Eve, either. It's the same typeface, and I think the same artist did the woodcuts. But they're more aimed against the up-time Lutherans in Grantville than they are against Ludwig and me. Against you and Ron. And Gary. Especially Gary."

"I know," Carol said. "Poor Gary. Even if he is Missouri Synod and as stubborn as an ox about it, he doesn't deserve this kind of filth."

March 1635

Oswald Griep stood looking at the Church of Saint Thomas the Apostle.

A New Testament saint, of course. Those were perfectly all right with Lutherans, unlike the jumped-up modern saints with which the papists indulged themselves.

Some people referred to Martin Luther as a saint, of course. But that was doctrinally incorrect. The need to pursue and extirpate superstition wherever it raised itself among the ignorant was unceasing. Which was one reason that he had his doubts about what might be going on over at St. Martin's in the Fields. Martin, even the original one, was not a New Testament saint. He had shown up as a bishop giving his cloak to a beggar somewhere during the *media aeva* and become the object of a cult.

Cults were also to be extirpated. That was as much an article of faith with Griep as *Carthago delenda est* had been for Cato the Elder. Not that he had as much practical experience with cults and sects as Tilesius had accumulated. In theory, though, sowing them with salt would be a splendid solution, if only it could be managed in these parlous modern times.

St. Thomas the Apostle. Otherwise known as Doubting Thomas.

Count Ludwig Guenther, somewhat frivolously, told him that he had chosen the name because, originally, he had harbored some doubts as how to best deal with Grantville and its people when a modern miracle appeared within his lands.

There was a lot still to be accomplished. Interior finishing. Construction on the school was behind schedule. The war would draw day laborers away, probably. They were generally an unruly lot and prone to become soldiers. The skilled craftsmen would stay, though. Count Ludwig Guenther paid generously for competent work.

But the bricks.... He wandered across the site to inspect the piles of bricks, neatly laid out on pallets. The bricks were magnificent.

The school before the rectory. Rahel and the children were comfortable enough with her brothers in Jena.

They needed the school by fall. The rectory could wait until next year, if it had to.

Rudolstadt

"We'll postpone the dedication for six months," Count Ludwig Guenther said firmly. "As a matter of respect to Mayor Dreeson and Reverend Wiley. We should not be sponsoring a festivity so soon after their deaths."

"I was hoping to start services much sooner than September," Oswald Griep said. At his most stiff-necked.

Which, the count had learned through trial and error, meant that the man's feelings were hurt. He sat silently for a few minutes. "Go ahead and do that. There's no regulation that requires the dedication to take place first. Please keep it...low key."

Griep knew that the consistory in Schwarzburg-Rudolstadt harbored suspicions as to why Saxony had been so active in pushing his appointment, until they had no graceful way to avoid it. But there was more to theological life than worrying about the aberrations of Ludwig Kastenmayer, aberrant though they might be. Aberrant though they certainly were.

Holz had been with Tilesius for several years, now. The consistory in Dresden considered it much more important to keep tabs on an influential ecclesiastical politician such as Tilesius than on Kastenmayer, who was, when one came down to it, an ordinary parish minister of no particular distinction. Even if Tilesius, too, was a Flacian. Especially though Tilesius, too, was a Flacian. The Bible itself provided the warning. "For the son dishonoureth the father, the daughter riseth up against her mother, the daughter in law against her mother in law; a man's enemies are the men of his own house." Micah 7:6. Once a town had decided to call a Flacian minister, then—which one would it call? A former student of Jena, or of Leipzig? A former junior minister in Erfurt or in Leipzig? The Philippists were merely opposition. Tilesius, even at his age, was...competition. So.

Griep looked at the pamphlet the head of the Saint Thomas board of elders had brought him. Not one of Holz', as unpleasant as Holz was. Not "low-key," either. He paged through it again.

He knew what Count Ludwig Guenther wanted. No more "stress" in Grantville in the wake of the demonstrations, the deaths.

Not one of Holz' but still—stressful.

The count had, no matter how reluctantly, consented to his appointment at Saint Thomas.

He went downtown to the law offices of Hardegg, Selfisch, and Krapp.

Johann Georg Hardegg sent the pamphlet, with Griep's comments, to his sister Christiana in Leipzig. Who gave them to her husband Georg Friedrich Krapp—the printer, not one of the multitudes of Krapp jurists. Who, as requested, produced an analysis of which firm had most probably done the printing and sent it all, as he had been asked to do, to Georg von Werthern in Dresden.

Who was the patron of the parish Oswald Griep left when he accepted the call to Saint Thomas the Apostle in Schwarzburg-Rudolstadt. The same parish Werthern had thrown Pankratz Holz out of some years previously, immediately before appointing Griep.

Dresden

The people in the room grouped themselves by age. Without anyone's organizing it. By the book cupboard, Zacharias Prüschenk von Lindenhofen. He was about twenty-five, von Arnim thought. Next to him, Georg von Werthern's two boys, Dietrich and Wolfgang. Both in their early twenties, only a year apart. The elector's two oldest sons, Hans Georg and August, who matched Dietrich and Wolfgang precisely in age, year for year. They had all been educated together.

On the other side of the room, Saxony's most prominent theologian, Matthias Hoë von Hoënegg, who was forty-five now, and Georg von Werthern, much the same age and Saxony's chief minister of state for the past two years. Werthern, with the assent of the two young dukes, was effectively setting policy now. The elector was...incapable most of the time.

Not, unfortunately, incompetent. "Incapable" was a statement of fact. "Incompetent" was a legal status, reached after extensive hearings, that determined a ruler to be mentally unsound. It was followed by the establishment of a regency—also an interminable process. One for which Saxony had no time in the spring of the year of our Lord sixteen hundred thirty-five.

In the middle, Nikolaus Gebhard von Miltitz and Johann Georg von Oppel, both in their mid-thirties and well aware that when catastrophe hit, the two of them, as working diplomats, under Werthern, would get the task of negotiating to save whatever might be saved out of Saxony's shattered ruins.

Presuming that any of them were still alive when the time came, of course, von Arnim thought. If not—then someone else. That fell within the providence of God.

Benedikt Carpzov, next to them. Same age. The best lawyer they had available.

By the door, looking like they were not entirely sure they should be present, Carpzov's younger half-brothers, both in their late twenties. One a lawyer, the other a theologian.

And himself, of course.

By age, he belonged with Hoënegg and Werthern.

By temperament, too. He had worked with both men for years. One theologian. One civilian councillor. One military man.

In agreement.

Von Arnim glanced across at the young dukes, who, with Werthern's sons, were flanking Prüschenk. Then at the diplomats. "Saxony can't afford the hatred he is stirring up," he said.

Carpzov started to say something.

Von Arnim looked at Hoënegg.

"The pamphlets are not about serious doctrinal issues. The rest of you don't need to worry about Holz—the church will take care of him, in time. These, though, have become Zacharias' own personal vendetta against the up-timers. Because the daughter of Chancellor Hortleder chose the other man. Thus standing in the way of his ambitions."

The youngest Carpzov, the theologian, started to say something.

Von Arnim nodded at him.

"Zacharias hadn't actually made an offer to Anna Catharina's father, yet," he said. "He was still weighing whether it should be Friedrich Hortleder's daughter or the daughter of the mayor of Naumburg, Dr. Romanus. Which of the two matches would bring him more advantages. He almost offered for Gertrud Romanus more than two years ago, but then he made the acquaintance of the Hortleder family and held off."

Von Arnim looked at Werthern.

"The jurisdictional issues in regard to the Altschulerin woman, the wife of Jarvis Beasley, are negotiable. The Henneberg inheritance is an exclave, an outlier, now within the State of Thuringia-Franconia. They have naturalized the woman. Saxony can afford to lose her. It has lost many more subjects than one during this war."

Von Arnim looked at Prüschenk. "Do you agree to be silent? In voice and in print?"

Prüschenk looked back. "No. It is an abomination, and I will not hold my tongue. Nor will...." He stopped abruptly.

Von Arnim raised his eyebrows at Carpzov.

"One more step, I think."

"In the best interests of our father," Duke John George the Younger started. "...and in the best interests of Saxony," Duke August continued.

Dietrich and Wolfgang each moved forward and took one of Prüschenk's arms.

"...we order your arrest and internment on charges of high treason."

Prüschenk looked at Carpzov. "Are you here to represent me?"

Carpzov shook his head. "As a member of the Leipzig *Schöffenstuhl*, I am here to issue the warrant. No hearing is necessary. He looked at his brothers, who began to produce paperwork out of the leather folders they were carrying."

"This is contrary to proper procedure."

"No it isn't," Carpzov said serenely. Perhaps you missed my new book. It came out quite recently. *Practica nova imperialis saxonica rerum criminalium.* Lovely title, if I do say so myself. I am now the premier authority on Saxon criminal law practice, and I concur with the measures the general has decided to take. As do the consistory—he gestured toward Hoënegg—and the elector's council—he gestured toward Werthern. Or, perhaps I should say, the *sanior pars* of both."

Von Arnim nodded. "Let him be interrogated in regard to that 'Nor will...' please. It would be of interest of us to identify his sponsor."

Carpzov nodded.

"Then, if you will excuse me, Your Graces," von Arnim bowed to the young dukes, "I must return to the war we are trying to fight."

"We'll follow you in less than an hour," Duke August said. "With Wolfgang and Dietrich. We have to consult with our mother before we leave.

Grantville

Holz’~~s~~ next spate of pamphlets, directed at Kastenmayer, focused on the proposed confirmation of seven up-time men, betrothed to girls at St. Martin’s, without, Holz argued, sufficient instruction.

Particularly in regard to Mitchell Hobbs.

Who managed the laundry.

Where Kastenmayer had baptized the Beasley child.

Where Hobbs’ fiancée worked. Who belonged to Saint Martin’s even before she became betrothed to the up-timer. And came from the village where Jonas Justinus Muselius had taught school before the Ring of Fire happened.

Muselius, who was now betrothed to the daughter of the up-time woman who had spoken as an equal at the Rudolstadt Colloquy. And who, in spite of 1 Timothy 2:12, “But I suffer not a woman to teach, nor to usurp authority over the man, but to be in silence,” was now providing instruction in a heretofore unknown discipline called “statistics” at the University of Jena.

Where Muselius had once been a student. That was before the Ring of Fire, of course, but it probably showed something. A premonition of future decay of biblical standards, probably.

Wasn’t another up-time woman, also teaching, the one at the medical school, actually living in the household of Dean Gerhard of the theological faculty?

The general theme ran along the lines of “something wicked this way comes.” There was certainly a conspiracy. Even if Holz couldn’t figure out precisely what it was, he issued a ringing call for the orthodox theologians of the Universities of Wittenberg and Leipzig to call the lax and incompetent figureheads now usurping positions of trust at the University of Jena back to order.

Griep kept busy. He pounded the streets, assuring the new and potential parishioners of Saint Thomas the Apostle that Holz was behaving in a sectarian manner, had no congregation to which he was properly assigned, and should not be in Grantville at all. If they were dissatisfied with the situation at Saint Martin's, they should not turn to Holz. They should join Saint Thomas, where they properly belonged.

He had five hundred copies of the decision reached at the Rudolstadt Colloquy reprinted and distributed them for free. He also bought space in each of the Grantville papers to have the decision republished on full-page spreads with borders around them.

Which required a significant subsidy from his juristic brothers-in-law of the firm Waffler, Wiesel, and Finck.

Which also, when it appeared in the *National Inquisitor*, caused a considerable amount of merriment among the regular readers.

April 1635

"I postponed the dedication, as you instructed me," Griep said. "Nevertheless, they had a really big party at St. Martin's last week. It wasn't low-key at all."

Count Ludwig Guenther thought. Then thought a little more.

"It has been more than a month since March fourth," he said, finally. "The public announcement to postpone the dedication at Saint Thomas came at the right time. It was received well. The families have been preparing for these seven weddings for a long time. The grooms are all up-timers, whose relatives participated, so it did not leave an impression that we, the down-timers, as a whole, were ignoring the grief of the...original Grantvillers, shall I call them here? Their grief at the deaths of the mayor, the Calvinist minister, the policeman."

"I thought you wanted to avoid this 'stress,'" Griep said stiffly.

"Sometimes a celebration can also relieve stress," the count said.

"At least I tried," Griep said. "Holz has made no effort to relieve stress. Is it my place to ask what you propose to do about him?"

"He isn't within my jurisdiction. Or within that of my consistory."

"Whose jurisdiction is he in?"

"No one's, technically. There is no Lutheran organization within the Ring of Fire. Practically...."

"Yes?"

"If he's within anyone's jurisdiction, he's Tilesius' problem. But that is personal, not geographical."

"Are you sure that Tilesius thinks of him as a problem? Not as a weapon aimed to, in time, destroy the authority of the consistory of Schwarzburg-Rudolstadt? And, through that, and through you, to destroy the ability of Gustavus Adolphus to impose some kind of unity among the Lutherans of the USE?"

The count looked at Griep sharply.

He shrugged.

"Your role in the colloquies has been a prominent one. If the compromises you have forged among Lutherans in the USE fall apart, how is Gustavus to control the Lutherans in the Union of Kalmar?"

Ludwig Guenther raised his eyebrows.

Griep shrugged again. "Ecclesiastical politics is still politics. Especially for an emperor who insists on having a state church. Who knows what Saxony will look like after everything that has happened, will still be happening, this spring?"

* * *

"Pastor Kastenmayer," Liz Carstairs, interim mayor of Grantville and West Virginia County and, in practically everyone's opinion, mayor-presumptive as well, since she was likely to win the upcoming special election, ran down the steps of city hall. "I was going to phone, but then I looked out the window and saw you. Do you have any idea what this is about?" She handed him a piece of paper.

"I have received a similar letter from the Erfurt city council this morning, protesting that Ezechiel Meth is active again. Being harbored again by the dowager countess of Gleichen-Tonna, who has left Ohrdruf and is residing within the jurisdiction of West Virginia County. I have no doubt that Pastor Griep has also received one, and Count Ludwig Guenther as well."

"Who is Ezechiel Meth and why do we care?"

That was certainly a question that opened up possibilities.

In regard to the issue of the status of members of cults and sects.

Of which she was one.

Not just in his personal opinion. Certainly in the opinion of everyone else who had received a copy of the Erfurt protest. In the opinion, for that matter, of all the up-time Lutherans who had been transferred by the Ring of Fire.

Henry Dreeson had been a Presbyterian. A Calvinist. Comprehensible to the mind of ordinary men.

Liz Thornton *verh.* Carstairs was what other people called a Mormon. They called themselves by a much longer name. He would have to look it up. Shortened to LDS.

She might not even care that the followers of the late Esaias Stiefel showed signs of becoming active again.

This would require careful handling. Delicate phrasing. Coffee.

He looked around. They were almost directly in front of Cora's.

"Shall we go in?" he asked politely. "I'm buying."

He hadn't explained anything at all yet, but Liz knew that whatever it was, she wasn't going to like it.

Cora thumped the cups down.

"Have you ever heard of *Schwärmer*?"

She shook her head.

He searched his English vocabulary and found it wanting. "We need Jonas. Whatever am I going to do without Jonas once he leaves to become director of the normal school in Amberg? –Not that it isn't a splendid promotion for him and that we aren't all proud and happy." He stood up. "Gracious and most kind Cora, may I use your telephone, with most hearty thanks?" He moved behind the counter.

Anne Penzey, waiting tables on another Saturday morning, leaned over and whispered into Liz' ear. "Isn't he cute? I bet his eyes were blue when he was young, even though they've faded to a kind of greenish-hazel. It's amazing that he doesn't have to wear glasses at his age."

Liz took a look. The pastor wore his wavy hair long, at shoulder length. It was mostly gray, with some lingering brown strands. No receding hairline, but it had gone thin on top. The goatee that covered his chin was even grayer. "Cute" was not precisely the adjective she would have chosen. "Amazing," she agreed. That seemed neutral enough.

They were well through their second cups of coffee by the time Jonas arrived via trolley.

"Enthusiasts. Spiritualists. Perfectionists. Sectarians. Cultists. Heretics. 'Enthusiasts' is probably the most direct translation into English, but it does not encompass all the connotations." Jonas paused to think. Carefully. *It would need mental gymnastics and verbal acrobatics to convey to Mrs. Carstairs precisely what the* Schwärmer *were—without in any way stating or even clearly implying that she was one.* Finally, he settled for, "people with really, really strange religious ideas. Not all the same strange ideas, of course, which is why most of the groups are small.

"Esaias Stiefel thought that he was the reincarnation of Jesus Christ, and a lot of people agreed. You would think that they would have changed their minds when he died. That was, um, about eight years ago. But some of them didn't. Meth did reconcile with the Lutheran church, but Countess Erdmuthe Juliana, the dowager countess, never gave up her strange faith. Meth is with her again, so it's likely he has returned to heresy." He looked at Kastenmayer, a little uncomfortably. "We probably ought to call Pastor Griep, too."

"Ah, how did he die?" Liz asked. "This Stiefel?"

"Peacefully in his bed. In Erfurt. Gispersleben, where the cult was centered, belongs under that jurisdiction. That's why the Erfurt council is involved, I guess, since it seems to be reviving."

Waiting for Griep to get downtown from Saint Thomas' on the trolley had the rest of them into third cups.

It didn't help that he walked into Cora's and said, "Too late." Before he even sat down.

"What's too late?" Liz asked.

"It was Tilesius in Langensalza who alerted Erfurt. So he's bound to have notified Pankratz Holz, too, that they have come here from Ohrdruf. It's going to be a big mess. Tilesius and the Stiefelite controversy go back...at least thirty years. Not quite before my time, but almost. I was in my first year at the university when they held the set of hearings that led to Stiefel's first recantation."

"First?"

"Yes, ma'am. There were several."

Liz had an impulse to say, "But I thought they just burned heretics in this day and age. This sounds a long-drawn-out as up-time legal proceedings." She managed to stifle it. Instead, she said, "All right."

Griep was frowning. "I don't want to cause you stress," he said carefully. "But perhaps we should also ask your chief of police to join our discussion."

Preston Richards listened carefully. "Look," he finally said, addressing both of the pastors and Jonas, "It sounds like you think we didn't have that sort of folk up-time. We did. Let me tell you about the Hare Krishna people who were right up Route 250. The Ring of Fire didn't miss their conference center by much. *Then* you'll have something to thank God for. Namely, that they aren't here with us today."

"But what are you going to do?" Griep asked.

"Unless they start making trouble? Nothing." That was out loud. His mental response was *go see Al Green when I get a chance and figure out what this is all about better than I know now.*

"Well," Liz said. "I'll send a polite letter back to Erfurt, I guess. Thanking them for their concern. After that—like Press says, unless they actually make trouble, there's nothing we can do. It's not against the law to have what Jonas calls 'really, really weird religious ideas.' "

She smiled at him. "So go finish getting ready for your wedding. And Dina and Phillip's. At this stage, you probably have a list of two dozen things to do that Carol and Salome think are more important than...what did you call them?"

"Stiefelites. Or did you mean 'enthusiasts' in general?"

CLOTHED WITH THE IMPERISHABLE

Grantville, 1 April 1635

It was beautiful for a Palm Sunday. Beautiful spring weather was far from guaranteed in Thuringia in the spring. On most April Sundays that Dina could remember, the congregation had been bundled up in cloaks and hats, not infrequently coats and hats that dripped water onto the floor of the church, plop, plop, plop, all the way through the service, while everyone smelled like wet wool.

But on this Sunday, which was actually the first day of the month, there was warm sunshine outdoors, and the floor was dry.

Her father proceeded calmly through the ritual of confirmation for the seven up-time men he had been instructing in the catechism. The confirmation had been set for today, of course, so they could take Easter communion next week. The ritual of marriage for them and their down-time fiancées followed.

For Ryan Baker and Magdalena Heunisch, it was following none too soon, as her stepmother had said.

Dina smothered a smile as a vision of young Baker proceeding up to his first communion next week, carrying along a new baby to be baptized, flitted across her mind. Magdalena wouldn't be there, of course—from a child's birth to the mother's churching was 40 days.

Dina pulled her shoulders back. She needed to concentrate on the service.

But it was over. Her mind must have been wandering for some time. The congregation, today an odd mix of members and non-members, down-timers and up-timers, spilled out into the driveway between the church and school for the celebration. A rather dampened celebration, in spite of the sunshine. The mayor and the Calvinist minister had been shot less than a month before; nobody yet knew by whom or why.

She stood to the side, keeping an eye on the children who were running in all directions while their parents happily gossiped, eating a wurst with mustard as neatly as possible.

Not that anyone would notice if I drop mustard on this dress, she thought. The least expensive dyes were always in the range of yellowish tans to muddy browns, which meant that her dresses were always in the range of yellowish tans to muddy browns as well. Frequently, pieced together from the better pieces of fabric that remained in dresses donated to the poor.

Not that anyone else in the family is more luxuriously clothed, she thought that evening as she helped her stepmother once more refurbish her father's everyday gown. *Nor is it because we don't toil or spin. Maybe I could turn into a lily of the field and be clothed as gloriously as Solomon without having to work for it. What's more, although preachers admonish us not to be concerned about our raiment, I suspect they would be highly disconcerted if we appeared in public without it.* She shook out the seam she was repairing and peered down at it. There were only so many times a garment could be mended before the cloth itself was too weak to hold the stitches. She added several rows of darning across a few inches of the seam.

As glorious as Solomon, she thought again the next day. She had bought the school supplies she needed. Surely she could take a minute to look into the dress shop. Just a little bit of a dream about a ruby red dress with embroidered bands on the cuffs and hem. A brief peek, surely, would not break the commandment not to covet. *It isn't as if the dress belongs to someone else*, she told herself. *I'm not coveting someone else's property. It's there to be sold.*

Except that it was being sold.

Which distracted her enough that she didn't see the squad of unruly children running at her.

Who knocked her into a collision with a man.

It was terribly embarrassing.

Now she had mud on her skirt. And probably chalk dust, too. Her skirts usually had chalk dust on them.

He had been so very kind for a member of the nobility. He must be noble, or at least a patrician from one of the imperial cities. His clothes were utterly magnificent.

Easter Sunday, 8 April 1635

Easter Sunday mass at St. Mary's was followed by a conclave. Not a conclave of theologians, but a conclave of interrelated and intermarried ladies of "Kubiak Country." Kubiaks and Drahutas and Baranceks; Onofrios and Zaleskis and, today, because of Richelle's betrothal, a sprinkling of non-Catholic Fortneys.

All of whom had financial interests in the alchemical enterprises of one Dr. (err, well, maybe *Dr.* and who were they to critique down-time academic practices?) Phillip Theophrastus Gribbleflotz.

Who wasn't here. Who was, it must be said, in Jena, presumably at HDG Enterprises, which was precisely where he was supposed to be on this particular day, although he had spent the last couple of weeks running back and forth from there to here in his most likely fruitless pursuit of aluminum. His absence didn't keep Tasha, Ted's cousin Bart Kubiak's wife, born a Drahuta, from going off on one of her tears on the subject of some "probably a gold-digging tart" girl that the clueless man had managed to get himself tangled up with.

Tracy Kubiak sighed. She had *not* grown up in a huge Catholic clan where the people lived in each other's pockets, day in and day out, week in and week out, month in and month out, year in and year out, from here to eternity. Nor had she deliberately joined one. She had bumped into Ted entirely by accident at a skydiving club in Pennsylvania, married him in a civil ceremony (though his relatives shortly afterwards "got that fixed up"), and rather firmly limited her offspring to two. With the addition of adopting the teenaged Richelle and her baby after the Ring of Fire.

Jonathan Fortney, Richelle's fiancé, said rather mildly that, actually, the girl was the daughter of the Lutheran pastor out at St. Martin's in the Fields. A school teacher.

That bit of data shut even Tasha up for the time being.

Tracy charged him with the duty of finding out more.

15 April 1635

Dina listened as her father read out the pericopes for the Second Sunday of Easter:

1 Corinthians 15:53-55: "...for the perishable must be clothed with the imperishable, and the mortal with immortality. When the perishable has been clothed with the imperishable and the mortal with immortality,

then the saying that is written will come to pass: 'Death has been swallowed up in victory. Where, O death, is your victory? Where, O death, is your sting?' "

* * *

"Are you sure about this, Dina?" Ronella twirled a stick of chalk back and forth through her fingers. "You hardly know him. And he's hardly...." She let her words trail to a stop.

"God is giving him to me." Dina leaned against the chalk board, even knowing that once more she would have to brush out her skirts. A person's feet were sore after a full day of teaching. "I prayed that if He was so gracious as to send me a husband, he would not be *exactly* like my father and brothers and husband, and He has."

"Um. Yeah. Phillip's a little different, all right."

"He may not be as handsome as a statue of a pagan god, or as beautiful as our Savior appears in a stained-glass depiction. But, honestly, who is?"

Ronella cast her mind around, considering the male inhabitants of Grantville. "We've got a few dozen who are pretty good-looking. You have to grant that, even if they aren't a hundred percent perfect."

"Phillip looks fine. He's healthy and has all of his teeth and most of his hair. Besides, he has the best quality of all in a husband."

Ronella's eyebrows rose up.

"He actually wants to be my husband. He isn't being pushed into marriage by his parents or by a vestry board who think that every pastor needs a wife or—as far as I know, anyway—by anyone at all. He's...." Dina tried to think of a comparison. "It's like the army. He's not a draftee. He's a volunteer."

Ronella groaned.

"His clothes are beautiful. You have to grant that, at least. He may not be the most handsome man in the world, but he sure does know how to dress. And...."

"And what?"

"If God grants us long lives, all of us, sons and daughters of the King though we may be, will as perishable mortals end up with gray hair and drooping jowls. A real sense of style, though...." Dina's eyes sparkled. "Even if loving pretty things shows that we are frail and subject to vanity—a real sense of style is something that's going to last a lifetime."

Ronella kept her opinion of Phillip's sense of style to herself. Dina must be besotted.

22 April 1635

Dina listened as her father read the second of the three sets of banns preparatory to the upcoming marriage of Jonas Justinus Muselius and Ronella Koch.

Everyone knew about that, of course. It was going to be the social event of the season in Grantville.

Then he looked up and smiled a broad smile, a smile entirely appropriate for a pastor whose dowryless daughter was going to marry a Lutheran man, certified to be capable of supporting her, following all the prescribed forms of the church. He read the first of the three sets of banns preparatory to the upcoming marriage of Phillip Theophrastus Gribbleflotz and Maria Blandina Kastenmayer.

Only a select few in the congregation had known that was coming. The announcement started a low buzz.

Dina knew that by the time everyone got out the doors, the buzz would be loud. The wives of the members of the parish board that oversaw the school would head for their husbands, demanding to know *why* they had not received advance notice of the departure of one of the teachers.

She thanked heaven that at least they would not be marrying right on the heels of the banns. She would have a couple of extra weeks to find something to wear.

She also had to find something to wear as one of Ronella's witnesses, which Ronella insisted on calling a maid-of-honor. As if she were some noble lady-in-waiting, which she most certainly was not. Ronella's brother Jake was coming back from Augsburg for a couple of weeks to be her other witness. She'd thought that Jonas might ask one of her brothers, but he had asked Gary Lambert and his fiancée to witness for him.

All of which was beside the point that she was avoiding: she had to get something to wear as a bride.

She didn't have anything suitable. Clothing, unfortunately, like human bodies, belonged to the realm of things perishable rather than St. Paul's realm of the imperishable. Mortal rather than immortal. Most of her clothes were perilously near to perishing, better suited for donation to the rag collector than anything else.

She said as much to Ronella during their lunch break the next day.

Ronella happened to mention the little joke to Anne Penzey at Cora's City Hall Café and Coffee House.

Anne repeated it several times to tables of lunching ladies, one table of which consisted of the formidable "ladies of a certain age" who constituted the Red Cross Sanitary Squad.

One of whom was Jonathan Fortney's Grandma Priscilla, who repeated it to his fiancée Richelle.

Who repeated it to Tracy and the other ladies of "Kubiak Country," who, most naturally, had an interest in the Gribbleflotz nuptials.

"I suppose she's too proud to accept charity." Erin Zaleski raised her eyebrows. "Genteel poverty and all that."

Richelle shook her head. "I sort of doubt it. She re-makes most of her clothes out of things that land in the poor box at the church."

They sat and chewed on that for a few minutes.

"And I know that she has accepted a gift from Ronella, to buy her maid-of-honor dress. So maybe she'll wear that for her wedding, too. The pastor didn't like it much, but Salome's a practical sort of person and talked him around. It's not as if everyone doesn't know that the Kochs have a lot of money and contribute quite a bit of it to St. Martin's."

"Imperishable," Belle Drahuta muttered. "Imperishable."

"Belle," Tracy asked, "what are you cooking up in that fertile mind of yours?"

"It's a wedding, so what she needs is a wedding dress."

"Yeah. So?"

"What's the most imperishable thing in your closet?"

Tracy blinked and thought a bit. "My hiking boots?"

"Oh, right. You and Ted got married at the courthouse."

Tracy nodded. "In jeans and a tee-shirt. I had a party dress for the dance that evening."

"Well, for most of us," Belle said with a somewhat grim expression on her face, "the most imperishable thing we have in our closets is a wedding dress. Cleaned, preserved with chemicals, boxed in non-acid cardboard, with a little acetate see-through window." She glared around at the others. "Don't we? It takes a major disaster before a used wedding dress perishes."

Tasha's little sister Katie stuck out her tongue. "Doyle wasn't a Catholic; we got married in the sacristy at St. Mary's in street clothes and then had a party at the VFW that night."

"The rest of us, though"—Belle glared around at the yard chairs and their inhabitants—"have wedding dresses contributing to our clutter collection, don't we?"

Irene Fortney protested, "I don't, and Dana didn't, either."

"All right, you don't. *But*," Belle continued, undismayed, "among us we ought to have enough unperished wedding dresses that we can find one that fits the Kastenmayer girl and lend it to her. It can be her 'something borrowed.' Can't it?"

"We can get that Englishwoman who's running Roth's jewelry store to provide a lucky sixpence, a real sixpence—not a dime."

"What about something blue?"

"Do Germans even have that superstition?" Irene asked. "That's all it is: a superstition. And both of them are down-timers, so maybe they won't buy in on it."

"She may not," Tasha said, "but Gribbleflotz is gullible enough to buy in on almost any weird idea that comes floating by. Especially if it involves blue. If we persuade him that it's the right combination, she'll do it to keep him happy."

The list of attendees at the "wedding dress party" expanded exponentially. They ended up in the gym at the high school.

"We're not having refreshments until *after* all the dresses are boxed up again," Belle announced firmly.

Since she had appointed herself as the mistress of ceremonies, nobody else argued.

"Ta-da!"

She waved a magic wand.

She actually waved a conductor's baton borrowed from the band director, but these things happen.

"First forward, Jana Voytek Barancek will offer her dress for inspection."

"First," Jana said wryly, "because the plastic window on my box is cracked anyway, so if it works, no one else will have to unbox hers and let the elements into the pristine and bacteria-free interior."

Dina stood as tall as possible.

Jana grinned. "Princess Diana floof from 1984," she commented as she pulled. Huge, puffed leg-of-mutton sleeves. Huge, puffed, ruffled skirt resting on six layers of crinoline.

"I thought Americans didn't have princesses," Salome whispered to Carol Koch.

"We didn't. England did, though, and American girls adored them."

Jana raised her arms, lifting the dress to its full height, "Aaaannd...the neckline of the dress is higher than the top of Dina's head."

"Back to the box with it," Belle said, grabbing her own box. "I'll be the first to sacrifice the sacred seal. From 1989 we have...more Princess Diana floof. In taffeta." The big, puffed, sleeves had puffed ruffles on the puffs. There were three layers of puffed ruffles at the hem. There was a little puffed ruffle around the neckline. "Ummm." She looked at the dress and looked at the diminutive Dina. "Probably not."

"Erin," she called as she stuffed it back into the box.

"I didn't even bring my box over," Erin Zaleski answered. "I just brought a snapshot to pass around, and labeled it, 'What the hell was I thinking?' From 1992, I offer up puffed sleeves, a ruffle on the turtleneck, *and* a mermaid skirt with no less than six layers of ruffles on the mermaid tail part." She started the snapshot off on its rounds of the room.

Belle looked around, "Next?"

"I was talking to Erin and just brought a snapshot, too." Ted's cousin Mary Rose Onofrio laughed. "Once I met Dina, there wasn't any point. From 1997, I have a large blob of white satin sized for a girl who was and still is twice as big around as she is."

Dina's hopes were beginning to fade.

Somebody blew a trumpet.

Jonathan Fortney's aunt Janelle Berry, who didn't weigh an ounce more than when she got married in 1976, bounced into the gym from the locker rooms wearing—an off-white crocheted mini-dress with a boat neck and long bat sleeves, no trimming beyond the fabric itself.

It was cute.

Janelle was cute.

It was an absolutely, utterly, one hundred percent perfect, Janelle dress.

It would even have fit Dina. Who, however, was not likely to get married on the porch of St. Martin's in the Fields with her legs bare below the mid-thigh level.

Tracy looked at it consideringly. "Maybe I could rig up an underskirt."

"Actually, no," Janelle said. "I couldn't resist showing it off again." She hugged her arms around her waist. "I was going to wear it for our twenty-fifth anniversary party, but then the Ring of Fire happened, and nobody was having parties that next year because everybody was sort of desperately trying to survive. It's hard to think that was almost exactly four years ago and now we'll all be eating cake in another hour, and even if it is more like baklava bars than layer cake, it's still good." She twirled around and the trumpeter—it turned out to be Jonathan—repeated the fanfare.

"I sort of had this idea," Jonathan's other aunt, Sylvia Partow, said shyly. She didn't bounce. "About the blue, I mean. And Tracy, if you were willing to add an underskirt to Jan's, I think you could add an overdress to this. A blue one. Because we were talking about 'something blue' the other day. Like this picture. I took it at a Renaissance Faire once."

She tiptoed in front of them. "My wedding dress isn't expensive. I made it from a Simplicity pattern. It only took four yards of 54-inch fabric, even with a floor-length skirt. And the lace was from a set of six little doilies that Mom had from her mother. I appliqued them to the dupioni."

Priscilla and the rest of the Red Cross Sanitary Squad beamed.

"What's a dupioni?" Salome asked suspiciously.

"A kind of silk. It's woven so it's quite sturdy," Carol Koch whispered back.

"One doily each on the sides of the sleeves and the other four around the neckline," Sylvia added anxiously. "From the shoulders down to the center of the neckline. They would show up. And the rest of the dress is plain enough that Tracy could make the overdress with the higher waistline that we see in pictures of fashionable ladies down-time."

Dina was looking at Sylvia's dress, enchanted.

Tracy waved her hand. "I move that nominations be closed."

Everybody ate honey cake that was really more like baklava bars, and she started thinking about blue fabric. Royal blue. Dina needed jewel tones to set off her coloring.

Ronella was going to have her dream wedding, which was a very up-time dream wedding. Ron and Carol could afford it, their daughter wanted it, and the groom, as far as they were concerned, didn't have any say in the matter.

It did occur to Jonas, as the preparations swirled around him, that for the sake of their long-term happiness, it might be that moving to Amberg with Ronella rather than staying in Grantville where her parents could easily continue to fulfill her slightest wish might well prove to be a divine blessing.

As May 15 approached, Pastor Kastenmayer considered that he might give a sermon on excessive luxury in dress after it was all over, The parable of the rich man and the beggar at his gates was widely applicable.

"Where did you get that?" he asked Dina one evening. "I know that I agreed that Ronella might furnish you with something that suited her, but surely *Frau* Carol Koch didn't give you enough money for something so...." *What was the right word?* he asked himself. *Self-indulgent? Sybaritic? Red?*

Dina beamed. "A real bargain, Papa. Honestly. It was in the window of the dress shop earlier this year. Elisabetha Schwentzel bought it, wore it a couple of times—she did, people *saw* her wearing it—and then decided that it didn't suit her and took it back to the shop, swearing that it was unworn. Herr Schneider knew better, of course, but he wasn't willing to embroil himself in a lawsuit."

Kastenmayer nodded. "Very proper of him. Christians should be wary of too much litigiousness in the secular courts."

"So Herr Schneider had it back and was willing to sell it to me second-hand, and even took a little more off the price when I said that I would do any cleaning and repairs that were necessary myself. There were some. It was too tight for Elisabetha across the shoulders and she ripped out one of the seams. And there was a small grass stain on the skirt, but I got it out. Also, since my wedding dress will be borrowed, and I'll have to give it back to Sylvia before Phillip and I leave for Jena, I can wear this for the trip, too. And for many other things, over time. Look at the quality of the wool." She reached the section of the dress with the repaired shoulder seam out for her father to finger the fabric, having discreetly folded the embroidered bands on the cuffs to the inside. "It will last and last."

He nodded.

She wandered off to her room, clutching the lovely dress that she had—she admitted it—coveted so badly.

22 May 1635

There would be no elaborate procession of the friends of the bride and groom through the streets of the town, escorting them from their homes to the church. After all, the groom was not from Grantville, but rather lived in Jena and had spent the previous night at the Higgins Hotel, while the bride only had to walk over from the rectory.

Pastor Kastenmayer checked over the marriage license issued by the state and county for what must be the tenth time.

"Everything is in order," his wife said.

"What about the witnesses?"

"The State of Thuringia-Franconia only requires two. The church only requires two. Jonas and Ronella will witness for the church."

"But they are both Dina's witnesses. Neither of Phillip's witnesses is Lutheran!"

Salome Piscatora *verh.* Kastenmayerin repeated patiently, once more, everything that had been agreed upon in relation to the ceremony through which Maria Blandina Kastenmayerin would become Maria Blandina Kastenmayerin verh. Gribbleflotz.

"For the purpose of the church, Jonas will act as Phillip's witness and Ronella for Dina. Then, for the purpose of the marriage license, so everyone gets to participate officially, Jonathan will witness for Phillip and Richelle for Dina."

It had taken a while to negotiate this arrangement, It wasn't the fact that Richelle Kubiak had an illegitimate child. Salome had been living in a war-ridden land for the past fifteen years and seen too many unfortunate girls with children of unknown paternity. No, the problem had been that a Catholic young woman and her semi-Calvinistic heretic up-timer fiancé were willing to show up as witnesses at a Lutheran wedding. And that the groom wanted them there. Had, in fact, been quite unyielding on this matter.

So the ceremony itself, on the porch, to obviate as much scandal as possible in the eyes of Oswald Griep, Pankratz Holz, and any other wandering Flacian who might be in the neighborhood, would be, besides the witnesses, family only. By invitation, at any rate. Since it was outdoors, there was really no way to prevent observers from wandering by to watch if they were so inclined.

Officially, though, it was a small, family-only ceremony. Family, of which Dina had a lot, particularly when one considered all the remote connections of the Selfisch family who somehow happened to be in Grantville that day. Phillip, apparently, had none at all.

The party that the parish threw for them in the driveway, on the other hand....

"It's still going strong," Dina said to Phillip when they finally got away from it and left for Jena. "There are going to be a lot of hangovers in the morning."

* * *

Kastenmayer sighed with relief when Salome signaled to him that they could go home now. She had sent her own boys to bed hours ago;

Matthaeus, Martin, and Cunz were adults and she would leave them to their own devices.

"Sit down," she said, as she pulled the bar across the door.

"If I sit down, I'll never get up again to go up to bed. Then in the morning I'll have a miserable crick in my neck."

"Should I rub it?"

"If you would. And my temples also."

"Then sit." She gave her husband's shoulder a gentle shove.

After a few minutes, during which he breathed deeply in relief from his aches, he said, out of nowhere, "I'm so glad that Dina didn't borrow an up-time wedding dress after all."

"But she did," Salome answered, puzzled. "She borrowed it from Sylvia Fortney. It made the white blouse and underskirt of her ensemble."

"Oh."

"Why?"

"At least it was underneath, then. I know that the Kochs spent a great deal of money at the up-timer bridal shop for Ronella's gown, but, really...." He paused. "Perhaps, in spite of all my efforts, I do not understand up-time clothing. Last week I stood there, in front of the altar. Because she was so utterly determined to have her 'walk down the aisle' with her father escorting her. Though why he should have done so, I have no idea, since she is well past the age of consent and I'm sure they had completed all the necessary contracts about dowries and such well before."

"Yes," Salome murmured.

"I stood there, and it took so long for them to reach the front of the church, it seemed. All I could think, looking at that white gown in such a flimsy fabric, was that Ronella was getting married in her underclothing. Which was very unsuitable of me, I am sure."

Salome forced down a giggle.

In all truth, she had thought the same thing.

THE TRUTH ABOUT THAT CAT AND PUP

PART II
Grantville, May 1635

"Things can *always* get worse."

Carol Koch looked at Pastor Ludwig Kastenmayer. "We've had an anti-vaccination riot. Somebody, nobody knows who, has assassinated two of the finest men who ever lived in this town. Not perfect men, no, but good men. Honorable men, who tried to do their best. And one of the anti-Semitic fascists killed Buster Beasley, who was...I guess he was okay...in his own way, so to speak. He was on the right side that day."

"The situation has been...unnerving...since last fall, what with the actions of the local Flacians also. Those are of more immediate concern to the parish."

"I think a lot of it's been as funny as hell," Ron Koch said. "What with Edgar Neustatter excommunicating Pankratz Holz last November. In a laundromat or something."

Kastenmayer shook his head. "There has been nothing amusing at all about the agitation that led, however indirectly, to Fred Jordan's death."

Rather reluctantly, Ron nodded.

"It could be worse." Kastenmayer went back to his original point. "Consider the pan-Lutheran theological colloquy in Magdeburg last fall. Count Ludwig Guenther maintains that not much was accomplished because Saxony and Brandenburg did not participate, as a result of which he anticipates another one in early 1636. At least, however, it averted a schism that would have torn the Lutheran churches in every province of the USE in half."

"Hah!" Carol exclaimed. "This particular count seems to be a nice enough guy as a person, but in both the colloquies, first in Rudolstadt, then in Magdeburg, I ended up thinking about the proverb." She reverted to English. " 'In democracy, it's your vote that counts. In feudalism, it's your count that votes.' Your ordinary, everyday, church member couldn't get a word in edgewise for all of the pontificating politicians, and he's one of them."

It took Ron a while to explain the joke to the pastor, who still didn't speak much English. The pun didn't work at all German, given that although *wählen* and *zählen* could be used, *Graf* and *Wahl* were not at all similar words.

"This is all well and good," Pastor Kastenmayer's wife Salome interjected, "but we are here this evening to complete the plans for two weddings."

“I met Superintendent Tilesius, once” Dina said at the Koch-Muselius rehearsal dinner. “The year before the Ring of Fire, he put on a really big celebration for the centennial of the Augsburg Confession in Langensalza. Three days long. Papa took us all. I had a wonderful time.”

Ronella swallowed. She was Lutheran, but.... “You had a wonderful time celebrating the centennial of when a great big thick theological book was published?”

“It was great,” Jonas said. “I was there, too. We took the whole Quittelsdorf village school on a field trip.”

“It does sound like it would have been fun,” Gary Lambert said. “If the Ring of Fire had only happened a year earlier, we could all have gone. We’re both too young to remember the bicentennial celebration for the American Revolution, but my parents used to talk about it. Almost every town in the United States put on a bash.”

“You wouldn’t have needed to go that far—as far as Langensalza,” Friedrich Hortleder said. “We had a big celebration in Weimar, too, as good as the one Tilesius put on, if you ask me. In spite of the marauding armies. Sometimes people need to focus on what’s really important in the long run, no matter what’s happening all around them.”

“I agree,” Salome said. “By the way, Carol, have you noticed that lately we’ve only been getting Pankratz Holz’s pamphlets. They’re basically topical attacks. The personal attacks on Ludwig and Gary aren’t coming anymore.” Nor were the personal attacks on her, but she was too modest to mention those.

“We always sort of thought that the worst ones—like the Christmas Eve set—were coming out of Saxony. Maybe the distribution network has collapsed because of all the military activity. If so, it’s the only actual blessing of war I’ve ever heard of,” Ron Koch commented.

* * *

"Two weddings down," Carol said. "A week apart. Oh, my aching feet."

"Have another cup of cider," Salome suggested.

Carol grinned. "At least they got Ron to church two weeks in a row. That hasn't happened often in our lives. He was born a Lutheran, of course—well, baptized as one, when he was a baby—so that's what he is, but he doesn't actually work at it. A lot of the up-time Germans I met were like that. Most of his friends thought I was a little odd because I actually went to church."

Rudolstadt

"Well, of course. If they won't do anything about Ezechiel Meth, they won't do anything about Pankratz Holz, either. This 'storefront church' of his is ursurping a great deal of what should be Saint Thomas' parish. The Philippists have kept going to Saint Martin's. Of course, Kastenmayer has known that St. Thomas' would be opening since the beginning, so their budget has allowed for this. He's shrewd enough to have determined the leanings of most of those who were attending there because they didn't have an option yet.

"For Saint Thomas, though, Holz is splitting the Flacians. Which means that we have obligations, bills to pay, but can't count on the number of members I expected."

"I will take up the question of a transitional subsidy with the consistory. However, you wanted this appointment, Pastor Griep. You went to a great deal of effort to secure it. All I can really recommend now is that you use persuasion to bring your flock into the fold. I certainly can't herd them there."

"But can't you *do* something?"

Count Ludwig Guenther, once more, pointed out that he and his consistory really did not have any jurisdiction over the ecclesiastical situation in West Virginia County. No more in regard to Holz than in regard to Meth. "Which," he finished, "only confirms my prudence in having erected both St. Martin's and St. Thomas' outside the boundaries of the Ring of Fire, within my own lands."

After dinner, Count Ludwig Guenther beamed down at his young wife. In accordance with the best medical opinion, both up-time and down-time, she was breast-feeding little Albrecht Karl herself. "It will all be to do over again, Dearest. You do realize that?"

"All what?" She winced. The baby had both top and bottom teeth as of the previous week.

"The theological colloquy. The one we held in Magdeburg last year, at the emperor's insistence. I told him, at the time, that there was little point in trying to achieve some lasting settlement without the participation of Brandenburg and Saxony. Especially Saxony. But he wasn't to be deterred by the power of reason. When he makes up his mind that he wants something, he wants it *right now*."

"So, when?" She detached the baby and handed him over to the waiting nursemaid.

"Not this fall, I think. That will be too soon. But, after things have rested a while during the winter. I predict that we will be going back to Magdeburg early in the spring of 1636."

Emelie giggled. "More days on a hard bench? So the delegates can't fight about who has a right to bring in what size or shape of cushion? You have mentioned the hardships of presiding over colloquies several times."

The count steepled his fingers against his mouth. "My explorations of Grantville have taken me into several of the up-time churches. Two of them have a device called an 'upholstered pew.' This obviates the cushion issue." He nodded decisively. "Our treasury can afford it. If I am called back to Magdeburg to preside over yet another theological colloquy, I shall have the benches upholstered—all of them—before the sessions begin."

Emelie giggled again. "Maybe you should have the upholsterers arrange things so the padding is removable. Take it away from the most long-winded and obstreperous ones. The longer they talk during the day, the thinner the covering on their sections of the benches will become during the following night."

He beamed down again. His wife. "Dearest," he said. "I'm really glad that you are on my side."

She reached one hand up and took his. "Always."

June 1635

Holz addressed the question of the Koch-Muselius wedding in three separate pamphlets. The first dealt with the processional, recessional, bridal gown, bridesmaids' dresses, and a level of expenditure appropriate, according to the sumptuary laws of every reasonable principality, for none but the upper patriciate and nobility. The general thrust of the content was "not the way we've always done it."

Since most down-timers figured that the up-timers in general belonged to the patriciate, if not to the nobility, they yawned. Even Oswald Griep said, to anyone who asked, that the issues were adiaphoral.

The second dealt with the music, which was, Holz proclaimed, awful. Since almost all the down-timers agreed, but there was no law anywhere, civil or ecclesiastical, against having bad taste in music, this did not resonate widely, either.

The third addressed the theology of Kastenmayer's having agreed to conduct a wedding ceremony before the altar, which gave at least an appearance of creeping papistry, since marriage was not, in the Lutheran scheme of things, a sacrament. Baptism, except in emergencies, took place at the font, before the altar. Communion took place at the altar. Marriage. No.

That was a more serious allegation. A lot more serious. Oswald Griep really wished that he had thought of it himself.

Wherefore his comments on the pamphlet were tart.

Holz' response was intemperate.

Truth be told, since their viewpoints on most matters were quite similar, they had only small grounds for disputes. Which caused them to hold onto those small grounds even more bitterly and tenaciously, magnifying them as large as they dared.

Increasingly, the longer he was at Saint Thomas, Griep became territorial. Resentful of the intruder.

His pamphlet accusing Melchior Tilesius of attempting, from Langensalza, to extend undue influence into what was properly the superintendency of Schwarzburg-Rudolstadt, was bitter.

June 1635

"Well, there they go." Ron Koch slapped Gary Lambert on the back as they watched Ronella and Jonas set out for Amberg and a new life in the Upper Palatinate. "Every way we looked at it, going over to the trade route, down to Nürnberg, and east on the Goldene Strasse is still the easiest way to get there. Not the fastest, but the easiest. And with Jonas only having one driving hand...."

He looked after the wagon that was heading out on the Badenburg road from where it joined Route 250. "There were times last fall when I thought the girl was going to pine away with longing. Go into a decline or something."

Carol swatted him lightly. "Ronella's not that kind of a wimp. She would have gotten him, one way or another. Eventually. Don't you think, Gary?" She turned her head. "Pastor Kastenmayer?"

They both agreed.

Gary took a deep breath. "Guys, while we're all here.... Not in the middle of a bunch of other people."

"What?"

"Um." He stopped, clearly uneasy. "I don't want you to think that I don't love each and every one of you. But now that Jonas has left.... He was my best friend. What was tying me to Saint Martin's, really. Since he's gone. Uh, doctrinally...." He stopped again, then motioned toward the tower a quarter mile beyond the boundary line. "Okay. I'm switching my membership to Saint Thomas. Theologically, I'll be more comfortable there. And I know that Anna Catharina will be. Her dad's pretty conservative. So I'm going to go ahead and do it. Get it over with before the wedding. But I wanted to tell you before I talked to Griep about it."

He searched their shocked faces. "I still want to be friends, but.... Well, I guess I'd better be getting to work." He turned around and climbed on the trolley that was about to start for the other side of the Ring of Fire.

"More changes," Carol whispered. "More of them, all of the time. Creeping up on us, after so many changes already the past few years."

July 1635

"Anne." Natalie Bellamy stood up and waved. "Anne, I want toast, please." She sat down again. "There's so much babble in here this morning that a person can't hear herself think."

"It's another 'creeping papistry' pamphlet," Orrine Sterling said. "It landed on the news stands in Rudolstadt day before yesterday. Before the distribution here."

"What is Holz going on about now?"

"Well, you know that Pastor Kastenmayer and his wife took some time off," Carol said.

"Since it's the first time in two years, they deserved it."

"Nobody's arguing about that. But they went to Erfurt. Not for some kind of a church thing, but because Dina's sister had a baby. Andrea and Tony Chabert. You know Tony—he was one of the guests at Tom and Rita Simpson's wedding. He joined the army right away and has stayed in. They had a boy and they named him Ludwig. Ludwig Anthony, even before the Kastenmayers decided to go visit."

"Maybe that's why he decided to go visit," Anne said, delivering the toast.

"I haven't seen the pamphlet," Carol said. "I guess I'll have to read it. Bring me my bill, please, Anne. I'll stop and pick one up on the way home."

"She looks sort of worn thin," Natalie said.

"With Ronella gone and Jake in Augsburg, I guess they call it 'empty nest syndrome.' "

"Whatever reason," Orrine said, "Holz is declaring that for a Lutheran pastor to visit a Catholic son-in-law who doesn't show any immediate signs of converting, even if he didn't actually go to the baby's baptism—Tony had it done in a Catholic church up there in Erfurt—is a sign of...well, something doctrinal that's bad. Even if he watched though the outside door and didn't go to communion or anything. What Holz wrote, in the English translation, is 'unionism,' but I can't imagine what it could possibly have to do with the Civil War. Or workers' rights, either."

Neither could anyone else who was still at the table.

* * *

"It doesn't matter what you think, Pastor Griep." The head of the board of elders elected by the congregation (confirmed male members, of course) of St. Thomas the Apostle stood there stubbornly. "Well, it matters. We took it into consideration. But we've voted. We know you don't like using the names of modern saints who aren't in the Bible, but that's just too bad, I guess. We're naming the school for Saint Guenther of Thuringia. He was the patron saint of the count's family for seven hundred years or more. Even if he's been de-patronized, so to speak, he's still in heaven, and we expect he still has considerable interest in what's going on around here. It was his job for a long time."

It was becoming clear to Oswald Griep that shepherding his new congregation into a fully reliable doctrinal stance might be a long-term project. At least he would have Gary Lambert's help.

He wrote a pamphlet and a flyer aimed at the vacillating Flacians of Grantville and West Virginia County, stating in no uncertain terms his views that Pankratz Holz was an unauthorized trespasser, engaged in stealing the Lord's sheep.

September 1635

"Ron and I went to the dedication at St. Thomas," Carol said. "As guests, of course. But you and the count were honored guests, up on the podium. We were sort of lurking in the back, trying to look as inconspicuous as possible, being from the wrong side of town, theologically speaking. As well as geographically."

Countess Emelie laughed. "You must at least be happy that Holz is now so angry at Pastor Griep that he has stopped writing pamphlets about Pastor Kastenmayer."

"I can't be glad. Not really."

"How come?" Count Ludwig Guenther asked.

Carol opened her purse. "I finally got this done. I had to have the illustrations copied by hand and with the move to Bamberg, Lenore Jenkins has been so busy that it took her forever to finish, and then I had to wait again until someone at the University Press had time to bind it. It's for your little Albrecht Karl. The book I was telling you about. The poem. Eugene Field. It somewhat says how I feel about all these disputes. I don't want to tell you. It all bothers me too much. You can figure it out for yourselves."

The count leafed through it. "It's a lovely book. We are grateful. The stuffed animals, the printed fabrics in the pictures, the floppy blue ears on the dog and the perky yellow ones on the cat are charming."

"What do you think she meant, Dearest," Emelie asked after she had gone on her way to Jena.

He flipped the book to the last page and read in the excellent English he had acquired in Oxford on his grand tour so many decades before:

The truth about that cat and pup,
Is this: they ate each other up.

"I have been called to the next colloquy. Sometimes, though, I start to think that the wish of Gustavus Adolphus, to achieve doctrinal unity among all Lutherans, is close to being Don Quixote's unattainable dream. Your friend Carol may think so, too. I suspect that she has become...discouraged."

Emelie reached up and took his hand. "All you can do is try."

THINGS COULD BE WORSE

Ohrdruf, May 1635

Catharina Diana Schlosser stood before the mayor and council.

"Five years," she said. "Five years. I have been teaching the beginners of this town for five years without any serious complaints. Not from the parents. Not from the children. Not from the other teachers at the school. Not...." She waved her hand. "Not from the pastor."

The mayor shifted in his chair.

She looked at him. Maybe his seat was uncomfortable. Maybe he was nervous. Maybe....

"Pastor Holz...," he began.

She realized that it would not be tactful to say that Pastor Holz was a lying shit.

A lying shit who, while over in this town causing many other troubles had also thought to question the orthodox Lutheranism of a father who would give each of his children a middle name chosen from classical mythology, and, by extension, the orthodox Lutheranism of a daughter who would bear such a name. A father who was currently teaching in Grantville, at a school sponsored by the Philippist parish of St. Martin's in the Fields.

Which the mayor, seriously irritated with Grantville because of their protection of the Stiefelite heretics who gathered around the countess of Gleichen—which, to speak the truth, she herself thought was more than a little peculiar—and the death of—what was he exactly? a constable of some kind, she supposed—the man who came to represent the SoTF, the one called Fred Jordan, in March, found...well...meaningful. Significant.

Or, Catharina grumbled inwardly, purported to find significant.

Unfortunately, it meant that her job was on the line unless the pastor developed a little more backbone than he was displaying at the moment. Which she didn't think was likely.

Grantville, May 1635

Thursday evenings at the Thuringen Gardens were usually slow. Thursday wasn't a big day for church stuff, either. The *Stammtisch* had pretty much expanded beyond the limits of Mitch Hobbs' hospitality, not to mention that his wife Walburga's patience with the messes they made had come to an official end the day after the wedding last month, so they had reserved a regular table.

"Ryan's not coming," Derek reported. "He says that David's being fussy, and Meg's feeling pretty wiped out. Maria's down at the adult education center, trying to find out if there's any way to combine classes with working at the bakery."

Errol Mercer looked up. "Education. That reminds me. Who *is* going to replace Dina at Countess Kate, now that she's getting married?" That was his main concern at the moment, given that most of his regular income came from the Lutheran school. "Not just Dina, but they're losing two at once. Jonas is headed for Amberg, which means that the high school has lost Ronella from the math department. For all practical purposes, Jonas has been something like a principal ever since they started Countess Kate up. He does the kind of work that a principal does, anyway, on top of teaching. Like paying me."

Walburga sighed. "Anna Piscatora, that's Salome's sister...."

"Yeah, she's married to Heinrich Schlosser. He's been at Countess Kate for more than a year, I think." Errol nodded. "He's got a lot of sense and doesn't put up with a lot of nonsense from either the kids or the parents. He could take over for Jonas. But he has to be close to fifty years old, one side of it or the other. I don't think he could work the kind of schedule that Jonas has been doing. Not in the long run. And the school keeps getting bigger. If they make him principal, they'll have to find one more new teacher, making three."

"*Anna Piscatora* says," Walburga continued firmly, "that their oldest daughter, the one who is still teaching in Ohrdruf, would be happy to take Dina's place."

"It seems a bit weird to me," Roland Worley said. "That they keep hiring one another's relatives, I mean. What do they call it? Incest?"

"Nah." Errol shook his head. "Some other word. It's not coming to me right now. But Heinrich Schlosser's a good teacher; I don't see any reason why the school shouldn't take a flyer on another of his kids, seeing that Hektor's already teaching one of the sixth-grade classes."

"Nepotism!" Roland slapped his hand on the table. "That's the word."

"But so what?" Derek Blount put down his beer. "Honest, I mean, Dina is the pastor's daughter! A niece of his wife isn't even that close of a relationship."

"*Anna Piscatora* says...." Walburga ignored the interruptions.

"Okay, what the fuck does she say?" Derek picked his beer up again.

"She says that their second daughter—her name's Anna Penelope, Denise Beasley's friend, the one you up-timers call Penny—will graduate from the high school this month, is almost eighteen years old now, and would be willing to split the vacancy. They're not going to find anyone else who will teach eighty kids the way Dina has been doing since her sister eloped."

Roland frowned. "Doesn't Penny have to go to the normal school before she can teach?"

"If she was going to teach in a public school, yeah, I think." Mitch leaned back. "But Vesta Rawls says that the state doesn't set the requirements for the church schools. Parochial schools. Didn't, even up-time. Can't, I suppose, if there's separation of church and state. I dunno. They have their own boards and stuff."

"I suppose...." Roland's wife Rahel doodled in the condensation on the table with one finger. "If the 'too many relatives' bit really bothers you, we could see if the middle school would hire Hektor. They always need teachers over there. What does Irma Lawler call children that age? Oh, *the pits*. The useless part of a fruit. Even so, teaching in one of the up-time schools might have a bit more prestige for him. They don't make the down-timers they hire to teach go to normal school if they teach subjects that the up-timers don't know anything about." She smirked a little. "Which turns out to be a lot of them, these days. Like German. Or Latin. That would get Salome's nephew out of Countess Kate and replace her daughter with two nieces. Fair enough trade."

"Who at the middle school would pay any attention if we asked? All of us were pretty much the dregs when we were that age," Mitch pointed out. "Yeah, *the pits*. The kind of kids who get middle schoolers put in that category."

"They're still going to have to find a new math teacher for the high school," Derek's wife Ursula said. "The board isn't likely to find one who can afford to teach practically for charity the way Ronella has, since she didn't need the money. And if Hektor moves to the middle school, that will make another vacancy at Countess Kate."

"Hey." Derek grinned. "Speaking of 'all in the family' stuff, isn't Jonas some kind of cousin of Mrs. Kastenmayer's, too? Things could be worse. If she didn't have a bunch of relatives, they'd hardly have anyone on the faculty at all. Anyway, none of us have any kind of 'in' with the board of education at the church, so it's really none of our business, is it?"

Rahel added a few flourishes to her doodle, thinking. She had an "in" because she worked for Irma Lawler, who was born a Vandine and was related to Charles Vandine, who was going to come back from Geneva and be the new Calvinist minister now that someone had shot the Reverend Wiley. And Roland managed the machine shop when Nat Davis, who was a friend of the famous Mike Stearns, was out of town. Roland had an "in" right there. If they both said something.... Well, it couldn't hurt anything.

Grantville isn't all that different from Quittelsdorf, really, she thought, as her busy finger added some scallops around the edge. Oh, the up-timers believed a lot of different things and had many strange ideas. But getting something accomplished was pretty much the same, once you figured out how the people connected together. *Making things work is still mainly a matter of who you know and then who they know.* Her doodle acquired three decorative swirls. *And I can live with that.* It grew four little feathers, attached to the top. *And I will give high odds that Walpurga can, too. Things could be worse.*

One side of the doodle sprouted a hand holding a crown. *If the war doesn't come back.* The war had taken away her father's prosperous leasehold in Quittelsdorf and thrown his fields away, probably to someplace called West Virginia, the up-timers thought; it had reduced Matthias Dornheimer from a full-holder to a hired hand on Johann Pflaum's farm in Lichstedt. He was past sixty, without the heart to start over. The Bible had something to say about that. The Book of Job, when a man did everything right all his life, but God still came along and dropped misery right on top of his head just to tease the devil. The moral of the story was supposed to be that Job had kept his faith and started over. Papa hadn't. Not with only one of his eleven children surviving and that that one a girl. Herself. *Everybody says that the emperor is going to invade Saxony and Brandenburg very soon. Next month, probably. If the war comes back, things will get a lot worse.*

* * *

"I had a letter from Lutz, today," Salome said at supper.

"Which Lutz?" The question was reasonable, given how many relatives on both sides of the Kastenmayer family were named Ludwig and nicknamed Lutz.

"My cousin, Reimarus. I wrote him last month. Aunt Margaretha died last August. You remember. She fell ill in Nürnberg and quickly died while in visiting relatives of her late third husband. You met him once, at least. The Flemish merchant she married after Papa died. That was when? Ten years before she died, at least. Van Sice died first, though, a couple of years earlier, and left her in a good financial position."

She took a deep breath. "Last August. Nine months ago. Nine months, and not a hair have I seen of the little bequest she left for me. I don't see how he can begrudge it—she surely left her own children more than she left to Anna and Ernst and myself, and she brought the three of us up as if we were her own children after Mama died. With her own children, as if we were brothers and sisters rather than cousins, in Papa's rectory."

"The love of money...."

"With all due respect, Husband. I do not believe that I love money unduly. But we do need it. However, Lutz did not even mention the matter in his reply. It was all about the *Concordance to the Lutheran Hymnal* that Chancellor Hortleder got from Gary Lambert last year and how prominently he himself is involved, as an organist in Weimar, in organizing the new Lutheran church music academy that the Saxe-Weimar dukes are sponsoring."

Pastor Kastenmayer could not deny that they needed money.

With Dina's marriage, however generously Phillip had offered house room to the boys while they studied in Jena, an ineffable boon, for the present they had lost the income, however small, that Dina's teaching had brought to the household.

"Perhaps...." He paused. Salome was right. The bequest was due to her and they needed it. Nevertheless. "Reply," he suggested, "without mentioning the money directly. Then keep writing, often enough that he can make no pretense that your existence has slipped from his mind."

"Very well."

Personally, she thought that her brother-in-law would be more reasonable in regard to taking firm measures and that Anna, therefore, could well do her part in reminding Lutz what they were owed. But when she wrote the next day, she provided him with a lively account of the "seven at one blow" up-time converts by marriage and a critical evaluation of the lack of merit to be found in one Richard Wagner's "Wedding March" from an opera called *Lohengrin*. That should be enough to spur Lutz to write back.

If that didn't work, if correspondence from Anna had no effect, if persuasions from Ernst in Wittenberg proved insufficient, then.... There was always Johann Georg Selfisch. However much the ghost of Ludwig's first wife had haunted their marriage, there was no doubt that her half-brother was a shrewd lawyer, nor that he could, because he was a relative, be persuaded to come up with a few appropriate words on his firm's new, modern, up-time style, letterhead stationery without charging for them.

June 1635

It looked like half the people who had bothered to attend the city council meeting had done their own informal adjournment to the Thuringen Gardens once Liz Carstairs brought down the gavel. Even Liz, although, of course, she didn't drink.

"Of course, I don't know exactly what to expect from the transition at the USE level." She heaved an exasperated sigh. "Nobody does. I've talked to Count Ludwig Guenther and to the duke down at Altenburg. They're as much in a fog as anyone else. At least we've already finished with the worst of the mess of transferring the SoTF state administration down to Bamberg."

Sorting that out, especially the issues of who would stay and who would go, as a result of the referendum the previous February, had been neither an easy task nor, in a lot of ways, a pretty one. More than a few up-timers had been privately, and sometimes vocally, of the opinion that Grantville should ignore these particular election results, more or less on the unexamined hypothesis that some animals were more equal than others.

Chad Jenkins tapped a finger on the table. "The worst of it, maybe. What with house sales and people who work for the state but don't want to sell their houses, not to mention the shortage of rental management companies, I don't think we'll have even the first-stage personnel transfer finished until next fall. There'll be stragglers even after that, Huddy Colburn says. It's worse than when so many folks took off for Magdeburg. Huddy, Thurman Jennings, Bunny Lamb—all of them say their office staff is run ragged."

Given that Chad had owned a bunch of rental properties even before the Ring of Fire, he knew what he was talking about.

Gary Lambert nodded. "Bamberg's really a done deal, though. It's a matter of making it work, now. But when it comes to the national election, we're just getting started. I heard that Ed Piazza thinks that the emperor and Wettin himself will lean heavily in favor of the Philippists. I'm not sure I agree with that assessment. The emperor, perhaps, but of course the dukes of Saxe-Weimar are the major patrons of the University of Jena. It was theirs, after all, before Saxe-Weimar got 'slid' into the NUS and then SoTF. The theology professors there, Gerhard and the others, are orthodox. Very sound views."

"If they do end up, for political reasons, favoring the Philippists...." Old Emmanuel Onofrio pursed his lips. "Which they may have to do, if they intend to extend the policies of religious toleration that were begun under Stearns.... As a Catholic, I have to hope that they will. As does Father Kircher." He looked at Nicholas Smithson, who nodded.

"It would be an understatement to say that the more extreme Flacians won't be happy," Gary admitted. "That's pretty hard for me to admit, being the up-time equivalent of a Flacian, so to speak. At least when it comes to doctrine. But we, every variety of Lutheran in America, had come to terms with separation of church and state a century and a half before the Ring of Fire hit. Here and now, state churches are still going strong. What we don't know yet is how vociferously unhappy they may be. But it hasn't happened yet, I'd point out. Even if the Crown

Loyalists do push an established church through the parliament...and I don't think they will, not on a national basis. The sensible ones realize that separate established churches in each province will work better. Several of the provinces are relatively homogeneous when it comes to religion. And there won't be persecution. *Cuius regio, eius religio* is not coming back on a provincial level. An established church won't mean much more than that part of some people's taxes go to support a denomination they don't belong to."

Ron Koch stroked his chin. "It's going a bit too far to say that the provinces outside of the SoTF are 'relatively homogeneous,' if you ask me. Everyone knows they'll have to carve some kind of an exception for the Upper Palatinate. Beyond that, think about the way the Congress of Copenhagen set up Westphalia. It's maybe forty percent Catholic and forty percent Lutheran, with fifteen percent Calvinists and a mishmash of everything from Anabaptists to Jews making up the rest."

Onofrio frowned. "I didn't realize that."

"Neither did I," Al Green said, looking at Ron.

"Hardly any of you—I don't mean 'you' as Catholics or 'you' as Baptists; I mean 'you' as the American-born up-timers, generally speaking—hardly any of you even think about it. If you think about it at all, you vaguely think that northern Germany equals Protestant and southern Germany equals Catholic, which is way too much of an oversimplification."

"The important question, though, is how it's going to affect us. Right here in Grantville. Whether we're up-timers or down-timers. And we just don't *know*." Liz pushed her hand through her hair.

"Right now, though," Mel Richards pointed out, "things could be worse. They *were* worse a couple of months ago. Press was saying that yesterday. They could get a lot worse again if a new war comes this way.

But we can't fix what's already happened and we can't predict what's going to come at us next. All we can do is deal with it."

Jena, June 1635

"Amberg is so close to the active war zone," Carol Koch fretted.

Johann Gerhard listened patiently to the woes of the University of Jena's so-valuable up-time teacher of statistics. No mortal man could change the fact that Amberg was in the Upper Palatinate and that the Upper Palatinate was close to Saxony.

"It has always been so," he answered, "even though that thought will bring you small enough comfort. Consider the first line of the eleventh chapter of Second Samuel. 'In the spring of the year, the time when kings go out to battle....' It was a truism, already for the divinely inspired authors of the Old Testament, that kings will march their armies out to war in pursuit of their ambitions, and that they consider the spring a favorable time of the year in which to do it."

Carol laughed a little weakly. "At least no king is likely to send Jonas to be killed at the front and steal Ronella to become one of his multiple wives. Maybe the world has made a little progress over the years. Not just between then and the up-time that Granville came from; between then and the here-and-now." She turned around. "At least, Ronella writes that the place that Duke Ernst's secretary, he's a nice guy, she says, named Böcler, and efficient...." She stopped. "Where was I? Oh, yes, the place that Böcler rented for them to live—he did it on behalf of the normal school, not Duke Ernst, but Duke Ernst has pretty much been managing the normal school so far—is fairly nice and was immaculately clean when they arrived. If empty. They don't have any furniture. They do have a cook. And a housemaid. So I guess that things could be worse.

"But...." She stifled an, "Oh, God" in deference to down-time views of blasphemy. "Dean Gerhard, I'm *so* miserable that Gary Lambert has switched his membership from St. Martin's to St. Thomas. He's been such a good friend, all along. And I can't like Oswald Griep over at St. Thomas. The count's consistory appointed him in February, and he turned up in Grantville in March, so I've had three months to try to like him. Even 'putting the best construction on everything,' though, I don't. Can't."

Gerhard pointed out that only God could search the depths of a man's heart. It was possible that Griep was, in his own way, a faithful steward.

After Carol left, he shook his head. Even though Griep was on the correct side of things, doctrinally speaking, he *was* sometimes a difficult man to like. Theologically, though, he could not himself find fault with Gary Lambert's decision. Which would, given Gary's upcoming marriage to Anna Catharina Hortleder, strengthen the ties of Grantville's Lutherans to Weimar. Which could not be considered a bad thing.

Grantville, July 1635

And then there was war.

"I haven't seen Edgar Neustatter and his group at church the past two Sundays," Pastor Kastenmayer said. "They're usually pretty faithful attendees."

"Didn't you see the newspapers?" Heinrich Schlosser raised an eyebrow. "They've been out of town on security runs. That's their business, after all. There was an article a week or two ago. Something involving an attack on the Schwarza Express that they were involved in."

Kastenmayer shook his head. He rarely had time to "stay on top of current events," as Carol Koch would put it. The parish still hadn't filled all the teaching vacancies at Countess Kate. The new term would start in six weeks. If they didn't locate a competent mathematics teacher for the upper grades, it was likely that a dozen or more families would transfer their children to the public elementary and middle schools. Schlosser was not optimistic that one could be found, given that industry paid much better than teaching. Industry, because of the war, was "booming."

The assistant principal at the elementary school, who happened to be the son of the Methodist minister, had let the parish board know—informally, of course—that he would be most appreciative if St. Martin's could avert this development, as Blackshire Elementary currently had no more available classroom space, and although he was hoping that Grantville would, in the near future, pass a bond issue to allow for expansion.... Several St. Martin's parishioners who worked there as "aides" confirmed that Blackshire was, as the up-timers said, "bursting at the seams."

Also through young Jones, a "guidance counselor"—Kastenmayer rather wondered what that might be, but not seriously enough to expend the time necessary to find out—at the Fluharty Middle School, who attended the Methodist church, a Moor named Avery, sent word that they were *already* holding class sessions in the attic, the gym, and, weather permitting, in the parking lot, so the last thing they needed was a good-sized batch of last-minute transfer students. More helpfully, Avery offered to cast around among students he knew at the new technical college to try to find someone who knew someone who would be willing to teach mathematics at St. Martin's for a one-year term. He might as well, he said, since the public schools were still frantically searching for someone to replace Ronella Koch and might well encounter a candidate who was not up to that standard, but would do fine for Countess Kate.

Heinrich Schlosser accepted with gratitude.

August 1635

When Colonel Derek Utt, the SoTF commander at Fulda, died of the plague at Merckweiller-Pechelbronn in the Province of the Upper Rhine, Pastor Kastenmayer didn't take much notice of it. His world did not overlap significantly with that of the truly near-noble up-time families such as the Riddles, Utt being married to the daughter of the chief justice of the SoTF Supreme Court. He did know that much. The funeral was Church of England. Ron and Carol Koch attended it, of course. Salome sent a proper note of condolence on the behalf of St. Martin's in the Fields. Otherwise there was no connection.

Not until they received a letter from Andrea saying that Tony Chabert had been designated as Utt's successor to command the Fulda Barracks Regiment. It was an important promotion for Tony, of course; he would now be a full colonel. It was a wonderful proclamation of the confidence that the leaders of the SoTF and commanders of its National Guard had in his abilities and competence. It....

"They're leaving Erfurt," Salome said to Carol Koch. "At least Erfurt is right in the middle of the USE and probably as safe a place to be as anywhere when there is a war. But now he's going to Fulda and Andrea will go with him. The baby's only a month old! We've only seen him once, and now that *man* is taking them into a plague zone, or at least perilously near to one. And a war zone, or at least perilously near to one. Ludwig, being a pastor, says that we must hold to our faith in God's divine protection and pray, which is true. Still...."

Carol rested her temples on the heels of both hands. "I know exactly how he feels."

September 1635

The war on the eastern front went on. Mike Stearns was now a great general, even if no longer the prime minister. Gretchen Richter was turning into some kind of a heroine.

Elector John George of Saxony, his wife, and one of their sons were killed by partisans in the Vogtland. That was too close to Grantville for comfort, in the opinion of most of the town's population. That the Committees of Correspondence were good guys was about an article of faith for most Grantvillers, but the local CoCs in practice, if a person could believe the newspaper reports coming out of Saxony....

A sister of the King Christian of Denmark, a woman named Hedwig—nobody in Grantville had ever heard of her before, but the newspapers made a lot of it—had been married to John George's brother, it seemed. That was a long time ago; she'd been a widow for nearly 25 years. Now the partisans had driven her out of her—well, it seemed to be a retirement home, as far as anyone could figure out—just because she was a relative of the late elector. Not because of anything particularly nasty she had actually done herself, as far as anyone could tell. The place was called Schloss Lichtenburg, near Prettin. She'd turned up at Halle requesting sanctuary in the USE.

"If you ask me," Liz Carstairs said, "if they let her out accompanied by close to fifty civilian attendants, mainly women, with a few elderly men and children, and also fifty competent riders, which is what Lyle Kindred is reporting in the *Grantville Times*, nobody was really after her scalp. Lyle actually sent a stringer up to Halle to take a look."

"The fifty competent riders may be why they let her out," Mel Richards said practically. "If the partisans weren't particularly well-trained, the thought of fifty fewer well-equipped opponents might have appealed to their commander a lot in a *let somebody else worry about them* kind of way. Press heard that the fifty weren't even all of her private militia; she left the rest of it behind to protect her dower villages. He says that she most likely did it to make sure that as much of her property as possible won't be raided, but it should have the sort of incidental effect of protecting the people who live on it. From both sides. John George's supporters and ours. Strict policies or no strict policies, Mike Stearns can't be everywhere at once."

"At least she's gone now, according to the *Times.* The railway people at Halle loaded her whole gaggle onto a special train for Magdeburg. Well, not the horses and riders, but the rest of the people who were trailing along with her. She paid her respects there, let the riders catch up, stopped in Brunswick to see Duke Georg's wife, who used to be her foster daughter, and headed west. She's planning to live with her nephew, the one who's the governor of Westphalia. If you ask me," Liz repeated, "everyone made too much of the whole thing."

In Wittenberg, Salome Piscatora's only surviving brother, Ernst, a pastor in Wittenberg who had hopeful eyes upon eventually becoming a professor at the university there, was considerably more familiar with the context of the above events than was the case of the honorable Mayor Liz in Grantville.

Their ongoing correspondence in the matter of Cousin Lutz and Aunt Margaretha's undelivered bequests over the past couple of months had brought him closer to his sisters than had been the case for several years.

Not every possible target of the campaign being waged in Saxony by the fairly well-organized but very radical CoCs and the ill-organized, often nebulously hostile to all forms of divinely instituted government authority, irregular bands of various types had a private militia conveniently to hand.

He expressed what he sincerely believed to be some well-founded worries.

There were other possible targets, possibly one could term them *symbolic* targets, upon whom the rebels against John George might focus their interest. For example.... Ernst pulled together all the things he had heard and overheard, confirmed and rumored, probable and improbable.

He reminded his sister of the success of the letter-writing campaign in the USE that had reminded the emperor and General Torstensson of the undesirability of attacking the castle doors in Wittenberg upon which Martin Luther had posted the Ninety-Five Theses in 1517. Doors which were, of course, dear to the hearts of all Wittenbergers.

And, speaking of the late, great, Dr. Luther, would his sisters be so kind as to bring to the attention of someone properly responsible, that one of the *symbolic* targets that he had heard whispered about....

Even in the middle of a war, the mail was still going through.

Salome tried to decide who the properly responsible someone might be, concluded that it was Count Ludwig Guenther, and forwarded Ernst's letter to him. He wasn't the ruler any more, of course. Schwarzburg-Rudolstadt was a county, an administrative unit of the SoTF now. He was more on the order of a county manager, which was, when you came right down to it, a glorified hired hand. But he was still the head of the consistory of the Lutheran church in what used to be his *Grafschaft*, because the SoTF insisted on separation of church and state and *somebody* had to keep things organized and rein in all the superintendents of the districts when they got above themselves and ahead of themselves, or *some* people (like Melchior Tilesius) would let *other* people (like Pankratz Holz) run wild.

Besides, the count knew the emperor, so maybe he could drop a word.

October 1635

Nobody was going to be dropping a word to the emperor for a while. He had been at a battle, one called Lake Bledno. Everyone pretty much agreed that he was injured and that the injury was serious. Nobody seemed to know exactly what the injury was.

But it looked like his Swedish chancellor, Oxenstierna, supported by the most reactionary of the Crown Loyalists, intended to take over the USE and revoke everything.

That, at least, was what Lyle Kindred said in his editorials in the *Grantville Times.* The various ragtag newspapers and broadsheets published speculation a lot wilder than that.

Salome talked to her sister Anna; then they talked to Ludwig and Heinrich; then they talked to the Kochs; the Kochs talked to Gary Lambert, because they still considered themselves to be friends even though he had switched his membership to St. Thomas.

Also because he was now married to the daughter of the chancellor of Saxe-Weimar, where Duke Albrecht was still running the Wettin private properties, albeit in the same rather ambiguous and ambivalent way the Count Ludwig Guenther ran his.

Duke Albrecht, who was becoming increasingly concerned about Oxenstierna's intentions toward his brother, Wilhelm Wettin, the titular USE prime minister.

The gathering that resulted was unofficial. Thoroughly off the record. Probably, it didn't even happen.

"I agree that the person we are meeting to consider may stand in some danger." Pastor Kastenmayer started with this point. "He's the head of the *Stift*, the collegiate chapter, in Zeitz, so is prominent to some extent, even apart from his grandfather, the Great Reformer. I would consider him to be an inoffensive man, but.... Given the close ties to

Naumburg...." He glanced over at Gary. "The diocese has been Naumburg-Zeitz for centuries, and since the middle of the last century it has been essentially secularized, managed by administrators appointed by the Albertine Saxon dukes. By John George, until his recent passing, which means that in the eyes of the CoCs...."

"Gotcha!"

"He married quite late in life," Salome said. "He was fifty years old, I think. So some of the children are still at home. The oldest girl is about Dina's age, but hasn't married. Then two boys, both at Wittenberg, I think."

Enlightenment suddenly sparked as half of the group realized who had probably been feeding information about potential problems in Zeitz to Ernst Piscator.

Salome meandered on. "Or did one of those boys die a couple of years ago? I'm not sure. Both of them were named Martin. Martin and Johann Martin, that is. But Wittenberg should be as safe as anywhere in Saxony right now, so he's all right. Or they are, if they are both still alive. Three more girls. The youngest must be about eleven or twelve now."

"In any case, I agree with Martin that his father could well be targeted by the radicals in Saxony," Pastor Kastenmayer repeated.

"Martin who? Your son in Jena?" Gary Lambert wrinkled his nose. He had lost track.

"No, of course not." Kastenmayer appeared to be faintly annoyed. "Martin Luther."

"Martin Luther is dead and gone."

"Not this one. He only finished his Bachelor of Arts degree recently."

"So who's his father?"

"Johann Ernst Luther." Kastenmayer looked a trifle more exasperated. "We've been talking about him for quite a while now."

"The people will not be so much the problem." Count Ludwig Guenther frowned. "*If* we decide to send an escort, people can walk, once the escort we *might* send reaches them. Is there a suitable escort?"

Pastor Kastenmayer didn't even have to think about it. "Edgar Neustatter. He runs something called a security service. Neustatter's European Security Service. Or Services? NESS. That's what they do. He's a church member, too, so I can ask him."

"I think," Salome said gently, "that, church member or not, he will expect to be paid. He has quite a few employees. It must cost him as much to run a business as it costs the parish to run the school. Or close to it." The meeting broke up with a rather vague consensus that something should be done.

Gary Lambert headed for home. He felt a little uncomfortable with the people from St. Martin's now that he wasn't exactly one of them anymore. Even if he was, really, sort of three times removed, providing input from Saxe-Weimar. Input from Duke Albrecht to Friedrich Hortleder to Anna Catharina to Gary. Rather than being there because he was himself, so to speak.

The rest of them lingered. Count Ludwig Guenther fingered his beard. "But what about the books? What about von Pflug's collection of rare books?"

"Who the hell," Carol Koch asked, "is von Pflug. I thought that a *Pflug* was a plow! Something that would fall in Willie Ray Hudson's orbit. Not Neustatter's."

"Julius von Pflug," the count answered, "was the fortieth and last Catholic bishop of Naumburg. He ascended the episcopal throne in...." He squinted his eyes. "I think it was 1547. In any case, he did a delicate balancing act between Emperor Charles V and the Protestant princes throughout his career. Managed to hold his position until he died. He was also," the count smiled, "a great book collector."

"What does this mean?" Carol Koch asked with a grin.

Kastenmayer frowned some slight disapproval at this frivolous use of the catechism.

"When the bishop died, he bequeathed his library to the Cathedral Chapter at Zeitz. Zeitz-Naumburg are really one. Which means that Johann Ernst Luther is not only the senior member of the Cathedral Chapter at Zeitz—he is also, by virtue of that position, curator of one of the most valuable libraries in the German world."

"You're thinking that books don't walk?" Ron Koch was fully aware that swiping someone else's library was considered a great sport by seventeenth century rulers. "The Vatican did it to the library of the Palatinate in Heidelberg. Gustavus Adolphus has swiped more than one in his day—mostly from the Jesuits here in Germany. That's what caused the SoTF to take precautions in regard to its own valuable collection housed at Calvert High School. No looting, not even by His Imperial Majesty."

"Hah!" Carol exclaimed when he finished. "Right on a par with the Cattle Raid of Cooley."

This, too, she had to explain.

Edgar Neustatter looked at the count's emissary suspiciously.

"Gary Lambert would have had qualms of conscience," Ron Koch said, "but nobody else does. So we're not going to tell him about the project."

Neustatter quirked his mouth. "You probably oughtn't mention it to Preston Richards, either. Where do you plan to put these prizes, once you get them? People and books both."

"Duke Albrecht has agreed to take the Luther family, to settle them in Weimar. Duke Johann Philipp avoided Gary and Hortleder; he talked to his cousin directly. They should be safe enough there. He also pointed out that since Johann Ernst has been in Saxony all along, pretty insulated from all the changes that have happened since the Ring of Fire, he might not know what to make of Grantville. Carol said that it would be 'culture shock.' I think she's right."

Astrid Schäubin had a pen and paper. "What about the money. Look, we belong to St. Martin's. I know there's no way that the parish can pay for this. Not even you can pay for this."

Ron nodded.

"Or the count, for that matter. Since the Ring of Fire, he doesn't get to collect taxes any more. Same for the dukes at Saxe-Weimar. This wouldn't be cheap, and none of them are dripping money right now, especially not when the rest of the Wettin income inside the USE may go under right along with Wilhelm. Ernst and Bernhard don't count; one's in Amberg and the other one's in Burgundy."

Ron smiled. "There's one Wettin who has been raking in pots and pots of money." He smiled more broadly. "Johann Philipp at Altenburg. Mining." He pointed to himself. "Mine safety engineer. We have a sort of understanding by now.

"Plus, he's like the rest of the dukes from the Ernestine line. They've never quite forgiven the Albertines for making off with the electoral vote last century. If they can score one off the Albertines, even if John George himself is dead, they're not going to hesitate to do it. Rescuing Martin Luther's grandson from the Evil Foe is going to count as a grand publicity coup, as far as they're concerned. Probably something they can use as political leverage, too, the next time the carousel goes around in a circle."

Astrid made a note. "So the people go to Weimar. Where do the books go? Rudolstadt? Since it was Count Ludwig Guenther who brought them up?"

Neustatter shook his head. "Not if the point is to get them to safety. It's too close to the Saxon border, and not enough security." He looked at Ron. "See if you can talk them into agreeing on Schwarza Castle. Some rich Englishman is funding an Academy of Conservators over there—people whose whole job is taking care of books and manuscripts. Maybe you could push it as being sort of neutral."

He stood up. "If we take this job, I'm going to have to make a condition. I want to contact Colonel Hans Heinrich von Hessler and arrange for a few men from the Saale Legion to be with us on this expedition. It's really von Hessler's territory; I don't want to poach on it. Not that he'll have any problem with relieving Saxony of a library, if the alternative might be letting John George's heirs get their hands on it. Or having Oxenstierna send a troop to cart it off to Stockholm."

"Uppsala," Ron said.

"What?"

"Well, probably. Sweden's put most of the books it has stolen since it intervened in the German wars in the university library in Uppsala."

"Please talk to them, then, about where they want the books to go. I'll need to figure mileage into the estimate," Astrid contributed.

Neustatter agreed. "Give us the number of people and books; what you can about the layout of the place. I'll get you an estimate by Tuesday.

To the great entertainment of Astrid's brother Hjalmar, it turned out that the normal way of transporting valuable books and manuscripts was to pack them in new, never-used, empty beer kegs. Those were not only sturdy and waterproof, but also, at the end of the journey, completely re-usable and therefore saleable.

So. Kegs. Wagons to haul the kegs. Horses to pull the wagons. Horses for riders accompanying the wagons. Astrid scribbled.

The low-voiced chatter circled around and around the office. With a half-dozen people working on a Tuesday deadline, nobody tracked the murmur and mutter.

"How many books?"

"Better check with the count over at Rudolstadt."

" 'A big room full of shelves of them' isn't really informative."

"How many books fit in a keg?"

"Well, what size are the books? Books aren't exactly standardized in size. How much margin should we build in?"

A quick check indicated that the count did not want one single book left behind.

"All right, then. Pretend the high school gym is a room lined with shelves, imagine how many books might go on the shelves. Build in maximum margin."

"Wouldn't it be easier for someone to go down to the library and count how many books they manage to get on each of their shelves?"

"Do we need to bring packing material with us—for the inside of the kegs, I mean, to keep the book pages from getting wrinkled—or will they have some there. At the *Schloß* in Zeitz?"

"Foraging?"

"No, no time for it; this is a quick in and out."

"No, we don't want to irritate von Hessler."

"Fodder, then. Calculate the fodder for me, would you?"

"Join Neustatter's men, they said to me. You'll have an adventurous life, they said to me; lots of shoot-em-up adventures. Nobody said anything about calculating fodder."

"Who on earth is supposed to be ordering this much beer for a bunch of monks?"

"They aren't monks. They're canons."

"What's the difference?"

"They get married and have kids. In the case of this guy, six of 'em. Not all of 'em are home, though."

"Are they old enough to walk?"

"Yeah."

"Is he the one ordering the beer? The canon, I mean?"

"He'll be the one responsible for accepting the delivery. The order's going to come from somewhere else."

"Not here!"

"Nah. Wittenberg, I think."

"Is there any possibility we'll have to fight our way into the castle at Zeitz?"

"Well, not if people keep a lid on it and they don't know that we're coming for any other reason than a beer delivery."

"How do you guarantee that?"

"You don't."

"In and out of the castle shouldn't be that much of a problem."

"How long is it going to take us to pack up these books, anyhow, once we're in? I've got a feeling they're going to want us to be careful. Is it a two-hour job or a two-day job?"

"Wait till Hjalmar gets back from counting books at the library."

"How heavy do books weigh? What grade of axle are we going to need on these wagons?"

"I don't think they weigh more than beer."

"Better check that."

"Fighting's more likely once we get out of the castle—getting through Saxony over to the border. If von Hessler can't finagle it for us."

"So we may end up hauling ammo that we don't need, both ways. That stuff's heavy."

"That's better than discovering that we need it but haven't hauled it."

"Still, if we'll be taking it, it has to go into the estimate."

"Mileage. Maps, guys. Somebody get me the maps. Did Koch, or anyone, get back to us about Schwarza Castle as the final destination?"

"It's fifty miles if we start from Rudolstadt; make it sixty if we start from Grantville."

"If Duke Johann Philipp is in on it, stage out of Altenburg. If the roads are decent, that's only a third or so of the distance."

"The roads are never decent."

"It will rain. We'll have mud. I swear upon my sacred honor. We're going to have mud."

"Things are pretty well frozen already."

"They'll thaw for us. Give us special treatment. Figure on mud."

"I say we go in from Altenburg; out to Weimar and leave the people, drop down to Schwarza and unpack the books; leave the kegs there; we can pick them up some other time; hire some other folks there to take the horses and wagons back to Altenburg and we walk home. Minimal connection to Grantville; none to Rudolstadt at all."

"Even if we stage at Altenburg, I want to use Lorenz and some of the drivers from the livery stable here. We know that they're reliable. No guarantees if we just pick some up over there."

"You can't *get* from Zeitz to Weimar. Not anything like directly, with heavy loaded wagons."

"Shit."

"I take it that we don't want to parade this menagerie through Jena?"

"Fucking right, we don't. Forget Altenburg and give me the map."

"I hate to tell you guys, but if you want to move heavy wagons from Zeitz to Weimar, it looks like all roads lead through Jena."

"Split up, then. Send some of us with the people to Weimar, and the rest of us bring the books back here."

"Why aren't there decent roads. Roads, roads, roads."

"The only decent roads around are in West Virginia County, which is where we are *not* going to be. This isn't a little jaunt on the train."

"If you definitely wouldn't want to go back to Altenburg, you could drop down to Gera. But that's still in the middle of nowhere."

"But if we get them as far as Gera, we *can* catch the train. Offload the kegs onto a freight car. Ditch the wagons."

"Lorenz and his teamsters can take the wagons back where they belong."

"Why are we headed someplace that's basically one you can't get into or out of? Remind me again, would you?"

"Gera's in Reuss, isn't it?"

"Ja."

"What kind of terms are we on with Reuss right now? Considering that they're part of the SoTF but their land is all mixed in with Saxony."

"Ticklish."

"Please tell me why we're even *thinking* of accepting this job."

"Um. Pastor Kastenmayer wants us to?"

"We're getting paid."

Zeitz, November 1635

"From what Martin writes," Martha Blumenstengelin said, "it is believed that the king of Sweden is still incoherent." She looked up from her son's letter. "That's what I think he means, at least. His wording is very cautious. As for the rest of it...."

"We wait until the beer wagons arrive." Johann Ernst Luther gave her a crooked smile. "Heretofore, I have not lived a very adventurous life."

"Which was," his wife retorted, "perfectly all right with me. I wish the girls weren't being so fussy the last couple of days. I'm worried that they're coming down with something. If they are, walking from here to

Weimar with three sick children to take care of will be an adventure, all right. I can't imagine that security guards will be of much help."

"Magdalena is sixteen. She is no longer really a child."

"She's young enough to whine and complain if she's sick. She *will* whine and complain if she gets sick. She always has, all her life. Then Susanna and Elisabeth won't want her to be getting more attention because she whines, so they will do the same. Even with Ännchen helping me...."

"Then let us hope that they aren't getting sick."

But they were.

Jena, November 1635

"Measles!" Carol Koch exclaimed to Dina. "What do you mean, measles?"

"Phillip has a telegram from Jonathan Fortney. Grantville is quarantined. Locked down hard. There's a major epidemic."

"How long do these last?"

"Until the disease runs its course, I expect. That's customary. It may be six weeks. Possibly more."

"Well, at least—Ron's working down at Altenburg right now, so he's not caught inside." She hesitated. "Is it all of the Ring of Fire? Or just Grantville? How far does the quarantine run?"

"As far as the industrial zone has spread, so beyond the Ring of Fire. St. Martin's is in the quarantine—several of the members have the disease seriously. So is St. Thomas."

"But where did the measles come from?"

"A traveler brought them, I guess. Probably. That's how diseases usually come into a town. There's measles in Weimar, too; some of

Philipp's employees reported that during the last few days. Carters and wagoners move around all the time."

Carol rested her chin on the heel of her hand. She wished she could ask whether the expedition over to Zeitz had returned safely before the lockdown, but she had no idea whether Dina was even aware that it had happened. "Oh, well. Only God knows what may be coming next."

February 1636

Pastor Kastenmayer delivered prayers of thanks. For the significant recovery of the emperor. That was easy. For the end of the epidemic and quarantine. That was heartfelt.

The next one had been more difficult to phrase appropriately. One could not really publicly thank God that Chancellor Oxenstierna was dead.

No even if those were one's genuine sentiments.

He had settled on a prayer that God might comfort the man's wife and children in their grief. Not that he knew whether or not they might, personally, be grieving. The nature of politics, however, was such that they would inevitably experience a great deal of grief throughout their lives as a result of their husband and father's fall from royal grace.

A man didn't need to understand the nuances of modern politics to know that. The one thing needful was to read the Old Testament. Samuel. Chronicles. Kings.

March 1636

The *Stammtisch* still met at the Thuringen Gardens. For the time being. Meg was constantly feeling poorly, so Ryan missed most of the time unless she was sleeping and he brought little David along. He'd made it this evening. David was old enough to throw food. Cutlery. Napkins. Toys.

Walpurga was eight months pregnant. Ursel wasn't and didn't plan to be for another two years at least, but she suspected that Maria just barely was. She had that look about her. Rahel might be; probably was; hadn't said anything. Lisbet was six months along. Sabina would never be, of course, but Lew's sister had died in September and she had her late sister-in-law Bernita's two unhappy children in her care out at the goat dairy. Not that she had ever come to the meetings, anyway. Ursel suspected that within a couple of years, there would be enough squalling infants to put the *Stammtisch* out of business for good.

"According to the latest gossip in the newspapers, at least, Mike Stearns told the emperor, speaking for the FoJP, that they'll go along if parliament passes a law that each province can decide for itself whether it wants an established church. Hugh thinks it will go through." That was Ryan pontificating, echoing the opinions of his boss.

"The Fourth of July Party is going along with *that*? *Our* guys?" Derek practically banged his stein down.

"The mainliners are. Don't freak out, though. The Committees of Correspondence dug in their heels, insisting that one of the legal variations of having an established church needs to be not to have one. So complete separation of church and state would be an established church, so to speak. That's what we'll get in the SoTF, Hugh says."

"Well, then on the other side...." Roland looked thoughtful. "The worst of the Crown Loyalists are out of the game, for the time being, at any rate. Lyle Kindred's latest editorial says that the landgravine of Hesse-Kassel will go along with it since she gets a concession that Calvinism can be established. Which the emperor doesn't really like at all. Then there's Duke Georg of Brunswick. He's in camp on the Polish front, of course, but his regents in the province surely check with him about anything important. Nobody knows exactly how he'll jump."

"Has the guy over at Rudolstadt given any hints?"

"Not that I've heard."

Mitch Hobbs groaned. "This is all the same stuff that people were saying *last* spring. Why doesn't anybody ever at least *decide* something, for once and for all? Instead of just talking and talking and talking about it?"

WAKING UP IN HEAVEN

February 1636

It started as such a simple idea. Really, as a classroom exercise.

Countess Kate had been holding classes for several years, but it hadn't been dedicated because the construction was never really finished, because the school kept growing, because more down-time Lutheran families with no particular interest in the miracles of up-time public schools kept moving into the Grantville area, which meant that St. Martin's education committee had to keep adding more classrooms. By spring, though. Give it until summer, for chances of better weather. Midsummer, after the frazzle of planting and before the hassle of harvest, when as many people as possible would be free to attend. Don't postpone it until autumn, when it would compete with every village harvest fair.

A dedication this year. Salome suggested it to Ludwig, who brought it to the board of elders who passed it on to the education committee. Everybody agreed it would be wonderful.

And...then young Peter Kastenmayer thought of something else and he was, after all, the pastor's son. So the third and fourth grade teacher had all of the children in her room, all eighty of them, write little invitations in their best hand, asking the granddaughter of Countess Katharina the Heroic to attend their school dedication.

The other teachers thought that it was such a nice gesture. That made, roughly, two hundred and forty more little invitations.

They decorated a nice box, put the invitations inside, wrapped it up in tough burlap, and mailed them off.

Then the teacher for the fifth and sixth grades remembered that Martin Luther himself had a living grandson, a retired pastor. He wasn't even as old as Countess Katharina's granddaughter and he didn't live so very far away, either. Because of the troubles caused by the Saxon uprising, he was in Weimar, which was right up the road, so to speak. If the school was Countess Katharina, the church was St. Martin's, named for Martin Luther's patron saint.

Another box of painstakingly written invitations went out.

Johann Ernst Luther replied right away, saying that he and his wife Martha would absolutely love to come, and Duke Albrecht of Saxe-Weimar and the duchess had been so kind as to offer to bring them in their own carriage.

That was the point at which it occurred to someone that they really ought to mention the invitations to Pastor Kastenmayer.

Who mentioned them to Salome.

Who contemplated the presence of a duke and duchess, much less Martin Luther's grandson, at their modest school dedication and nearly collapsed. But Duke Albrecht and his wife were very kind and unpretentious. She had met them before. It could be done, with supreme effort.

The principal swallowed and broke the news that there was another invitation outstanding, issued but not yet responded to.

April 1636

Sebald Fischer's brother Thomas delivered the mail shortly after noon. He was a new member of St. Martin's, come from Nürnberg to join his brother, and a new hire at the post office. The town was constantly expanding, it seemed.

Salome Piscatora, wife of the Lutheran pastor at St. Martin's in the Fields, waved to him and then sorted it while she wondered a bit. Nürnberg was an independent enclave within the USE, prosperous and flourishing in its own right as an industrial center. Sebald was working at Lothlorien; what better way to learn who was where in Grantville, doing what, than delivering the mail? Should she mention anything to Phillip about whether he should say something to the Stones, or whoever was in charge out at the dye works, about keeping an eye open for industrial espionage?

She only went back to the table where the letter lay sixteen times between the delivery and her husband's return home from a meeting at the city hall. On the sixteenth trip, she stopped and stared.

She would so like to open it. But it was addressed to Ludwig, after all. She had some vague idea that in West Virginia County it was illegal to open a letter addressed to anyone other than yourself. Had that been in the lecture about privacy rights or in the lecture about something else? Johann Georg Hardegg gave the parish so *many* lectures about the status of what one could and could not, or should and should not, do under the laws of the county, state, and nation. He was so—conscientious. His lectures were so beneficial, and so boring....

That was not the correct attitude for a pastor's wife to have about a prominent member of her husband's congregation.

The letter was addressed to Ludwig, as was only proper, but the whole dedication project had been *her* idea. And the invitations had been little Peter's idea.

But it all depended on the countess, and the countess was so old—more than eighty years old. Hof wasn't so very far—as the crow flies. Being driven in a carriage on the existing roads was a different matter.

Would she come?

"Why don't we leave the mail until after supper?" Ludwig Kastenmayer's pale blue eyes twinkled. "Pleasure before business."

Salome clasped her hands behind her back. It was her duty to set a good example for the children and the maid.

Yes, it really was.

"Or, perhaps, we should see now. Then we could discuss the plans during supper."

She nodded in agreement.

"Alternatively...."

"We have fresh pork for supper, and new onions. One of Heydman's piglets got its head caught in that 'chicken-wire fence' that Irma Lawler put around her vegetable garden and strangled itself. Mathias brought us some meat and carried my newest goddaughter along for a little visit. Irma sent the onions."

"Kind of him. I'll thank him next time I see him. Especially kind of Frau Lawler, considering that she is a Calvinist. How is the baby Salome?"

"Flourishing. The picture of health. Some happiness for Heydman, finally."

"For which we should all thank the Lord." The pastor looked down at the letter in his hand. "As for the mention of pork at this juncture, I'm sure that my wife would never resort to bribery." The corners of the pastor's eyes crinkled up.

"Ludwig!"

"You would like to know if Her Illustriousness will deign to visit our modest school?"

"It *is* named after her grandmother—Katharina of Henneberg, countess of Schwarzburg."

"Ach! How could I possibly have forgotten?"

"You *couldn't* possibly have forgotten, Papa," the nearly-nine-years-old Peter objected. "That artist is painting a great big picture of Countess Katharina heroically defying the Duke of Alba in the passageway between the church and the school, and Mama has been talking about it ever since Christmas." The two youngest boys nodded solemnly.

"Respect your elders, my son."

"Yes, Papa. I'm sorry, Mama."

"All forgiven." Salome gave him a quick hug. "Ludwig," she said, a trace of wistfulness in her voice.

"Well, I suppose...." He made a great show of prying the seal off (they could always melt the wax and re-use it, after all). Then he unfolded one flap. Then the second. Then the third. He reached for his reading glasses as he unfolded the fourth flap.

"Anna countess of Mansfeld, widowed Reuss, to...."

Salome held her breath.

"...is delighted to accept the invitation tendered by Countess Katharina the Heroic Lutheran School in Grantville, State of Thuringia-Franconia, to inspect the facility named in honor of..."

Peter jumped a foot in the air and shrieked.

Salome could only wish that she was that young.

"...expects to arrive on...and would appreciate it if the parish of St. Martin's in the Fields would provide her with accommodations suitable to her status at the Higgins Hotel, of which she has heard excellent reports...."

"At the hotel?" Salome frowned. "It's very expensive. But, I suppose, the parish can manage it. The formal dedication ceremonies for the school will only last for two days. We did invite her, after all."

"...for the space of a month. As the countess, because of her age, rarely travels, she has decided to spend some time familiarizing herself with the situation in central Thuringia on behalf of her stepsons...anticipated entourage of twenty-four persons in the following ranks, stabling for twenty-two horses, garaging for her coaches...."

"Why don't her stepsons pay for it, if she's staying on the help them?" Peter asked.

"Rich people don't get rich by spending their own money," Pastor Kastenmayer answered. "Nor, really, is Reuss all that prosperous."

"Neither is St. Martin's in the Fields. And they're 'prosperous' enough to send twenty-four people and twenty-two horses with her." Salome sighed.

"What does 'prosperous' mean, Papa?" Peter asked.

"Wealthy," his father answered

"Rich."

"Yes, rich."

"Well." Salome took a deep breath. "I'll think of something."

"More likely, someone, Mama," Peter commented. "Write Dina a letter and tell her you need some of Phillip's money right away. If you offer to introduce him to a genuine countess—even better, offer to introduce *Dina* to a genuine countess—he'll pony it right up. If they're going to be in Jena when this lady comes. Probably even if they won't be able to attend. When they got married, I heard Cunz telling Martin that he's nuts about her and she leads him right around by his...."

"Peter!"

"Sorry, Papa. Sorry, Mama."

The family trailed in to the supper table, with Peter whispering to his brothers, "But that's exactly what Cunz said."

"How long has the countess been a widow?" the insatiably curious Peter asked the next Sunday.

"Since 1608. Almost as long as her grandmother, who lived as a widow from 1538 until her death in 1567," John George Hardegg answered. "Technically, she is from the sub-line called Mansfeld-Mittelort."

"Her husband was named Heinrich?"

Hardegg laughed. "All of the men of the Reuss line were, are, and apparently evermore shall be named Heinrich. Her husband was the second Heinrich of his generation. He had four brothers and cousins named Heinrich, who are also dead. Her stepsons are the second and fourth Heinrichs of the current generation, the first, third, fifth, and sixth having predeceased her. The two still alive must be pushing sixty. Given the rather odd relationship between Reuss and the SoTF, we can anticipate that they will be succeeded by Heinrichs I and III of the next generation if nothing disastrous happens to them, numbers II and IV already having died."

Peter thought about it. "That's odd. All those Heinrich names, I mean. What's odd about the SoTF?"

"Shall we say that Reuss is sort of in the SoTF, but not precisely of it. Not exactly one of our state's counties. The various Heinrichs acknowledge our governor as their governor, send themselves to the House of Lords, and let the Reussians, or whatever they call themselves now, elect members to the lower house of the SoTF congress. Inside their own lands, though, unless there's a direct contradiction with a new statewide law, they've kept on managing things pretty much the way they used to. Given where Reuss is located, all scattered in bits and interspersed with what were John George of Saxony's lands, and the military units running around there...."

Peter frowned. "What will she find to do in Grantville for a whole month?"

Salome had an answer for that. She smiled at her son. "She has an old friend who's coming to meet her. One of the Schwarzburg countesses. Not young Emelie, of course, nor Anna Sofie over at Kranichfeld, who's in Magdeburg, anyway right now, I think. Still in Magdeburg? In Magdeburg again? Another childless widow, I'm pretty sure."

Hardegg started to count something down with his fingers. His firm handled a lot of estate settlements and probates. "Ja! The widow of old Count Wilhelm of Schwarzburg, at Frankenhausen, who died in 1597. Clara, her name is. She holds the castle at Heringen as her dower and was born a duchess of Brunswick. She's a sister of Duke Georg of Brunswick at Calenberg[8], who is such a good ally of our emperor, and her mother was an aunt of the king of Denmark. The counts of Schwarzburg at Rudolstadt will be her heirs when she dies—even though Count Ludwig Guenther descends from Count Wilhelm's younger brother rather than his older brother brother at Sondershausen, because the reversion was set up thusly."

Salome drew a deep breath and resigned herself to a complex genealogical excursus.

Once, before Ronella Koch had married Jonas and gone to Amberg, she had quoted an up-time proverb about *all politics is local.* Maybe all up-time politics had been local. In the here and now, a lot of politics was

[8]Duke George of Brunswick-Lüneburg.

genealogical, and she had better understand it before all of these people arrived.

The number of *faux pas* permitted to pastors' wives was, essentially, none at all.

* * *

When the manager of the Higgins Hotel found that the first elderly lady, with entourage, would be supplemented by another old lady—not quite so old—with an additional entourage of twenty-two people, seventeen horses, and three coaches, also for a month, he wavered between fiscal delight and nervous prostration. At least, all of them were Lutheran, which would cut down on the number of theological disputes likely to break out in the lobby.

* * *

Caspar Schulthes came to Grantville and found far cheaper lodgings quite a way outside of the *up-time core*, as real estate agents now referred to it. Grantville was a matter of indifference to him, except insofar as it might finally give him a chance to get at the old lady.

A half-dozen years earlier, Clara of Heringen, as the countess was generally called, had dismissed him with a bad character for embezzling from the tithes paid by her tenants before he delivered them to her. Since then, he had been living in the nearest good-sized town from her dower lands in Heringen, suffering from disgrace and poverty, and plotting his revenge.

He became Caspar Schmidt from Nordhausen and got a job as dishwasher at the Higgins Hotel.

* * *

"I think," Salome suggested tentatively, "that in addition to what we have received from Phillip and Dina, perhaps you might mention to the elders that it couldn't hurt to check whether Herr Hortleder might be willing to bring up the situation with Duke Albrecht. The manager is willing to carry us on credit for a while, since we can pay in advance for all of the Reuss entourage for the first week. Beyond that, though, the parish could be facing bankruptcy.

"There will be the special collection at the dedication."

"That's designated for the school."

"At least, by the mercy of divine providence, Countess Clara is paying her own expenses. I suspect that Count Ludwig Guenther or Countess Emelie, more likely Emelie, had a word with her. She's quite well-off and travels a lot, even though this is the first time she's included Grantville on her itinerary."

* * *

Friedrich Hortleder, wife in tow, came in on the train a week or so later, eyed all the excitement, and parked himself in his son-in-law Gary Lambert's office at the Leahy Medical Center, while Catharina loaned her enthusiastic support to whatever Ludwig's wife and a massive contingent of middle-aged ladies were doing.

"Up-time," Gary said. "There was a book. It was supposed to be funny, but it got a skewer right through the target. *Lutheran Church Basement Women* was the name. St. Martin's doesn't have a basement, but otherwise.... You can't believe how glad I am that I switched my membership over to St. Thomas' on the other side of town, and Anna

Catharina isn't involved. Not that she should be, so close to her time. She keeps insisting that she's perfectly well and it's perfectly natural, and.... And I am frantic with fear for her and the baby."

"Have more confidence in your own hospital and doctors," Hortleder advised. "And in the providence of God."

"I want to thank you, again, so much, for letting her mother stay with her until after...."

"It's not an inconvenience, truly. It's not as if I'm even going to be home. As soon as the dedication is over, I'm up to Jena and from there will be following Johann Gerhard back to Besançon. Funny, I'd never been there before in my life; never really even heard of the place. Then I was there to see Bernhard installed as grand duke, and now I am going again to fill the role of 'one who stands inconspicuously in the second row back' for Gerhard. The outcome should be interesting. At least, I think, it won't drag on interminably the way Trent did, if only because the pope has invited representatives of all confessions, who won't have that much patience.

"In any case, I'll stop back in on my way home to check on my two girls before I go back to Weimar and resume my duties as chancellor."

"One thing I wanted to mention," Gary said. "About the new music school. I'm on the board of elders at St. Thomas' now, and our music program is not at all where it should be yet. We've been thinking that if we could hire, perhaps for a couple of months, a capable young man...."

They sorted out the capable young man.

"And, if you could drop in at St. Martin's—if you have time, of course. It's not my business, but I know that Kastenmayer is hoping to speak to you about some problem connected with the school dedication.

Hortleder mentally translated *problem* into *money*. "Love of money may be the root of all evil. No one loves it less than Ludwig

Kastenmayer, to be sure, but even he can't exist without it. Nor can parishes, nor schools."

"I don't understand how the countess can get away with sticking St. Martin's with her bills," Gary said, his exasperation clear in the tone of his voice.

"She probably couldn't, as a legal obligation," Hortleder said slowly. "They aren't her subjects. Talk some time to the Quiney boys about how the late Queen Elizabeth, in England, used to control her over-powerful subjects by visiting them, whether they had invited her or not, and reducing their influence by forcing them to support her court for a period of time. It was called a 'procession' around the country and has been a useful technique for rulers for a long time."

He steepled his fingers together. "Here, in this instance, it's more of what we, we down-timers, would consider a moral obligation After all, the parish issued the invitation, without placing any limits on it. The teachers and children weren't considering the financial implications, I'm sure. I'll stop at St. Martin's on my way out of town."

Hortleder saw to arranging a contribution from the Wettins, caught the train to Jena, and went off to Burgundy with Johann Gerhard, returning long before he was expected. Owing to something that happened at the conclave, still being held tightly under wraps, it had lasted barely a week.

June 1636

Hortleder stayed with Gary and Anna Catharina for a week, attended the school dedication with its unexpectedly large collection of celebrities (Count Ludwig Guenther and Countess Emelie came over from Rudolstadt for the day, and the duke of Saxe-Altenburg caught the train from Saalfeld), gave his wife a peck on her cheek, and went back to Weimar to get some work done.

Regional officials and local clergy dispersed.

Old Pastor Luther had such a fine time that he came back twice more, visiting both St. Martin's and St. Thomas' during his visits, but he didn't expect anybody to make a fuss over him.

The elderly countess from Reuss, her visit most thankfully subsidized in part by Duke Albrecht, stayed a month, poked into everything that was to be seen in West Virginia County, inspected the city hall, the telephone exchange, the mine (the manager would only let her into the upper levels), several churches of various denominations, Calvert High School and its famed library, the museum, and the Leahy Medical Center, among others. Everybody who was anybody in Grantville invited her to dinner. Then she went home again, to the general relief of her hosts and hostesses. Not to say of the Higgins Hotel.

Caspar Schulthes managed to drop occasional little pills containing this and that, which he had picked up from an unethical apothecary, into Countess Clara's room service trays. Not every day, but often enough. That was the joy of such a large hotel; if he had tried it when she was at home, her kitchen staff would have recognized him right away.

Countess Clara became ill and was hospitalized at Leahy. Dr. Adams diagnosed it as a stroke.

That was good enough for Caspar. He quit his job.

He didn't give up his lodgings, though.

Celle, Brunswick
June 1636

"Sorry to hear that she's sick," the treasurer of Brunswick said. He didn't sound very sorry. He'd never met the woman, and she was way down on his list of concerns as compared to, for example, keeping the Brunswick regiments in the field supplied and paid. "Duke Georg's sister Clara, I mean. What do I need to be thinking about?"

"Well," his subordinate said, "some of us down in the ways and means section have been discussing the lands that she holds as dower from her late husband. If she's likely to die, is there any way that, on her death, we could break the partition agreement of 1599 and get her possessions for her natal family in here in Brunswick rather than letting them go to her marital family in Schwarzburg-Rudolstadt."

The treasurer mulled this over for a while. Yes, both Duke Georg and Count Ludwig Guenther were in the USE, both were close allies and supporters of the emperor, and both were generally cooperative with the up-timers.

That did not signify an absence of internal rivalries. Especially not when it came to one's revenue stream.

"I'm not familiar with the particulars; that settlement was made long before my time. It can't hurt to have one of your clerks take a look at the papers and make a précis." He moved on to other topics.

The clerk looked a little worried. "Shouldn't we notify Duke Georg? I know the lady has been here for visits several times. She's quite a bit older than he is, but they get along well, as far as I know. There's no family estrangement."

"Don't bother," the bureaucrat from ways and means said. "He's out on the Eastern Front with more important things on his mind, and they weren't that close. She was gone from Brunswick, married already, by the time he was ten years old, I think."

July 1636

Young Friedrich Wayne Lambert was delivered at the Leahy Medical Center with no problems at all, if one discounted near nervous prostration on the part of his father. His mother, the cheerful little Anna Catharina Hortlederin, sailed blithely through the whole experience, even though it was a first birth. The midwife congratulated her and assured her that she could easily bear ten more with no trouble and probably would. That was when Gary fainted.

Pastor Kastenmayer called on mother and baby, even though she and her husband attended St. Thomas' now.

"They are friends," he said quietly to Oswald Griep when the pastor from St. Thomas' remonstrated with him. "If not parishioners, still friends."

Then he made his rounds among the other patients from St. Martin's parish.

Then, as usual, he called in at the registration desk asking for the names of those who had no or few visitors and called upon them as well, including Countess Clara.

A young nurse-in-training observed his visits quietly.

The band playing at the Thuringen Gardens was moving slowly, and the singer was even slower, probably by about a half beat.

An out-of-town visitor complained to the manager that he'd come to hear up-time music and wasn't getting what he'd paid for.

The manager shook his head. "Ninety percent of the patrons, now, are down-timers and we're not getting all that many out-of-towners any more. Most of my customers are local, and except when they're being deliberately trendy, on the Fourth of July or something, they honestly would rather listen to these plaintive eighteenth and nineteenth century Irish ballads than late twentieth century American music. Unless you come on Friday or Saturday evening, this is what you'll hear."

"I came to hear up-time music."

"Look, fella," the manager protested. "It's still up-time music that you're hearing. It's just not quite as far up-time as you maybe were expecting."

The singer moaned:

'Tis the last rose of summer,
Left blooming alone;
All her lovely companions
Are faded and gone;[9]

Yes, moaned. That was as far as the visitor was prepared to go in declaring that...thing...to be music, or the singer a musician. Moaned. At least it was up-time English. But, then....

Letzte Rose, wie magst du
so einsam hier blühn?
Deine freundlichen Schwestern
sind längst, schon längst dahin.

No, no, no. This was not what he had paid good money to visit the fabled Grantville to hear. He swallowed the last of his beer, pushed his chair back, dropped a skimpy tip on the table, and departed in search of better entertainment.

At the next table, a bunch of nursing students were sitting, listening with more interest.

"I don't care what kind of a spin you put on that song," one of them said. "No matter what the theory of the poem is, if you think about it, the subject is euthanasia. Pay attention."

I'll not leave thee, thou lone one!
To pine on the stem;
Since the lovely are sleeping,
Go sleep thou with them.
Thus kindly I scatter
Thy leaves o'er the bed,
Where thy mates of the garden
Lie scentless and dead.

"Listen. The guy picked the rose, who was probably perfectly happy where she was, and tore her into pieces."

A lively student-type dispute ensued while the singer persisted in his wailing.

"What on earth brought euthanasia to your mind?"

---

[9]Moore, Thomas. *The Poetical Works of Thomas Moore.* A. D. Godley, ed. New York: Oxford University Press, 1910.

"We've got this little old lady in the hospital. She's got the money to pay, and had a batch of servants with her at the hotel, but her steward sent them back where they came from to save on expenses. As I understand it, she's been a widow for close to sixty years, doesn't have any kids, and there's some guy who claims to be her stepson who, if you ask me, is trying to make off with whatever she has. She keeps trying to talk to me, and what I think she's saying is that he's no relative of hers."

Warum blühst du so traurig
im Garten allein?
Sollst im Tod mit den Schwestern
vereinigt sein.

The first speaker finally slammed his fist down. "I don't care what the rest of you think. The song still reminds me of that poor old lady. She hardly has any visitors except her steward and that one guy, and every time he comes she's a little worse the next day. There's something wrong, and I'm going to talk to someone about it."

"Who'd care?"

"I'm going to start with Pastor Kastenmayer."

Fulda, August 1636

"I can't stand it anymore." Andrea Kastenmayerin looked at her husband. "We've been here over a year now. When we were at Erfurt, I at least saw Stepmama and the little brothers occasionally, even if Papa had not forgiven me for marrying you. And Dina and Martin and Cunz more often; not Matthaeus, he has to follow Papa's lead. But we've been here more than a year now...."

"We had to come," Tony Chabert pointed out. "I'm in the army, and after all the losses to the plague at Merkwiller last year, Fulda was about totally stripped of personnel."

"I don't blame you. I know that's the way it has to be, and it is what it is. But I thought maybe, when we named little Lutz for him, right before we left.... But he didn't even stand by us at the baptism."

"It was a Catholic baptism. He'd have been in big trouble if he did. He did at least *come* to Erfurt with Salome and the boys after Lutz was born, before we left."

"I know." Andrea picked up her pen. "But I'm going to write him. Again. Tell him that he'll have another grandchild before Christmas. Probably, possibly, almost right at Christmas."

Grantville, August 1636

Pastor Kastenmayer took the nurse's worries to Johann Georg Hardegg, who said that Count Ludwig Gunther and Countess Emelie were in Magdeburg again because of politics, which is why they hadn't come over to see her, but that no way did Clara von Heringen have a stepson, and specifically not one named Caspar von Heringen, which was the name the pastor had found on the hospital visitors' log. Heringen was the name of the countess' dower estate; not the name of her late husband!

Armed with this information, Kastenmayer took the worries to Gary Lambert, because, he –said anxiously, while a Christian should not be averse to being called to eternal bliss, and the countess was a thoroughly good and charitable Christian, a woman of faith, an excellent lady who had practiced conscientious stewardship, had taken in foster daughters and cared for them well, still, it was not right for anyone to deliberately shorten her life. That was contrary to both the commandments of God and the civil law.

Lambert took the worries directly to the police.

The police, coming full circle, took the worries to Count Ludwig Guenther via radio. He got on the train in Magdeburg and arrived back in Grantville as fast as modern transportation could move him, leaving Emelie to take care of notifying everyone in Clara's extended family.

Caspar Schulthes observed the growing amount of traffic in and out of the countess' room, gave up his lodgings, and left town, hoping heartily that *the persnickety old bitch would die.*

At the end of it all, Press Richards admitted that it wasn't a very satisfactory solution, but pointed out to Count Ludwig Guenther that a small department like his couldn't be expected to solve every crime that occurred, or even come close to it. "It's not like we have the resources, or the personnel, an organization like the FBI did up-time. I'm grateful that most criminals are dumb, because it's a lot harder to catch the smart ones."

He picked up his coffee cup and sighed to find it empty. "You have to realize that 'crime rate statistics' were always bullshit. The baseline for them was an accounting of how many crimes came to the attention of the authorities in the first place. We never had any idea how many crimes were committed so successfully that no one even noticed that they happened. If it hadn't been for the sharp eyes of that boy over at the hospital, no one would ever have noticed this one. The countess would have been another old lady who died of what everyone thought were natural causes."

By the end of it, which had to be done on top of everything else, Pastor Kastenmayer looked at Salome one evening after supper and said, "I'm tired, my dear. Very, very, tired."

October 1636

"Does the pastor have a heart condition," the young nurse asked a group of his friends. "He's never missed a sermon, I know he's keeping up with the adult catechism reviews because I'm stuck in one of them, he's still doing all his hospital visits and calling on the homebound, and I know it isn't any of my business, but it seems to me that his skin is grayer than it was earlier this summer. Waxy looking. I think it's like something we learned about last year."

"It's definitely none of your business," one of the others said. "He's got people a lot more important than we are to look after him."

Fulda, November 1636

"I wish," Andrea said to Tony, "that I could have Stepmama here with me when I have the baby. I really wish it. Do you suppose that Papa would let her come? It would be like heaven to have her here with me."

"All you can do," Tony said, "is ask. Write him again. Nothing ventured, nothing gained."

Grantville, Eve of the feast of St. Andrew

Pastor Kastenmayer dropped into the chair next to his writing desk and picked up a *clipboard* that Gary Lambert had given him. He felt he was being lazy, but somehow it had become so much less exhausting to deal with his extensive correspondence when he was sitting down rather than standing at his desk like a normal man.

He picked up the letter that had come from Andrea the day before and read it again.

Taking out his new fountain pen, a gift from Carol Koch and really a shameful luxury for a man of the cloth to indulge in, but so much simpler than a quill, and fastening a sheet of paper under the clip, he wrote.

I am sorry for our estrangement.
I was wrong.
I am sorry that I did not attend the baptism of the child whom you and Tony so generously made my namesake.
I don't know if your stepmama can come to you this year; it is late in the season for travel. I will inquire what can be done.
I hope that I may see you, your husband, your son, and the child you are expecting very soon and ask for your pardon for my lack of a generous spirit in person.
Your loving Papa

He sealed it, put it on the pile of outgoing mail on the table in the entryway, and went upstairs to say his evening prayers and go to bed.

30 November 1636 (Feast of St. Andrew the Apostle)

Salome Piscatora roused at her usual hour and was surprised to see that Ludwig was still lying in their bed. The hour before breakfast was the time of day he devoted to his morning prayers. She reached over and shook his shoulder.

She dressed, checked on the activities of their current trainee kitchen maid, sent her to set the table, and got the boys who were still at home up for their daily routines. It was only the four little ones any more:

Joseph, Fritz, and Phillip were in Jena; even Salomon was boarding in Rudolstadt so he could attend the Latin school there. She shooed them in to the breakfast table.

"Where's Papa," Peter asked. "Why isn't he at breakfast? Is someone in the parish sick? Or some other emergency?"

She was tempted to look down at the bread she was slicing rather than at their faces, but resisted.

"Your Papa woke up in heaven this morning," she said. "You must go to school as usual. You may tell your teachers. Tell them also that I will come over to the school to access the telephone as soon as I have made a list of everyone who will need to be notified."

Within the hour, she walked across the drive that separated the rectory from the church and school.

Thomas Fischer, seeing nothing amiss or out of routine as the rectory was a busy place and routinely left the front door unlatched during the day, stepped into the entryway, dropped off the day's incoming mail, picked up the outgoing pile, and proceeded on his way.

ANGELS WATCHING OVER ME

Grantville, May 1637

"There's no sense in blaming yourself for it, Ryan," Dr. Jeff Adams said. "Meg has a congenital heart defect. Nobody is doing open heart surgery down-time. Nobody will be for decades. That's the way it is."

"But if I hadn't gotten her pregnant...."

"If she had died a virgin, she would still have died before she was twenty-five."

Ryan Baker looked down at his boots.

"That little boy has given her a lot of joy for the last two years. Take care of her. Keep her comfortable. There's nothing else to do."

Meg kept getting smaller. Ryan could see it.

The next time he took her to Leahy, turning to the others in the room, he said, "Out." Once they were gone, he slipped off his boots and climbed into the bed with her. She tried to move her head to where she liked to have it, tucked against his neck, under his chin. He helped her. Her light brown hair was smooth and slick.

After a few minutes, she opened her eyes and said, "I have been so happy."

A few minutes after that, Ryan realized that he might as well let the rest of them back in.

July 1637

It hadn't been his intention to tear apart the congregation of St. Martin's in the Fields. He'd just wanted a monument for Meg. The biggest one he could afford. The biggest one that anybody in Grantville could carve. With angels and Bible verses all over it.

So he'd gone to the Ugolinis, of course.

They owned the stone monument works, didn't they?

What difference did it make that they were Italian Catholics? Had never made any difference to anyone before.

Not until Pastor Griep at St. Thomas had attacked the board of elders at St. Martin's for creeping unionism because they had permitted a Catholic-carved monument in a Lutheran graveyard. Church yard. Right next to the church. Not that Pastor Griep didn't think of every possible reason to criticize St. Martin's, anyway. That had been going on ever since he came to town. He had disliked Ludwig Kastenmayer. In the interregnum since the old pastor's death, with the deadlock on choosing a successor, he had taken aim at the lay officials and, through them, at Count Ludwig Guenther.

A guy named Holz added plenty to the mess. He was a spokesman or something for a Lutheran superintendent named Melchior Tilesius from Mühlhausen, up in the northern part of Thuringia, who was locked in a turf battle with Johann Rothmaler, the Lutheran superintendent in Schwarzburg-Rudolstadt. Tilesius had a son-in-law in need of a good job. That might be relevant. It might not.

Then there was *Frau* Susanne Maria Brömel, the widow of someone named Elias Scheffel. Ryan had never met Scheffel; he had died a couple of years before Meg came along and turned him into a Lutheran. He'd been the chancellor for Count Ludwig Guenther. The widow had intervened. She had a pet candidate. She was also the stepmother of Pastor Rothmaler's wife.

After that, a guy named Wolfgang Radtke—the newspaper articles usually turned it into Latin and called him Ratichius—who was now secretary of education for the SoTF government down in Bamberg, got involved, as did his widowed patroness, Count Ludwig Guenther's aunt-by-marriage, who lived over at Kranichfeld and appeared to know every other influential old lady in the USE. They thought a different guy would be preferable.

So now, it seemed, after a vacancy of more than half a year, about a quarter of St. Martin's congregation had stalked off and joined St. Thomas.

The others were hanging in there, but not having a pastor available got harder every week. One came over from Rudolstadt to give a sermon on Sundays, but as Joanie Smith complained, it wasn't the same thing at all.

Ryan stood there, looking at the monument, holding little David's hand.

* * *

"As far as I can tell, being here in Jena and not in Grantville, it's not even as if someone were out to deliberately sabotage the parish at St. Martin's," Ludwig Kastenmayer's widow wrote to her son. "On paper, every single one of the candidates is qualified. I haven't met them, but their resumes could be duplicates. Triplicates. Whatever. It's simply a case of, 'it's not what you know; it's who you know.' "

* * *

"Joanie Smith keeps moaning that the vacancy is going on and on and on, and finding a replacement seems to be going nowhere, which is bad for the parish and worse for the school," Ryan summed up. "She's been teaching English at Countess Kate for a couple of years—those two girls from Suhl, Veronica and Mathilde, who are living with Joanie and Hank while they go to school here...their father sent them up from Suhl, he's that bigshot gunsmith Georg Weiss...talked her into joining."

"Let me think about this overnight," Hugh Lowe said. He was Ryan's boss at the -Grantville-Rudolstadt-Saalfeld Railroad and Tramway Corporation. He wasn't Lutheran; he was Methodist. The former Chevy dealer now had an iron in every ground transportation fire in the SoTF and in quite a few in the rest of the USE and had no difficulty coming up with the math of *Joanie Smith = Hal Smith's daughter-in-law; Hal Smith = a hook into air transport that I don't have yet.* Hugh had been the president of the Grantville Chamber of Commerce, way back when.

He had one strong religious conviction (the others being, he admitted to himself, rather flexible, not to say nebulous): church fights weren't good for local business.

Young Ryan was coming along well, really well. He'd moved from trainee to junior executive in four years, even with all the time off he'd taken for poor little Meg's illness.

Through transportation, Hugh had connections. A network. Who in that network was Lutheran?

First he talked to Burton Vandiver at the office. Burton wasn't Lutheran, but his wife was a down-timer and a member out at St. Martin's.

Then he phoned Gary Lambert at the hospital. They'd gotten to know each other on the ambulance board. Gary was an up-timer and had switched his membership over to St. Thomas on the other side of town, but he'd probably have heard some things.

"Give me a couple of days to get back to you," Gary said. "I'd like to run this past my father-in-law, who's the chancellor up at Weimar."

Gary duly got back to Hugh, who then phoned his probably biggest contact who might have a fish in this pond, Duke Johann Philipp of Saxe-Altenburg.

* * *

Meanwhile, Ryan was talking to the guys. The ones Ms. Mailey had tagged as the Group of Seven. They'd all joined St. Martin's on the same day and for the same reason. *Flirt to convert*, as someone put it. One of Al Green's sons, he thought. The clever one.

"I asked Hugh for input," Ryan said, "but I don't know if anything will come of it. Since then, I've got this idea. It looks to me that the main problem is that we have to wait for Count Ludwig Guenther to make up his mind. If we didn't have to wait for that, the board of elders could get a move on."

"Isn't it Count Ludwig Guenther's church?" Mitch Hobbs asked. "I've heard about *cuius regio* and all that."

Roland Worley shook his head. "They abolished that in the USE with the new Constitution. It, *cuius regio*, meant that the count got to tell everybody that they had to be Lutheran. What we're dealing with here is *cuius ecclesia* or something, which probably isn't the right Latin. He can't tell people in what used to be his principality to be Lutherans any more. But he's still running a church synod, or whatever you'd call it, for the Lutherans who live in what used to be his principality. St. Martin's is built on his land, and he built it with his money. It's literally his church, so his superintendent gets to appoint the new pastor. Which I guess he would, except for all the outside meddling."

Roland knew exactly as much about the organization of down-time Lutheranism as he had learned in the catechism class he took two years earlier so that Rahel Rosina Dornheimer would marry him: *i.e*, nothing at all.

But, then, the other guys didn't know a jot or tittle more about it, so they accepted his analysis.

"This is what occurred to me," Ryan said. "If he can appoint the pastor because he owns the church, I was thinking that if he would agree, the parish could buy itself from him. We'd have to work out an installment plan and take out a mortgage. Which would mean finding a bank that would give us a mortgage, but if we can stop the bleed-off of people to St. Thomas, the congregation is big enough that there's plenty income to pay it back on a reasonable schedule. We've already broken the news to the down-timers a long time ago that without a state church in the SoTF, none of their taxes come back to support the parish, and they have to make it off the Sunday offerings. Every member might have to dig into their pockets a little deeper, but St. Martin's could make it work.

"That way, though, if we owned ourselves, the elders could can look around at the various territorial churches and ask one of them for the kind of pastor we want. Not be held hostage any longer."

"That kind of complicated idea is beyond me," Derek Blount said. "But if the rest of you want to try it, I'll sign on. Ursel might have some ideas."

"I'm positive," Mitch Hobbs said, "that Walpurga will have some ideas. Jim Fritz is still up in Erfurt and you all know what he's like. He won't do anything about this, but do you think Maria might sign on for him?"

"Probably, if Ursel asks her to," was Derek's answer. "They're cousins."

"Lisbet and I aren't exactly pillars of the parish," Errol Mercer said. "Except for playing music when they ask us. Then, all of a sudden, we're in good standing again in spite of our tendency to stay up late on Saturday night and sleep late on Sunday morning. Our names are on the membership list, though. I'll sign. What about Lew Jenkins?"

"Still in Erfurt, but as soon as his enlistment is over, he'll be back next year. He and Sabina have been saving every cent and will go into partnership with Manning and Myrna to expand the goat dairy. I'm sure Sabina will sign on for him."

They all thought about it for a while and then put Ryan and Roland on the train for Jena to talk to Carol Koch, on the theory that since she was teaching math at the university there, she had more connections to influential down-timers than any of the other up-time Lutherans.

Carol said that she would see what she could do. As an up-time ELCA Lutheran, she had felt a bit stranded among the proponents of Lutheran orthodoxy during her years teaching mathematics at the university. She remembered what she could and picked up a few concepts from Dean Johann Gerhard.

"I have, of course, also been fascinated to read the debates that surrounded the organization of the Missouri Synod in the eighteen forties. C. F. W. Walther must have been a remarkable man." Gerhard smiled. "I doubt that there's a Lutheran academic alive and awake today who hasn't read those papers from *Herr* Lambert's foot locker. I like that hymn, too. *Erstanden, erstanden!*[11] A scholar and a poet."

Then she got in touch with Duke Albrecht of Saxe-Weimar, who commented, "That's odd. My cousin Johann Philipp down at Saxe-Altenburg wrote me a letter about this problem last week."

* * *

"If what you are really looking for is a pastor will try to get along peaceably with all the other factions and all the multiple religious denominations in Grantville," Duke Johann Philipp –recommended, "write to the faculty at Helmstedt, up in Brunswick. Ask them to recommend someone who's been a student of Georgius Calixtus and Conrad Horneius. Someone they'll sponsor."

His advice was not, oh, surely not, in any way, affected by the long-time (as in several centuries of time) irritation of the Wettins at having the counts of Schwarzburg and their allodial landholdings mixed in amid his family's own Thuringian holdings.

Carol did more than write to the faculty at Helmstedt. She sent her up-time German-born husband to talk to them. Ron was as detached from ecclesiastical matters as most run-of-the-mill up-time Germans who were technically Lutheran but actually secular, but he was entirely willing to do his wife a favor. He was pretty well-known as a mining engineer by now. People were willing to talk to him if he asked.

Justus Gesenius went from Helmstedt to talk to his good friend David Denicke at Herzberg. Who was at Herzberg because that was still the principal residence of the dukes of Brunswick, current events having

[1]10 https://www.youtube.com/watch?v=6QKdyCQ5-jU

greatly delayed their plans to build a larger and better palace at Hannover. David was the tutor of the sons of Duke George of Brunswick-Lüneburg. Who in turn was a supporter of the emperor and fighting on the Eastern Front in the emperor's wars.

The duke was very protective of his university at Helmstedt. Very proud of it. When Denicke's letter reached his military headquarters, he leaned his camp chair back, propped his booted feet up on the table, and smiled.

Helmstedt had experienced hard times in the past decade. Up to 1625, it had counted about 500 students. Then the plague hit, and the town lost a third of its population. The university had to close temporarily; it had never entirely recovered, but the new oil leases were certainly helping. Students were still going elsewhere, but soon they would be coming back, if only because of the remodeled and modernized dormitories. A few more prominent faculty members wouldn't hurt anything, either.

He smiled to himself. A man could certainly get a bit of payback against the orthodoxy of Wittenberg and Jena by placing a candidate from Helmstedt at St. Martin's. Right under the noses of the Jena theological faculty. In Grantville, the city of up-time miracles. Or, at least, very close to Grantville. He directed his ecclesiastical officials at home to get directly involved and be very, very, very cooperative with St. Martin's.

* * *

Count Ludwig Guenther, who had been spending most of his time in Magdeburg, deeply absorbed in federal politics, with only occasional visits home to Rudolstadt, bestirred himself to ask what was going on. Johann Rothmaler waffled. So did the Schwarzburg-Rudolstadt consistory. By the time they admitted what had been going on, the count's response was, "There's no point in digging ourselves a deeper hole than we're already in. Offer them a 99-year lease on the land and purchase of the buildings."

St. Martin's board of elders accepted the deal. The buildings might need to be moved or sold back to the count's heirs in 99 years, but all of them would indubitably be dead by the time the reckoning came due.

* * *

The University of Helmstedt faculty got curious enough to send a delegation to St. Martin's, including Calixtus.

He enjoyed meeting Gary Lambert, the source of so many fascinating documents that had been in circulation since the Rudolstadt Colloquy. "I find it interesting, in an odd kind of way, to find myself so vehemently vilified by the supporters of strict Lutheran orthodoxy for things that I will not have done for another decade or more. For the time being, I count myself fortunate that Abraham Calov is still only in his early twenties, so no one takes him very seriously."

To welcome the visitors, the ladies of the parish put on a huge outdoor combination picnic/potluck in the driveway between the empty rectory and the absolutely packed school.

Athanasius Kircher, from St. Mary's downtown, dropped by to shake hands. Upon being introduced to Calixtus' teenaged son, he said wryly, "I understand from my biography that we'll be friends in twenty years or so, and that I'll provide some letters of introduction when you make a visit to Rome. Be sure to drop me a note when you need them.

Charles Vandine also stopped in to introduce himself and demonstrate that, "Presbyterians don't all have horns, a forked tail, and carry a pitchfork."

Calixtus laughed. "It appears to be my concurrence with that view that caused about half of my life's tribulations. The other half having been caused by my belief that not all Roman Catholics do, either."

While the professors glad-handed, Denicke met with the board of elders and the alleged "group of seven."

"You don't need an academic type, I think. You need a parish pastor. Preferably not an elderly man, this time, or you'll have the whole thing to do again in a few years. Not that a long-continued earthly life is certain for those of us who are in our thirties, but it is more likely than for those who are in their seventies."

Generally, the board agreed.

"I have a good friend," Denicke said.

They winced.

"No, hear me out, please."

Duke Georg counted a bit of coup when St. Martin's voted to join the territorial church of Brunswick and extended a "call" to a Helmstedt alumnus to be their pastor. He recommended that the Helmstedt faculty send out feelers to see if any other congregations in the SoTF might be interested.

"The icing on the cake for the parish," Martin Kastenmayer informed his sisters Andrea and Dina, is that this young man, Simon Horst is his name, went along with Denicke on his grand tour. He couldn't have afforded it on his own; he went to Latin school on a scholarship and –barely scraped together enough money to attend the university at Helmstedt right next door to his home village. But Denicke at age 19 did want a grand tour, didn't want a tutor, and Denicke's father thought that a nice young man almost guaranteed not to get young David into trouble was the best alternative companion, so he covered the costs. Dear old dad also specified 'Protestants only.' Off they went. Visited a few Huguenot strongholds in France. Passed through Holland for a few months. Then plopped themselves down in England for the rest of the time. Simon Horst's completely fluent in down-time English and having no trouble adapting to the up-time accent."

* * *

Even old Count Anton Heinrich, who was the working manager of Schwarzburg-Sondershausen, came down for the installation, probably for the purpose of experiencing a little *Schadenfreude* at the discomfiture of his cousin of Schwarzburg-Rudolstadt. Also, possibly, to acquire a bit of insight as to what strange things could happen to one's administrative set-up when one was no longer precise a ruling count any more: a count, still, if one had not renounced one's rank, but not ruling.

Salome came down from Jena to help with the final preparations for the installation. "He's sixty-five if he's a day," she said anxiously to the ladies of the parish, "so make sure that there's a comfortable chair. Also, treat the lady on his arm as if she were his legal wife, and give her a chair. The whole thing has been terribly embarrassing for the Offeney family for the past thirty-five years, so we shouldn't do anything to make them feel worse now. He'll probably never stop trying to get their children legitimated and ennobled."

Count Ludwig Guenther and Countess Emilie attended to be gracious. Superintendent Rothmaler attended because the count told him to. The superintendent's wife's stepmother, who still had a protégé to place, attended in order to eyeball the health of the remaining pastors in the superintendency so she could calculate where the next vacancy would most likely occur.

She had her chance. In addition to another delegation from Helmstedt, there were over sixty pastors, or their substitutes or deacons, from the Schwarzburg-Rudolstadt superintendency bidding farewell to a parish that had been, however briefly, one of theirs. Several of them were quite elderly, so the parish borrowed enough chairs for all of the above.

The installation also featured music by the students of Countess Katharina the Heroic. To down-time ears, something over two hundred and fifty children from the first through eighth grades, on bleachers in the driveway, letting loose, at full volume, on "Standing on the Promises"[11] as accompanied by Lisbet Hercher's dance band, was sheer cacophony. Pretty much, for the ears of listening up-timers, it was also sheer cacophony as well.

The rest of the rite was thankfully held indoors and featured better musical taste. There was still no organ in the church, but they borrowed a piano. They honored C. F. W. Walther by assigning their best soloist to his hymn.[11] The only thing missing was a clerical family to welcome. Pastor Horst, never having received more than a minimum stipend in his previous assistant-pastor assignments, had never felt free to raise the hopes of any young woman by the slightest proffer of courtship.

The women of the parish had started to mention various possible ideal brides to one another even before the new pastor moved into the rectory. There were quite a few suggestions.

Joanie Smith introduced him to her charge Veronica Weiss and stood back to see if things would take their natural course. Veronica's

---

[11] https://www.youtube.com/watch?v=OF8wWlPYPpk

[11] https://www.youtube.com/watch?v=STN9K1U64TM

father wasn't a pastor or teacher, of course, but as far as Joanie was concerned, that was a good thing. These Lutheran clergy families, all marrying each other's daughters and sisters for the last century, were starting to get as inbred as the nobles, if you asked her.

Ryan Baker, little David in his arms, came up to Salome Piscatora, asking if *Frau* Kastenmayer would please come with him to see Meg's monument.

"I never meant to start this ball rolling. I only wanted there to be angels watching over her for all of eternity."

Back in Jena, Salome shook her head sadly at her stepson Martin. "He is doing very well, you know, financially, young Baker is. Logically, he must marry again. He will need a wife to run his household and care for the boy."

"And?" Martin raised his eyebrows.

"I feel so sorry for the second wife he chooses. Whoever she may be. However soon. He would soon have outgrown little Magdalena, if she had lived. Later on, if she had lived longer, I am afraid that their marriage might have had problems. But since she has died so young, she will always be there in his heart. Close to perfect. Competition that no living woman can hope to match."

She shook her head again and turned back to the hearth.

AFTERWORD

This is mostly a small bibliographical essay. The historical characters who appear in the Pastor Kastenmayer story sequence (identified as hi d-t in the Cast List) were not, by and large, major players on the European scene. You will not find them mentioned in general textbooks on European history; most of them won't even be mentioned in general monographs on seventeenth century Germany.

More significantly for most fans of the 1632 series, you will not find most of them mentioned in anything written in the English language—any more than, for example, you would expect to find the people who led the county where you were born in Minnesota or Missouri mentioned by in books written in German and published in Germany. There's a little, but not a lot. So bear with me, please. Here are some examples of what is available.

For a sense of how social and economic unrest manifested:

Schindler, Norbert, *Rebellion, Community and Custom in Early Modern Germany* (Cambridge, England: Cambridge University Press, Past and Present Publications, 2002).

For the near-poverty in which most Lutheran parish pastors lived, though by the sixteen-thirties (except when caused by the ongoing war) it was no longer the miserable, grinding, poverty of the first generation of them a century earlier, see:

Karant-Nunn, Susan C., *Luther's Pastors: The Reformation in the Ernestine Countryside. Transactions of the American Philosophical Society, Volume 69, Part 8* (Philadelphia: The American Philosophical Society, 1979).

For the dukes of Saxe-Weimar, there is a thick and beautifully illustrated overview that begins in the fourteenth century and continues until World War I:

Hoffmester, Hans, and Wahl, Volker, eds., *Die Wettiner in Thüringen: Geschichte und Kultur in Deutschlands Mitte* (Arnstadt and Weimar, Rhino Verlag, 1999).

Duke Ernst, who appears not only by passing mention in these stories but also as a secondary or supporting character in several Eric Flint's mainline novels, has a good recent biography:

Jacobsen, Roswitha, and Rüge, Hans-Jörg, *Ernst der Fromme (1601-1675): Staatsmann und Reformer. Veröffentlichungen der Forschungsbibliothek Gotha Heft 39* (Bucha bei Jena: Quartus-Verlag, 2002).

For the counts of Schwarzburg-Rudolstadt, the equivalent book starts after our period of interest, but provides some information, starting with the regency of Count Ludwig Guenther's widow, Emelie:

Fleischer, Horst, ed., *Vom Leben in der Residenz: Rudolstadt 1646-1816. Beiträge zur schwarzburgischen Kunst- und Kulturgeschichte, Band 4* (Rudolstadt: Thüringer Landesmuseum Heidecksburg, 1996).

The available book for Saxony, which has the charm of being in English, is slightly before our period of interest, but again will provide a visual impression of how John George and his family lived:

Syndram, Dirk, and Scherner, Antje, eds., *Princely Splendor: The Dresden Court 1580-1620* (New York and Dresden: The Metropolitan Museum of Art/Staatliche Kunstsammlungen Dresden, 2005)

With far fewer illustrations, but also in English and including the 1632 series period of interest, there is:

Watanabe-O'Kelly, Helen, *Court Culture in Dresden: From Renaissance to Baroque* (London and New York: Palgrave, 2002).

Hedwig of Denmark, widow of Christian of Saxony (John George's older brother), whose escape from the events recounted in Eric Flint, *1636: The Saxon Uprising*, has a section in the following:

Essegern, Ute, *Fürstinnen am kursächischen Hof: Lebenskonzepte und Lebensläufe zwischen Familie, Hof und Politik in der ersten Hälfte des 17. Jahrhunderts: Hedwig von Dänemark, Sibylla Elisabeth von Wurttemberg und Magdalena Sibylla von Preußen. Schriften zur sächsischen Geschichte und Volkskunde Band 19* (Leipzig: Leipziger Universitätsverlag GMBH, 2007).

For the Stiefelite heresy and Ezechiel Meth, with whom the Grantvillers found themselves dealing in Ohrdruf. Coming in at 640 pages, this book will, I assure you, tell you everything you ever thought you might need to know about the topic and probably much more:

Weiß, Ulman, *Die Lebenswelten des Esajas Stiefel, oder, Vom Umgang mit Dissidenten. Forschungszentrum Gotha fur kultur- und sozialwissenschaftliche Studien der Universität Erfurt. Band 1* (Stuttgart: Franz Steiner Verlag, 2007).

For Clara, born a duchess of Brunswick, the unfortunate elderly lady who is poisoned by a disgruntled ex-employee, with her relatives, foster-daughters, travels, and even mourning customs after her husband's death:

Kuhlbrodt, Peter, *Clara von Schwarzburg: Eine geborene Herzogin von Braunschweig-Lüneburg in Heringen (Helme). 2 vols.* (Heringen-Nordhausen: Friedrich-Christian-Lesser-Stiftung, Band 20/1 and 20/2, 2009).

More generally, for the role of noble widows, see another monograph that, at 768 pages, will probably tell you more than you wanted to know or even dreamed that there was to know:

Kruse, Britta-Juliane, *Witwen: Kulturgeschichte eines Standes in Spätmittelalter und Früher Neuzeit* (Berlin and New York: Walter de Gruyter, 2007).

If anyone among you is curious about sources of information about any of the other historical characters, please email me at virginiademarce@yahoo.com. I will be happy to try to satisfy your curiosity.

Made in the USA
Las Vegas, NV
10 August 2021

27927754R00171